P9-CEP-408

Sam ended the argument by tucking Victoria's arm in his. "I'll escort you home. As you said, it's only a few blocks. And it gives me a chance to talk to you about what happened last night."

The warmth that had coursed through Victoria moments ago was nothing compared to the fiery heat that suffused her now. Not for the world would she admit that the last thing she wanted was to *talk* about last night. What she wanted, rather desperately, was to repeat it.

"I want to apologize, Victoria."

"Apologize?"

"You were a guest in my sister's home last night. I shouldn't have abused her hospitality by trifling with you the way I did."

Victoria would hardly classify that shattering kiss as a mere trifle. That Sam viewed it as such stung. Rather badly.

"As best I recall," she returned, "it was *I* who kissed *you*. Perhaps I'm the one who should apologize."

"Perhaps you should," he agreed with a quick grin that almost—almost!—disarmed her. "As I said, you took me by surprise last night. That's no excuse, however. I'm sorry. I assure you it won't happen again."

That wasn't at all what she'd hoped to hear him say. The fool! The blind, chug-headed fool!

Also by MERLINE LOVELACE

THE COLONEL'S DAUGHTER
THE HORSE SOLDIER

And watch for MERLINE LOVELACE'S
newest historical romance

A SAVAGE BEAUTY

coming September 2003

MERLINE
LOVELACE

The
Captain's
Woman

MIRA®

If you purchased this book without a cover you should be aware
that this book is stolen property. It was reported as "unsold and
destroyed" to the publisher, and neither the author nor the
publisher has received any payment for this "stripped book."

ISBN 1-55166-649-9

THE CAPTAIN'S WOMAN

Copyright © 2003 by Merline Lovelace.

All rights reserved. Except for use in any review, the reproduction or
utilization of this work in whole or in part in any form by any electronic,
mechanical or other means, now known or hereafter invented, including
xerography, photocopying and recording, or in any information storage or
retrieval system, is forbidden without the written permission of the publisher,
MIRA Books, 225 Duncan Mill Road, Don Mills, Ontario, Canada M3B 3K9.

All characters in this book have no existence outside the imagination of the
author and have no relation whatsoever to anyone bearing the same name
or names. They are not even distantly inspired by any individual known or
unknown to the author, and all incidents are pure invention.

MIRA and the Star Colophon are trademarks used under license and registered
in Australia, New Zealand, Philippines, United States Patent and Trademark
Office and in other countries.

Visit us at www.mirabooks.com

Printed in U.S.A.

This book is dedicated to the nurses
and Red Cross workers I served alongside—
with my most profound respect and admiration.

1

Whenever Victoria Parker looked back on the cold, snowy night that plunged her into a wrenching passage from girl to woman, her heart would ache at the absurd arrogance of youth.

She supposed more generous souls might excuse her conceit that blustery February night. After all, she'd celebrated her seventeenth birthday only a few months before. Not only did she stand poised and eager on the brink of womanhood, but she thrilled to the promise of the new century about to dawn.

The old world was rapidly giving way to the new. Electric lights now flickered in most major cities. All across the country, female suffragettes were demanding the same right to vote that the state of Wyoming had granted its women two decades before. Railroad tracks and telegraph lines now spanned the American continent, once so vast and seemingly limitless. And for just a few pennies, eager patrons could enjoy rousing concerts, touring vaudeville acts or that incredible new invention, the moving picture show. With the utter confidence of the young, Victoria quite honestly believed the coming century held only the promise of grand adventures and great passions.

Not that she was unaware of the dark clouds gathering on the horizon. After thirty-five years of peace following the War Between the States, a strident call to arms was once again sounding across the country. It had begun three years ago, when Cuban rebels mounted yet another insurrection to throw off the yoke of their hated Spanish masters. To deny the rebels their supply and support base, the Spanish military governor had moved hundreds of thousands of peasants off their farms into recon-centration camps. There they died, day after day, week after week, from sickness and starvation.

American businessmen with interests in Cuban sugar plantations had raised the initial alarm. With their profits threatened by the continuing turmoil, they'd become increasingly vocal in their demands for intervention by the United States. American reporters in Havana had added to the urgency by detailing in their dispatches the atrocities committed by Spain. Some of those stories, to be sure, contained as much fiction as fact. But moral outrage over the situation in Cuba ran high, and newspaper giants like Joseph Pulitzer and William Randolph Hearst shrewdly continued to fan the flames with story after story. Victoria herself had contributed to the war fever by helping her papa draft indignant editorials about the abysmal situation.

Her thoughts that fateful February evening weren't centered on war or female suffrage, however, or even on the plight of the Cuban peasants forced into *reconcentradas*. Her most pressing concern as she sat before the dressing table in an upstairs bedroom at the Double-S ranch was her hair.

"Wherever is that maid?"

Grimacing at her reflection, Victoria struggled to tame her strawberry curls into the smooth, pouffy chignon made so popular by Charles Dana Gibson's sketches. At the same time, she kept an ear tuned to the faint sound of laughter and the chink of glasses drifting from the floor below. Elise Sloan's birthday party was already underway. If Victoria didn't hurry, she'd miss the festivities completely.

She and her parents had intended to arrive early, but a sudden fall of snow had made the eight-mile carriage ride to the Sloan ranch outside Cheyenne an exercise in sheer determination. Elise and her mother, Suzanne, had escorted the late arrivals upstairs to thaw out and change. Unfortunately, the maid who had delivered a pitcher of hot water and promised to help the young miss dress must have been diverted by other duties.

Eager to get downstairs, Victoria snatched hairpins from the dressing table and stabbed them into her scalp. The chignon slipped precariously to one side.

''Botheration!''

And here she'd so wanted to look her best tonight!

Ordinarily, Victoria didn't concern herself unduly with her appearance. She didn't have to. Her mother's inherited wealth and her father's prominence as owner of one of the city's leading newspapers assured her place in Cheyenne society.

Her parentage aside, Victoria could, quite without conceit, take satisfaction from her natural attributes. The nipped-in, hourglass fashions of the day perfectly suited her narrow waist and generous curve of bust and hip. Her sparkling, china-blue eyes and Cupid's-bow mouth had inspired some rather wretched, if enormously flattering, poetry. But it was her dancing smile, disguising as it did the hint of obstinacy in her nature, that enchanted every unattached male within two hundred miles.

Except one.

Elise's handsome young uncle, Samuel Garrett. The former cavalry officer who persisted in treating Victoria with careless, big-brotherly affection. The

man she'd known most of her life but only decided
to marry a year ago.

She remembered the date exactly. March 22. Sam
had just resigned his cavalry commission and returned to Cheyenne to take over management of the
Garrett family's business affairs.

Victoria had barely turned sixteen and was thoroughly enjoying the attentions of her many admirers. She'd also just begun scribbling quaint little
stories for her father's paper and was quite puffed
up with her own importance. Yet she'd taken one
glimpse of the tall, broad-shouldered officer who
stepped off the train and experienced the most ridiculous, most intense quivers in the pit of her
stomach.

In the months since, the odd sensations had intensified every time her path happened to cross that
of Elise's uncle. Since Sam and his parents, like
Victoria and hers, lived in town, that occurred with
satisfying frequency.

Not that Sam had any inkling of her tumultuous
emotions, of course. Although spoiled outrageously
by her doting mama and papa, Victoria was Wyo-
ming-bred and range-smart beneath her sugar-spun
beauty. She possessed far too much intelligence to
let Sam Garrett know he set her pulse to pounding
whenever he handed her into a carriage or took her
in his arms for a waltz.

But tonight, Victoria thought, stabbing another

hairpin into the soft, shining swirl, she intended to bring the man to his knees.

"There! That will have to do."

Satisfied that the loose chignon would hold, she swung around to survey the dinner gown hanging on the wardrobe door. A small, feline smile curved her mouth. If the yards of exquisite lace decorating the sapphire velvet didn't start Sam sweating beneath his frock coat, the scandalous neckline would surely do the trick. No doubt the icy winds rattling the windowpanes would raise gooseflesh all over her arms and chest, but she considered the chill a minor inconvenience in her carefully planned campaign.

Now she needed only to squeeze into her new, straight-front corset, lace up her petticoats, pull on the deliciously wicked gown and float downstairs to join the party.

The sound of footsteps brought her off the dressing stool. She could manage the corset strings herself if necessary, but needed the assistance of another woman to achieve a truly wasplike Gibson Girl waist. Hoping it was the maid, Victoria threw her flowered silk robe over her chemise and knickers and peeked through the door.

The sight of a slender, black-clad female making her way down the hall brought an exclamation of relief.

"I've been waiting for you. Do, please, come and help me with my corset strings."

The young woman who turned in response to her summons looked nothing like the Irish maid who'd delivered the hot water earlier. Instead of a snub nose and slightly crossed blue eyes, she possessed the unmistakable features of a Plains Indian. Her broad cheeks and dark eyes bespoke Sioux, or perhaps Cheyenne, blood. So did her raven hair. She wore it parted in the middle and braided into a heavy knot at the back of her neck.

Victoria couldn't remember seeing her at the Sloan's sprawling ranch house before, but servants arrived and departed with regular frequency in the West. Particularly young, attractive females like this one.

"I'm rather late," Victoria admitted with a rueful smile. "Will you assist me?"

"Yes, of course."

The reply was low, melodious and surprisingly cultured. Her skirts rustling, the woman glided back along the hall. When she stepped into the light thrown by the electric sconce, the glow cast a rich sheen over her dress. The black gown might be plain and rather too large for the wearer's slight build, but it had been cut by the hand of a master. As had the jet choker encircling her slender throat.

Victoria was just beginning to suspect she'd mistaken another late arriving guest for a servant when footsteps pounded up the stairs behind them.

''There you are!''

The rich, deep baritone spun her around. Her pulse leaping, she watched Sam mount the last few stairs and hurry toward her. He was so tall, so weathered by both his native Wyoming winds and his years in uniform. And so strikingly handsome in the white tie and tails he'd donned in honor of his niece's birthday! Below his thatch of light brown hair, streaked by the sun and rigorously pomaded into a neat part, his eyes gleamed with eager anticipation.

Shivers of delight raced across Victoria's skin. He'd never looked at her with such warmth before. Of course, he'd never seen her in only a chemise, knickers and a thin silk robe before. A blush heated her cheeks, but she retained enough presence of mind to tilt her head to a coquettish angle.

''You must excuse my—''

''They just told me you'd arrived!''

Startled, she realized Sam wasn't addressing her. Or even looking at her.

His entire attention was fixed on the black-gowned woman. Catching her about the waist, he swung her in high, exuberant circles. Victoria jumped back, flattening herself against the wall just in time to avoid a sturdy boot square in the chest.

''Sam!''

Laughing, the recipient of this rough-and-ready treatment braced her hands on his broad shoulders while she was swung in yet another circle.

"For pity's sake! You'll make me dizzy."

"It would serve you right for slipping upstairs without so much as a hello."

"I peeked in the drawing room. You were surrounded by Elise's friends. All of whom appeared quite taken with her handsome uncle, I might add."

He lowered her to her feet, a crooked grin slashing across his face. "There's no accounting for the tastes of silly schoolgirls, is there?"

Silly schoolgirls?

Victoria went rigid against the wall, but Sam remained too engrossed with the other woman to notice. His gaze roamed her upturned face with a hunger that slowly shaded to worry.

"You've lost weight. You're thin. Too thin."

Since his hands still circled her waist, Victoria thought waspishly, he was certainly in a position to accurately assess her condition.

"It's been almost two years since John died," he said, his voice gentling. "Do you still grieve for him?"

"I will always grieve for John Prendergast. He was my friend and my teacher as well as my husband."

Prendergast! Victoria's eyes widened. She'd

heard that name many times from her friend Elise. So this must be Mary Two Feathers Prendergast.

Elise had told her all manner of stories about the woman. Her mother, Bright Water, had been an Arapaho healer and a close friend of Elise's own mother. Supposedly, Suzanne Sloan had wrangled an invitation for Bright Water to go East and study medicine with a Philadelphia physician. After an outbreak of typhoid decimated her tribe and took Bright Water's life, her daughter had gone in her stead.

A mere slip of a girl, Two Feathers had taken a Christian name, trained with the gruff John Prendergast and eventually married him despite the wide disparities in their ages and backgrounds. Widowed several years ago, she'd returned to treat those of her tribe who still lived on the Arapaho reservation.

But why had she traveled to Cheyenne, so far from Wind River? And in this weather?

Evidently the same questions occupied Sam's mind. Scooping up the coat the young widow had dropped when he'd spun her off her feet, he tucked her arm in his.

"Let me escort you downstairs to join the rest of the company. I'm anxious to hear why you're traveling through the snows of winter."

"I must wash my hands and tidy my hair before I'm fit for company," she protested, drawing free.

"And," she added with a smile for Victoria, "I must help this young lady finish her toilette."

Sam acknowledged her presence for the first time. "Oh, hello, Victoria."

To her sudden, sweeping fury, he actually reached out and chucked her under the chin.

"You'd better hurry into your dress. There's a young lieutenant from Fort Russell downstairs who's been pestering Elise for the past half hour, wanting to know where the devil you're hiding yourself."

"Indeed?" she said frigidly.

"Indeed," he echoed, grinning, before his glance returned to the widow. The teasing light Victoria so detested faded from his eyes. "I'll make sure my sister seats us next to each other at dinner. We've some catching up to do."

"Yes, we have," she answered, skimming a glance down his elegant frock coat and shirtfront. "I'll tell you what brought me to Cheyenne and you must tell me how you find life now that you no longer wear a uniform."

He hesitated for the barest fraction of a second before giving a careless shrug.

"Well enough. I'll see you ladies downstairs."

Their gazes on his broad back, neither woman moved. Still smarting from his avuncular and wholly patronizing caress, Victoria quietly seethed.

Mary watched him with a more thoughtful expression.

"He has a warrior's heart," she said softly, almost to herself. "Like his father."

"I beg your pardon?"

With a little shake of her head, the widow turned aside the question. "Shall we do up your corset so you may find this lieutenant Sam speaks of?"

"Thank you, but I shall manage. I don't wish to delay you when you have your own toilette to attend to."

"A few more moments won't matter. Come, let's strap you in."

Victoria's entrance into the drawing room some ten minutes later went a long way to soothing her pique over Sam's cavalier treatment.

Heads turned. Eyes widened. The buzz of conversation slowed, then petered out altogether. The faces of the guests crowding the high-ceilinged room registered a variety of reactions.

Victoria caught flashes of envy from some of the younger women. Surprise and perhaps a frown or two from the older matrons...including her mother, who hadn't been consulted by her daughter concerning the alterations to the sapphire gown.

If the women eyed her with varying degrees of approbation, the males appeared universal in their wholehearted approval. Victoria couldn't help but preen a bit under the admiring stares of the young men and smile saucily at the older gentlemen. A wink from her papa won one from her in return. Even Sam, she saw with a stab of smug satisfaction, broke off his conversation and swept her from head to toe with a startled look.

Head high, her pulse fluttering under the black velvet ribbon tied around her throat, she glided into the room and made straight for her host and hostess. Elise's parents stood near a round, claw-footed table draped with lace and filled to overflowing with canapés on silver trays, crystal champagne flutes and a towering ice centerpiece sculpted by the Hotel Sheridan's French chef, who'd driven with his minions through the whirling snow to cater the birthday fete.

"I'm sorry for taking so long to dress," Victoria apologized prettily. "I do hope I haven't held up dinner."

"Not at all," Elise's mother assured her. "We're still waiting for another of our guests to come downstairs."

Almost twenty years of marriage and four children had added a glow of maturity to Suzanne Sloan's beauty. Her soft brown hair, so like her younger brother Sam's, showed only a few strands of silver.

The man who stood beside her wore his years a bit harder. Once a notorious gunslinger, Black Jack

Sloan was now a prosperous horse rancher and an elected member of the Wyoming state legislature. Although he could still the antics of his lively offspring with one piercing look from his steel-gray eyes, they held a distinct twinkle tonight as he surveyed his daughter's closest companion.

"You look lovely, my dear. And rather, er, grown-up."

Victoria gave him her most brilliant smile. "Thank you, sir."

"Yes, you quite take the shine from me," a willowy brunette declared as she joined the group. "You always have, you wretched, wretched excuse for a friend."

"Not tonight, Elise."

Victoria spoke only the truth. She'd never seen the brunette sparkle so vivaciously. Or appear to such advantage. The dratted girl much preferred to spend her time in horse barns instead of drawing rooms, and usually had to be forced into ball gowns and dancing slippers. Tonight, however, she looked positively radiant in a stylish creation of rich, ruby velvet. Diamonds winked at her throat and ears, and a delicate touch of pink tinted her cheeks.

"Lieutenant Duggan's here," Elise informed Victoria. "He's been asking for you."

"Has he?"

"Yes, and he brought a friend with him." The

color in her cheeks deepened. "A new lieutenant, just out of West Point."

Good heavens! Had a male with two legs instead of four finally captured her friend's interest? Intrigued, Victoria murmured her excuses to the Sloans and tucked her arm in Elise's.

More than one male glance followed them as they crossed the room. They made such a contrast, Victoria knew. One so dark and slender, the other so fair and well curved, each kissed with the bloom of budding womanhood. Her spirits gratifyingly restored after the way Sam had all but ignored her upstairs, she allowed Elise to draw her toward the two eager lieutenants from nearby Fort Russell.

She had to admit they presented a rather splendid picture in their dress uniforms. The belted dark blue jackets sported gold epaulets and ropes. Long silk tassels dangled from their sabers. With their hair parted rigorously down the middle and their mustaches waxed to sharp points, they represented the flower of America's military establishment.

The look of almost slavish adoration that came over Lieutenant Charles Duggan's face as Victoria approached raised her spirits even more. Charles was really a delightful young man. Quite polished and so very anxious to please.

Graciously, she allowed him to fetch her a glass of champagne and laughed merrily at the tales he and his friend shared of their days at the Point. Others drifted over. Within minutes, Victoria and Elise were surrounded by their wide circle of friends.

She let several moments pass before she slanted a look over her shoulder. Sam caught her provocative glance. Grinning, he lifted his champagne flute in silent salute. A delicious heat raced through Victoria's veins and she was feeling a flush of feminine satisfaction at having snared his full attention when his gaze shifted to her left.

The hunger she'd glimpsed so briefly upstairs flitted across his face again, quickly come and just as quickly gone. With a sudden, hollow feeling in her stomach, Victoria sensed Mary Two Feathers Prendergast had entered the drawing room.

The gay atmosphere around her seemed to deflate. All at once the air seemed thick and stuffy. When Suzanne Sloan ushered her guests in to dinner a few moments later, a dull ache throbbed at the base of Victoria's skull.

2

Twenty-eight sat down to feast at the Sloans' mahogany dinner table. An elaborate chandelier with cut-crystal globes hung overhead. The pools of light from its many bulbs cast a golden glow over a sideboard laden with serving dishes. Silver gleamed, and the tall crystal stemware purchased during the Sloans' recent trip to Europe gave off a brilliant luster.

Once his guests were seated, Jack Sloan exercised his privilege as host to toast his daughter on the occasion of her birthday. The hard edges of his face softened for a moment, just long enough for the assembled guests to glimpse the man behind the once-legendary gunslinger.

"To you, Elise. May you find as much joy in the years ahead as you've given your mother and me the past seventeen."

A rousing chorus of "Hear, hear!" colored

Elise's cheeks again. The murmured comment of the young lieutenant beside her turned them even pinker.

Victoria was seated directly across from her friend, with Charles Duggan at her right side. Sam, she noted, occupied the chair next to Mary Prendergast near the foot of the table. He'd obviously made good on his promise to rearrange the name cards tucked in delicate silver filigree holders. With something dangerously close to a sniff, Victoria bestowed a smile so brilliant on the young man seated to her left that he almost dropped his soupspoon.

Course followed course, but in the heart of cattle country, the main dish could only be beef. The Hotel Sheridan's imported chef had outdone himself with his artistic presentation of four-inch-thick tenderloins baked in a sherry mushroom sauce and flaky pastry shells.

The gastronomic delights, free-flowing champagne and well-traveled guests made for a lively dinner party. As always at any gathering of Cheyenne's elite, the conversation ranged from ranching to the activities of the state legislature to the upcoming visit of one of Italy's noted tenors. Inevitably, the talk soon turned to the Cuban situation and the very real possibility of war.

"Dashed bad luck, that horse rolling on your father," a whiskered gentleman huffed to Sam. "Andrew Garrett should be the one to lead our Wyoming regiments into action when the call to arms comes. Where is the general, anyway?''

"He and my mother are in Denver. They're consulting a surgeon, a specialist just out from Boston who has some expertise with crushed spines.''

The portly gentleman huffed again and shook his head. "Let's hope this sawbones knows what he's about. Hard on a man like your father to be reduced to wheeling himself around in a chair.''

"Yes, it is,'' Sam replied evenly.

Too evenly, Victoria thought. And in almost the same tone he'd used upstairs, when Mary asked him how he liked being out of uniform. As he turned the conversation away from the accident that had crippled his father and brought him home to manage the Garretts' business affairs, Mary's soft observation came back to Victoria in a rush.

Like his father, Sam was a warrior at heart. He'd been raised on army posts, had attended West Point, had served in uniform for almost eight years himself. Yet Victoria had never thought to ask him if he missed army life. She'd been too titillated by his return to Cheyenne, and too infatuated to look beyond the lazy grin he habitually presented to the world. Chewing on her lower lip, she sat silent while his sister raised the question that burned in everyone's mind.

"Do you really believe it will come to war?''

"After the insults the Spanish ambassador gave

our president?'' the same portly gentleman said indignantly. "I should think so!"

A vigorous chorus of agreement rose from others at the table. All America was incensed by the contents of the letter stolen by the Cuban junta in New York and published just last week in newspapers all across the country. In the missive, the Spanish ambassador had labeled President McKinley weak and vacillating—mild adjectives indeed when compared to some of the epithets those same newspapers regularly hurled at the president. Yet the incident added another spark to Americans' smoldering dislike of the Spanish.

"Spain has apologized and vill recall her ambassador," Victoria's papa pointed out in the heavy German accent that flavored his speech despite almost five decades in the States. "Perhaps the pacifists vill prevail, after all."

"I for one sincerely hope not," Lieutenant Duggan put in. "The army hasn't seen any real action since that little fracas at Wounded Knee eight years ago."

"It was hardly a 'little' fracas," Mary countered quietly, entering the conversation for the first time. "My people call it a massacre."

The young officer reddened. In his war zeal, he'd forgotten that a full-blooded Arapaho sat three chairs down from him. Taking pity on his obvious embarrassment, Mary picked up the thread of the conversation.

"I, too, think it will come to war." Her glance shifted to Sam. "That's why I left Wind River. I'm on my way to Washington."

"Washington?"

"Yes. I leave Cheyenne on the eastbound train tomorrow."

"The devil you say!"

He made no attempt to hide his displeasure, Victoria noted. The ache at the base of her skull grew sharper.

"Surely you can stay longer," Sam protested.

"Unfortunately, I cannot. I'm on my way to consult with a colleague of my husband's. Dr. Anita Newcomb McGee. Perhaps you've heard of her?"

"No."

"She's a very prominent physician and currently vice president of the Daughters of the American Revolution. She, too, is concerned about the possibility of war and the potential casualties it will bring. She's suggested that the War Department establish a Hospital Corps and recruit women nurses to fill the positions."

The quiet pronouncement captured the attention of the entire table.

"Do you mean the army would put women in uniform?" Elise asked, astounded by the concept.

Smiling at her astonishment, Mary nodded.

''Countless number of women volunteered their services as nurses during the War Between the States. Some acted as couriers, spies, even saboteurs. But they worked individually, never as part of an organized corps. Dr. McGee's proposal would give the army the surge capacity it needs to augment the male nurses.''

''And give the nurses the protection of the Army,'' Sam put in.

''Exactly.''

Sensing an interesting piece for the next edition of the *Tribune,* Victoria's papa leaned forward and caught the widow's attention.

''If I may be so bold, vhy does Dr. McGee vish to consult vith you?''

''I have some little skill at organization as well as medicine,'' she replied modestly. ''My husband and I helped train volunteer nurses during the great typhoid epidemic that swept through Philadelphia in '93.''

Deitrich Parker's bushy gray brows twitched like a rabbit's, a sure sign that he'd unearthed an exclusive.

A newspaperman to his bones, he'd learned typesetting from his father before immigrating to the United States as a boy of ten. After landing a job as a runner at a New York daily, he'd worked his way up the ladder to senior editor, married the owner's very beautiful and quite wealthy daughter and subsequently moved to Cheyenne to establish his own paper.

"May I talk mit you after dinner?" he asked, his accent thickening in his enthusiasm. "I vould like to print a story about your trip to Vashington."

"Better you should print one about Dr. McGee. She's truly a great physician."

"*Ja, ja,* and so she is! Victoria shall write a piece on her. My daughter, she is good mit words."

"Is she?" In an obvious attempt to shift attention away from herself, Mary addressed the author in question. "Do tell me what you've written."

"Nothing very profound, I assure you. Mostly little anecdotes about the social events here in Cheyenne. Fourth of July picnics and such."

"You're being too modest," the loyal Elise protested. "What about that serial you did on Queen Victoria's Diamond Jubilee last year? *Victoria Regina,* by Victoria Parker. Your vignettes about the queen's life enthralled us all."

"I merely collected bits of information and arranged them in chronological order."

"Don't listen to her," Elise advised the young widow. "She has the keenest wit. Everyone in Cheyenne looks forward to her amusing stories each week."

"Perhaps she should do a piece on the 'cowboy cavalry' our esteemed Senator Warren wishes to organize," one of the guests suggested. "That's as interesting around these parts as Britain's doddering old queen.''

From the corner of one eye, Victoria caught the smirk the two lieutenants exchanged. Elise's father noted it as well. Leaning back in his chair, Sloan put the topic on the table for general conversation.

''You don't agree, Duggan?''

Chagrined at being caught in the smirk, the young officer nevertheless answered truthfully. ''At the risk of putting my foot in my mouth again, I can only echo the opinions of the regulars at Fort Russell toward volunteer infantry regiments. They drill irregularly, if at all, and sorely lack experience in the field. Yet those sentiments are mild indeed compared to our feelings concerning volunteer cavalry regiments.''

Jack Sloan grinned. ''The idea of a regiment composed of rowdy wranglers, undisciplined bronc busters and broken-down old scouts gives you the willies, does it?''

''Well…yes.''

''You'd better get used to it. Despite the army's objections, the congressional delegations from both Wyoming and North Dakota are in favor of it. I'm in favor of it, too,'' the outlaw-turned-horse breeder added with a grin. ''A volunteer regiment such as Senator Warren's talking about will need a good twelve hundred head of prime horseflesh. My guess is he'll push his regiment through.''

"So will the assistant secretary of the navy," Sam put in quietly. "Theodore Roosevelt is as enamored with the idea as Senator Warren and he carries even more clout in the War Department."

Sam should know, Victoria thought. He'd spent two of his eight years in the army on staff duty in Washington.

She decided on the spot that the cowboy cavalry would indeed make for an interesting piece. And the perfect person to lend his perspective was Captain Sam Garrett, but recently discharged from the United States Cavalry.

Victoria decided to ask Sam for his opinion during the lull after dinner, when the ladies went upstairs to refresh themselves. At least that was the reason she gave herself for detaining him before he could join the men in the library for brandy and cigars.

"May I ask you something?"

"Of course."

"Privately."

He hooked a brow, but followed her into the small room just off the dining room that Elise and her mother had claimed for their own. An embroidery tambour was tilted to catch the light, and one of Elise's split-legged riding skirts lay draped over the sewing machine, awaiting repair.

Folding his arms, Sam leaned against the door

molding and waited while Victoria ran her fingers around the tambour. If the move put her in a wash of soft light, that certainly wasn't her intent. Nor did she consciously angle her chin a few more degrees to give him an unobstructed view of her profile.

He, evidently, thought otherwise.

"A very pretty pose," he said with amused approval. "You'll have to try it on your lieutenant."

Her chin came down with a snap. There it was again. That patronizing, almost paternal attitude she thought she'd vanquished forever with her grand entrance and daring décolletage.

"What was it you wanted to ask me, Victoria?"

With some effort, she kept from snapping at him. "I've decided Senator Warren's proposed volunteer cavalry would indeed make a good subject for an article. As a former cavalry officer, I'd like your views on the concept."

"Better you should ask my father. The general spent a good deal more time as a horse soldier than I did."

"I will, when he returns from Denver. But you spent almost eight years in the cavalry yourself. What do you think of the concept?"

"What do I think?" His shoulders lifted. "The army has only a little more than twenty-eight thousand men in uniform at present. If we go to war with Spain, we'll require ten times that number."

"As many as that!"

"As many as that. And we'll need them quickly. That means recruiting men, putting them in uniform and teaching them to ride and shoot, all within a few months."

"A process that might take less time," she said slowly, "if they already knew how to ride and shoot."

"Exactly. Unlike your devoted young swain, I think volunteer cavalry regiments make perfect sense. In fact, I—"

Catching himself, he bit off whatever he'd intended to say.

Victoria was too much her father's daughter to let it go at that. "In fact what, Sam?"

"Nothing. You have my opinion, for whatever it's worth. Now, don't you need to go fluff your petticoats or find your fan or do whatever you girls do before you're besieged by eager young subalterns hoping for a dance?"

She came very close to grinding her teeth together. Really, the man was insufferable. And blind as two bats tied back to back!

"Since you apparently don't wish to share more of your thoughts," she said icily, "I might as well join the other silly schoolgirls."

"Uh-oh. You heard that, did you?"

"Obviously."

Chuckling, he tried to make amends. "Well, I'll

admit neither you nor Elise resemble schoolgirls to-night.''

''Indeed?''

''Indeed,'' he tossed back in that teasing tone she hated. Scraping a hand across his chin, he eyed her up and down. ''The truth is, you rocked me right back on my heels when you waltzed into the drawing room in that gown.''

That was better. Much better.

''Ooooh.'' Oozing syrupy sweetness, Victoria batted her lashes. ''I can't tell you how gratified I am that you've realized Elise and I have put our dolls behind us. In fact—''

She let the pause string out for a long, tantalizing moment.

''All right,'' he said with a grin. ''I'll take the bait. In fact what?''

Perhaps it was the three glasses of champagne she'd consumed that made her so reckless. Or the fact that she was coming of age at a time when women were throwing off the shackles of the old century and demanding rights and privileges in the new that shocked their parents. Or perhaps it was just the thrill of being closeted alone with the man she ached for with a secret, shameful passion. Whatever caused this giddy sensation, it propelled Victoria slowly across the room.

''In fact,'' she murmured, placing her gloved palms on his chest, ''I chose this dress with you in mind. I hoped it would open your eyes and make you see I'm a woman grown, with a woman's desires.''

Sheer surprise blanked his face. "Good Lord!"

"It's all right," she murmured, astonishing even herself with her daring. "You won't be the first."

"The devil you say!"

His shocked exclamation took her aback for a moment, but she'd gone too far now to ignominiously retreat. Her palms glided upward, slipped behind his neck.

"It's true. I've been kissed before. A number of times, if you must know. You won't be the first."

The relief that burst through Sam was so sharp and profound he almost laughed aloud. For a moment there, he'd actually believed… Had thought…

What a dog he was for even imagining that Victoria had bedded with a man! The very idea was absurd. The girl was barely out of hair ribbons and pinafores.

Although…

The lush curves displayed so enticingly by that damned gown certainly didn't belong to any girl. Nor did the red, ripe lips mere inches from his own.

Still, Sam had no intention of claiming the kiss she was so obviously offering. She was his niece's playmate, for pity's sake. He wouldn't trifle with

her here, under his sister's roof. Hell, he wouldn't
trifle with her at all.

No sooner had that thought formed than he discovered that he'd seriously underestimated the little
minx. Rising up on tiptoe, Victoria pressed her lips
to his.

It wasn't much more than an awkward fumble.
A crooked slant of mouth against mouth. Yet for
the second time that night, she rocked Sam right
back on his heels.

She tasted so sweet, so warm. So damned delicious. Like a light, sugary pastry fresh from the
oven. The greedy desire to steal a deeper taste hit
Sam with a punch. Unthinking, he wrapped an arm
around her waist and drew her up against his chest.

With a little moan, she fit her body to his. Her
mouth opened under his. Rich. Ripe. Promising
sensual delights that sent a shaft of heat straight to
his groin.

For a few moments, Sam forgot who she was.
Forgot where they were. With her corset stays digging into his ribs and her breasts plump against his
shirtfront, he came close, damned close, to forget-
ting that it was another woman whose lips he ached
to cover with his own.

With a little grunt, he jerked his head up. Her
lids fluttered open. Shame stabbed into him when
he saw the dazed confusion in her cornflower eyes.
So much for her claim of having been kissed be-

fore! He'd bet she hadn't experienced more than a few chaste pecks on the cheek by that fuzz-faced lieutenant.

Sam had to admit this kiss had been anything but chaste. She wore the marks of it on her face. Her lips were swollen, and his chin had scratched a red patch on hers. There wasn't much he could do about that, but he could at least repair some of the more obvious damage.

Feeling like the vilest lecher alive, he gently set her away from him. "Your hair's come down."

"What?"

"Your hair. Turn around."

Still dazed, she submitted to the gentle pressure of his hands. To Sam's consternation, the line of her neck and shoulders sent another spear of heat straight to his belly. The glimpse over her shoulder at her high, full breasts almost bent him double.

Thoroughly disgusted with himself, he lifted the tumbled strand. It curled around his fingers like a living thing, warm and soft as a summer breeze. He couldn't decide whether the color was more copper or gold.

Not that the color mattered, dammit! Victoria Parker was a guest under his sister's roof, for God's sake. He had no business playing with her hair. Or any other part of her! With more haste than skill, he shoved the strand in place.

"Shall we rejoin the party?"

She blinked, confused by his abrupt withdrawal. Calling himself ten kinds of a fool, Sam took her elbow and urged her toward the door. One step into the hall, they almost collided with Elise.

"Here you are! I've been looking for you everywhere." Her curious gaze darted from her uncle to her friend. "Whatever were you doing in the sewing room?"

A blaze of red rushed into Victoria's cheeks. Calmly, Sam answered for them both.

"Victoria was asking my opinion about the cowboy cavalry."

"Was she indeed?"

A sly smile curved Elise's mouth. Sam ignored it.

"Did you come to tell us that you're ready to crank up the gramophone and begin the dancing?"

"Oh! No!" Recalled to her mission, the brunette poured out a hasty explanation. "I came to tell Victoria that her papa wishes to leave at once. He's asked for your carriage to be brought up from the barn."

"Papa wants to leave? But why?"

"You'll never believe it! Ed Jernigan sent a rider out from town with the most awful news."

The news must be terrible indeed for the *Tribune*'s senior reporter to send a rider all this way on such a cold, blustery night.

"What's happened?"

"You can't imagine!"

"Elise!" Sam snapped. "Tell us at once!"

"The Spanish just blew up one of our ships in Havana harbor! The USS *Maine,* I think it was. Reports are it went down with all hands."

Victoria could only stare at her in shock, but Sam uttered an oath he would never have used in front of two young ladies under less portentous circumstances.

"Your papa wants to rush a special edition of the *Tribune* into print. He's waiting for you in the vestibule. I was sent to find you and tell you to get your wraps immediately."

Almost as dazed by the stunning news as by Sam's shattering kiss, Victoria rushed out. Suddenly, irrevocably, the war that had hovered for so long in the distant future was upon them.

3

Ten hours later, an exhausted Victoria was sure she would remember that February night as long as she lived.

It was well past midnight by the time the Parker carriage pulled up in front of the brick building on the corner of Seventeenth Street and Carey Avenue that housed the offices of the *Cheyenne Daily Tribune*. Not to be confused with the *Weekly Tribune*, Deitrich Parker's newspaper was only one of six that vigorously competed for circulation in Wyoming's bustling capital. The *Tribune*'s arch rival, the *Cheyenne Daily Sun-Leader*, dominated the scene, but readers were so hungry for news and entertainment that Victoria's papa deposited a very respectable profit into his accounts each month.

Lights blazed from every window of the *Tribune*'s offices when Deitrich hurriedly kissed his wife on the cheek.

"I don't know how late ve vill be," he warned as he climbed out. His boots squishing in the snow, he handed his daughter down.

Both he and Victoria braced themselves for a stern lecture, but Rose Parker merely nodded. Like her husband, she took pride in her daughter's cleverness with words, but had come to disapprove of the amount of time Victoria spent at the newspaper offices. Composing stories was an acceptable pastime for a well-brought-up young lady. Sitting down at a Linotype machine and actually transferring those stories to print, as Victoria had been known to do in a pinch, took matters a step too far in Rose's considered opinion.

"Do wear a smock," she adjured her daughter.

"Yes, Mama."

"Although I cannot approve of the alterations you've had made to that dress—which is a matter we shall discuss later!—I shouldn't like to see it covered with ink."

"No, Mama."

Not at all fooled by the demure reply, Rose harrumphed and settled back on her seat.

Hanging on to her papa's arm, Victoria plowed through the drifting snow. Once inside the offices, the familiar stink of sawdust, rag paper and printer's ink enveloped her. Most of the staff was already there, she saw, roused from their beds by the senior editor.

In addition to the three hefty immigrants who worked as bundlers and distributors, the *Tribune* employed two full-time reporters, one part-time contributor besides Victoria, a free-lance sketch artist and aged Mr. Woodbury, a master at the fine art of typesetting. Fortunately for the newspaper industry, but unfortunately for Mr. Woodbury, the recent invention of the Linotype machine had rendered his centuries-old profession obsolete. He'd forced himself to learn how to operate the newfangled machine, but sat down at the keyboard with great and obvious reluctance.

"Vhere's Jernigan?" her father asked, throwing off his overcoat. It landed on the scarred oak counter separating the front area from the offices beyond and slipped, unheeded, to the floor.

"Right here." The tall, gangly senior editor popped out of his office. "The telegraph wires are burning up," he informed his boss.

Holding open the swinging gate in the counter for Victoria and her papa, he followed them back to his office. The news staff crowded in behind.

"I've sorted through the dispatches we've received so far and tried to make sense of them," Jernigan said, "but every report that comes in contradicts the last."

"Haf ve heard from AP?"

Like most newspaper owners with the proper credentials, the correct political affiliations and pockets deep enough to afford the steep costs, Deitrich Parker subscribed to the Associated Press. The news cooperative had been founded mid-century by New York newspaper magnates anxious to pool resources and collect the latest news from Europe, while at the same time minimizing the exorbitant Trans-Atlantic telegraph costs. In the forty years since, it had grown to a vast network of newspapers stretching from New York to San Francisco, with its own leased telegraph wires to flash news rapidly over a 26,000-mile circuit.

"Yes," Jernigan confirmed. "AP and INS. Hearst's people were right there, on the scene."

Unlike the AP, which made a claim to serious news reporting, the International News Service founded by William Randolph Hearst a few years ago provided the lurid, sensational stories that so appealed to the masses. In his running battle with Joseph Pulitzer for increased circulation, Hearst had sent a small flotilla of INS reporters to Havana to cover the Cuban insurrection. Several of these gentlemen, Jernigan related, had been sipping rum and puffing cigars on the veranda of the Inglaterra Hotel in Havana when a massive explosion rocked the city.

"They sprinted to the harbor and hired a boat." Admiration for the reporters' enterprising spirit colored Jernigan's voice. "Came within yards of the twisted, burning wreckage."

Her heart in her throat, Victoria peered over her papa's shoulder to read their terse, gripping dispatches.

AP's F. J. Hilgert reported only that the United States battleship *Maine* was blown up in Havana harbor, but Harry Scoval of the *New York Journal* indicated that many aboard had been killed or injured. The reporter himself had helped pull several bodies from the water.

Victoria gulped. Like so many of the reporters in Cuba, Scoval had long had a reputation for becoming immersed in the news he reported, but this was direct involvement indeed.

She stood silent while her papa skimmed the dispatches a second time. His brows twitching wildly, Deitrich faced his staff.

"What do ve haf on the *Maine?*"

"I pulled some of the dispatches that were filed when she steamed into Havana." Shuffling through the papers stacked on his desk, Jernigan snatched one from the pile. "She's a man-of-war, commissioned in 1895 and—"

"*Ja, ja,* this I know! How many men vas she carrying vhen she dropped anchor in Havana?"

"Three hundred and fifty-four."

"*Mein Gott!*" Shaking his head, Deitrich put aside all personal feelings. "Ve vill lead with the explosion. Ed, you must glean vhat details you can from tonight's dispatches. Remember, ve don't know yet who or vhat sank the *Maine*."

The tone of the dispatches had left no doubt in Victoria's mind. It was the Spanish. It had to have been the Spanish. They'd long resented U.S. interference in Cuba. Had threatened repercussions over the money and arms shipped to the rebels by Americans. Had lodged a strong protest when a U.S. battleship steamed uninvited into Havana harbor.

When Ed Jernigan presented essentially those same arguments, however, Deitrich offered another view of the matter.

"Ve can't discount the possibility that it vas an accident. Or," he added after a moment, "that the Cuban rebels blew up the ship."

"No, I suppose we can't," the editor conceded. "The Cuban junta in Washington's been agitating for years for the United States to send more than just money and arms. They'd have to know an incident like this would propel us into war."

"There are powerful men in this country who might think so, too," Deitrich reminded him grimly.

Shocked, Victoria opened her mouth to protest. She clamped it shut again as she recalled the rumor that had floated around the news community some months ago. Supposedly, Frederick Remington, who'd been covering the Cuban insurrection for the *Journal*, had cabled Hearst that things were quiet and there would be no war. Rumor had it that the powerful publisher had wired back, instructing the artist to remain in Havana. Hearst would supply the war if Remington would supply the pictures.

Victoria had thought the story just a bit of juicy gossip at the time, but now... She swallowed another gulp as her father stated emphatically that they must let the facts speak for themselves.

"Ve vill not address who or vhat caused this tragedy until it is known. Thomas, I vant a sketch of the *Maine* for center page."

"Afloat or going down?"

"Going down. Banks, you and Dobbs vill describe the ship and her armaments. I myself vill remind our readers of the sequence of events leading up to this black, black night."

"What about me, Papa?"

He turned to his daughter, his lips pursed. "If it doesn't distress you too much, *liebchen*, you may write about the captain and his crew. Pull the information from previous dispatches and try to put real people to the names on the ship's roster. Do you think you can do this?"

"Yes."

"*Gut.*" Turning, he clapped a hand on Mr. Woodbury's stooped shoulder. "I hope your bones don't ache too badly tonight, my friend. Ve haf much to do."

* * *

The rest of the night passed in a whirl of frantic activity. Dispatches going as far back as two years were picked apart for details about the *Maine,* the ongoing war in Cuba and the United States's increasingly strained diplomatic relations with Spain. Stories were written, revised, edited. Ed Jernigan's red pencil flew, and Deitrich's brows waggled continuously as he clasped his hands behind his back and paced the floor like a man awaiting the birth of his first child. As soon as Ed approved each piece, it was rushed to Mr. Woodbury, hunched over the Linotype keys.

Around 4:30 a.m., the elderly compositor's aching back and arthritic hands began to protest. At five, Victoria donned a canvas duster and took his place at the noisy machine with its hissing steam cylinders, clanking rotary press and overhead loom feeding a continuous roll of paper. At seven-fifteen, the four-page special edition of the *Tribune* rolled off the press.

With her hands stained by ink and her hair tumbling around her shoulders, Victoria stood beside her papa to view the first sheets off the press. In three-inch letters, the banner headline screamed the tragic news.

**USS *Maine* Sunk In Havana Harbor
Many Aboard Feared Lost**

"Gut!" Deitrich declared. *"Sehr gut!* Get them bundled and put out as soon as the ink dries. Our readers vill snatch them up!"

When the first copies of the *Tribune* hit the street an hour later, Cheyenne was already abuzz with wild rumors. Citizens anxious for news had lined up outside the *Tribune*'s offices, as well as those of the *Sun* and the *Eagle*. Bundled against the cold, they waited impatiently for the first editions while a bright sun slowly melted the previous night's snow to slush and the carriage horses on busy Carey Avenue threw up clumps of mud.

Victoria dragged off the stained duster just after 9:00 a.m. She was exhilarated by their success in putting the special edition on the street, yet sobered and saddened by the news it conveyed. To clear their heads of ink fumes, she and her papa elected to walk the few blocks to their home on East Seventeenth Street. They made an odd sight, she was sure, with him in his top hat and beaver-trimmed overcoat and her in the boots and the warm cloak she'd hurriedly pulled on last night over the sapphire ball gown.

As they threaded through the crowds milling about on the crowded streets, it seemed as if every one of Cheyenne's ninety thousand citizens had congregated to discuss the sinking of the *Maine*. It also became very clear that they didn't share Deitrich Parker's wait-and-see attitude concerning the perpetrator of the vile act.

"We'll have at those dastardly Spanish now!" a bewhiskered dry goods merchant declared to the group gathered outside his mercantile. "Our boys will make every last dago in Cuba pay for this outrage."

"You can count me as one of them boys," announced a bleary-eyed wrangler who'd obviously spent the previous night in one of Cheyenne's twenty-two thriving saloons. "I'm heading down to the armory this morning to volunteer."

"I'm for the navy," a burly railroad worker proclaimed. "I can shovel coal into a boiler with the best of 'em. Them pointy-bearded Spaniards mighta sunk one of our ships, but I'm aguessin' we'll soon send ten more steamin' right into Havana harbor."

Their patriotism won unanimous approval from the rest of the crowd.

"That's the spirit, boys!"

"We'll show 'em, by jingo!"

Edging around the crowd, Victoria hooked her arm in her papa's. "Not everyone shares your sense of caution before ascribing blame," she observed.

"The country is ripe for var. People *vant* to believe the Spanish committed this terrible act."

"It certainly seems so. I shouldn't have thought that— Oh!"

With a thump, she collided with an overcoated

figure just turning the corner. His strong hands caught her before she went off the board sidewalk and into dirty slush.

"I do beg your pardon, Victoria."

One look into Sam's face instantly erased the long hours at the *Tribune*'s offices. With a rush of heat, those stolen moments in the sewing room filled her thoughts. Her belly tightened, and it was all she could do to keep a most ridiculous breathlessness from her voice.

"What are you doing back in town so early?" she asked. "I was sure Elise told me you planned to stay the night out at the ranch."

"I brought Mary in to catch her train. I left her at the depot while I came in search of a newspaper."

The sparkle of the sun on snow dimmed a bit.

"Yes, of course. Mrs. Prendergast did mention that she intended to continue her journey this morning."

"*Auch du lieber!*" Her papa slapped his forehead under the tip-tilted top hat. "I forget she leaves so soon. I vanted to hear more about her trip to consult with Dr. McGee."

"You still have time," Sam advised. "The train isn't due in for a good half an hour yet."

"*Gut!* Come, Victoria, let me escort you home so I may hurry down to the station."

"Go ahead, Papa. I can walk two blocks on my own."

"And haf your mama skin me whole! No, no, a young lady doesn't valk the streets unaccompanied."

"But that same young lady can stay at the newspaper offices all night to help her papa put out a special edition," his daughter teased.

"*Ja,* and I shall hear about that from your mama, too."

Sam ended the argument by tucking Victoria's arm in his. "I'll escort her home."

"Thank you, Samuel!"

Feeling rather like a sack of potatoes tossed from one porter to another, Victoria barely restrained a huff as her papa hurried back the way he'd come.

"My parents sometimes forget that we *are* on the brink of a new century. I apologize for taking you out of your way."

"As you said, it's only a few blocks. And it gives me a chance to talk to you about what happened last night."

The warmth that had coursed through Victoria moments ago was nothing compared to the fiery heat that suffused her now. Not for the world would she admit that the last thing she wanted was to *talk* about last night. What she wanted, rather desperately, was to repeat it.

Her pulse skipped erratically as Sam steered her

around another clump of excited citizens and across Central Avenue, where modest clapboard houses gave way to the more elaborate brick and stone homes of Cheyenne's wealthy bankers and businessmen. The fanciful, turreted Nagle mansion loomed directly ahead when Sam slowed their pace and turned her to face him.

"I want to apologize, Victoria."

"Apologize?"

"You were a guest in my sister's home last night. I shouldn't have abused her hospitality by trifling with you the way I did."

Victoria would hardly classify that shattering kiss as a mere trifle. That Sam viewed it as such stung. Rather badly.

"As best I recall," she returned, "it was *I* who kissed *you*. Perhaps I'm the one who should apologize."

"Perhaps you should," he agreed with a quick grin that almost—almost!—disarmed her. "As I said, you took me by surprise last night. That's no excuse, however. I'm sorry. I assure you it won't happen again."

That wasn't at all what she'd hoped to hear him say. The fool! The blind, chug-headed fool! Wondering how much this apology had to do with the woman waiting for him down at the railroad station, she tossed her head.

"You can't *imagine* how very much you've reassured me, Mr. Garrett. Now, if you don't mind, it's been a rather long night. I should like to get home, have a hot breakfast and tumble into bed.''

Sam wasn't prepared for the jolt that went through him when Victoria spun on her heel and flounced down the walk. The thought, the mere thought, of this nubile young female tumbling warm and tousled into bed raised the kind of erotic images a grown man had no business entertaining about a gently reared girl.

Woman.

Girl!

The fact that he couldn't decide exactly how to categorize Victoria Parker after last night irritated the hell out of him, along with just about everything else this morning. He'd woken up feeling as friendly as a bear with a sore tooth, a feeling that only intensified during the drive in from his sister's place.

The plain truth was that he didn't like the prospect of Mary leaving Cheyenne so soon after her arrival, any more than he liked the thought of her going off to Washington. And he was still trying to accept the fact that she hadn't yet laid her husband's memory to rest. She'd made that plain last night. Sam had had to bite his tongue to keep from saying things she wasn't ready to hear.

Adding to his edginess this morning was this

business about the *Maine*. War was coming. Sam could feel it in his bones. The regulars from Fort Russell would assemble and ride off, leaving only a skeleton force to man the post. Boys like Lieutenant Duggan and that wet-behind-the-ears shavetail friend of his would answer the call to arms.

As would the eager volunteers who thronged Cheyenne's streets this morning. A long line had already formed down to the armory. The ranks of the First Wyoming Volunteer Infantry would swell to overflowing by this afternoon. And every wrangler, buffalo hunter and tracker worth his salt would rush to sign up for the cowboy cavalry regiment Wyoming's own Senator Warren was urging Congress to authorize.

After eight years in uniform, Sam had a damned good idea of the incredible challenges the army would face in the days and weeks ahead. Mobilizing a peacetime military establishment filled to bursting with ranks of untrained volunteers would severely test the leadership abilities of every officer and noncom. And despite his eight years in uniform, Sam wouldn't be one of those officers. With all his training, all his experience, he'd sit on the sidelines and watch his friends and neighbors ride off to war.

If he didn't love his father so much...

If his mother hadn't been so devastated by her husband's accident...

If Sam didn't know deep in his heart that he could serve the war effort as well by helping his brother-in-law supply the horses and equipment the army would so desperately need for its rapidly expanding cavalry regiments…

Blowing out a long breath, he followed Victoria the few steps to her parents' stone-and-stucco mansion, bid her a curt good day and left to rejoin Mary at the train depot.

4

For Victoria, the next weeks were a whirlwind of dramatic events and ever more sensational headlines.

The sketchy initial reports from Havana soon gave way to an avalanche of longer, far more detailed dispatches. Captain Sigsbee, commander of the *Maine* and one of its few survivors, could not offer any definitive explanation for the explosion that sank his ship. Theories abounded, ascribing the destruction to everything from Spanish torpedoes, to one of the old mines that littered the bottom of Havana harbor, to spontaneous combustion in the *Maine*'s coal bunker, causing a fire that spread to the magazine.

A few of the more dignified papers like the *New York Times* adopted the same deliberate attitude Victoria's papa had. Like the *Tribune*, these papers cautiously withheld judgment until the navy concluded its hastily launched official inquiry into the tragic event. The more sensational papers like William Randolph Hearst's *Journal* and Joseph Pulitzer's *World*, however, enflamed the passions of their readers by trumpeting their own conclusions with banner headlines. As early as February 17, a mere two days after the explosion, Hearst's *Evening Journal* screamed:

War? Sure!

A small army of American reporters rushed aboard ships to augment those already in Cuba. Once on the island, they scrambled for any and every story. Gruesome, on-the-spot reports of the charred bodies fished from the harbor were followed by detailed coverage of the solemn honors and burial the city of Havana accorded the dead American sailors. Several newspapermen even hired their own divers to swim down into the murky depths of the harbor alongside those of the Spanish and American navies attempting to determine the cause of the explosion.

A number of more daring reporters slipped past Spanish patrols to make direct contact with the rebels, who stepped up their deadly attacks with a new infusion of arms and supplies shipped to Cuba by outraged Americans. The armaments were paid for by Congress, which, acting on its own initiative, authorized a fifty-million-dollar war chest.

Victoria spent more and more hours at the *Tribune,* helping decipher the torrent of dispatches that flowed over the wires, composing stories and relieving poor Mr. Woodbury on the Linotype machine. She wasn't too busy to attend the fancy dress ball held at the Cattleman's Club on the first of March, however, and dance half the night away in the arms of her many admirers—whose numbers did not include Sam.

She hadn't seen him since their chance encounter in the street, wasn't sure what she would have said to him if she had. As Elise confided that night at the ball, her uncle had also been kept busy since his parents' return from Denver with disappointing news.

"The surgeon in Denver suggested Grandfather must resign himself to spending the rest of his days in a wheeled chair."

"Oh, Elise!"

Victoria couldn't help but remember General Garrett before his horse went down and rolled on him, crushing his spine. He was as tall as his son, but leaner, and every bit the commander despite the fact he'd been retired from active service for some years.

"How tragic," she murmured.

"It is, indeed," her friend said glumly. "He says

doctors don't know everything, but it hurts to think he may never walk or ride again.''

"Surely there's still hope?"

"I suppose so. Grandfather insists on keeping a pair of crutches near to hand, but every time he's tried to use them so far he's fallen on his face."

"Oh, dear."

"Grandmama keeps reminding us that he took a ball through the hip during the War Between the States, and had the same hip shattered by rifle butts while he was a prisoner in Andersonville. He recovered from those injuries. She's confident he'll recover from this one, as well."

"But if he doesn't?"

The tall, willowy brunette sighed. "If he doesn't, Grandmama says it doesn't matter one whit. He's the same man he always was. And Sam says—"

Irritated by the way her pulse fluttered, Victoria arched a brow. "Yes? What does your uncle say?"

"He says the same," Elise replied with a curious glance at her friend. "What happened between you two the night of my birthday, anyway? You can hardly say his name since without screwing up your face as if you've just bitten into a sour pickle."

"Nothing happened."

Nothing of any significance, anyway. At least according to Sam. Victoria hadn't been able to wipe the memory of his kiss from her mind, yet *he* had shrugged it off as a mere trifle. Annoyed all over again, she turned the subject.

"Are you coming into town on Friday to see the kinetoscope?"

"I wouldn't miss it!"

"Good. Let's go together, shall we?"

Friday dawned bright and sunny, hinting at the spring that had yet to take a firm grip on the plains. Most of the snow had melted and only a few dirty piles of slush leaned up against walls in shady corners.

Elise drove into town with her younger brother and left the carriage at Victoria's house. The three then walked downtown and joined the long line already formed in front of the Cheyenne Light Opera and Vaudeville House. Everyone within a hundred miles, it appeared, was eager to see the sensational kinetoscope entitled *Remember the* Maine!

Rushed into production by an enterprising master of the new art of moving pictures and being shown at the major cities along the transcontinental rail line, the stirring drama contained no actual footage of the *Maine*. Instead, it used images of an older battleship scuttled by the U.S. Navy during artillery practice. But the film was so cleverly pieced together that audiences hissed and booed at every flickering image of Spaniards, shed copious tears when the unidentified ship went down and shouted

"Huzzah!" at a finale showing grimly determined American soldiers marching off, presumably to Cuba.

"Golly!" Elise's younger brother Matt declared as they exited the theater. "I wish President McKinley would stop dithering and declare war!"

"Why?" his sister teased. "Do you think Mama's going to let you shoulder your rifle and march off with the men?"

Offended, he puffed out his chest. "Why shouldn't she? I'll turn fourteen in a few months. And I'll wager I can shoot a damned sight better than that fuzz-faced lieutenant from Fort Russell you're so sweet on."

Just in time, he dodged a sisterly slap.

"Let Mama catch you saying 'damned' and you'll feel the butter paddle on your backside, fourteen or not."

"Sam says it," the would-be warrior offered in his defense. "A lot! Mostly when he thinks no one's around, but I've heard him plenty of times just in the past weeks. He's grouchier than a stuck hog these days."

"That's true," Elise agreed with a sidelong glance at Victoria. "I wonder why?"

"Papa says it's because he can't go off to war, either," Matt confided.

"Or perhaps it's because he's sweet on someone

and can't bring himself to admit it," his sister suggested slyly.

If he was, Victoria thought, his secret love had dark eyes and hair the color of night.

And yet...

The memory of those moments in the sewing room rushed back. Despite his apology, Sam couldn't have kissed her the way he had if another woman claimed his heart. Victoria was woman enough to sense his interest in both her and Mary Prendergast, and feminine enough to be peeved by it.

She hadn't quite recovered from her pique when she and her parents turned out with the rest of Cheyenne for a change-of-command parade at Fort Russell some weeks later. The lieutenant general commanding the army of the West would officiate. Wyoming's Senator Francis E. Warren, who had himself earned a Medal of Honor during the War Between the States, would grace the reviewing stand, as would Brigadier General Andrew Garrett, the legendary horse solider who'd commanded the fort until his retirement some years ago.

Victoria couldn't help but feel a thrill as she and her parents were escorted to the viewing stand constructed for the grand occasion. The officers and enlisted personnel of Fort Russell had outdone themselves. Bunting draped every building, flags flew and the silver-and-brass accoutrements of even the lowest-ranking troopers gleamed from hours of energetic polishing.

Miraculously, the unpredictable Wyoming weather cooperated. After the bitter February cold, March was proving exceptionally mild. A brisk breeze fluttered the horsetails adorning the soldiers' Prussian-style spiked dress helmets, but the first tender shoots of green peeked through the saw grass covering the vast, open plains beyond the fort.

With the sun beaming brightly, the ladies had felt confident enough to throw off their dark winter coats and don cheerful spring colors. Victoria felt quite smart in a new walking suit of leaf-green broadcloth, lavishly trimmed with red braid. A rolled parasol, tan kid gloves and a modish hat anchored securely with a lethal, six-inch hatpin completed the ensemble.

The Garretts had already arrived when Victoria and her parents joined the guests on the viewing platform. She thought the general looked quite resplendent in his dress uniform, his chest almost obscured by row upon row of brightly colored medals. That he was forced to remain seated when everyone else stood milling about in no way detracted from his commanding air. His wife was beside him, her blue-black hair wreathed in a crown of braids and showing only the faintest traces of silver.

While her parents chatted with Sam's mother, Victoria paid her respects to his father.

"How good it is to see you, sir."

"You, too, Victoria. May I say you look quite ravishing in that particular shade of green?"

"You may indeed." She hesitated, loath to bring attention to his disability but quite sincere in her sentiments. "And may I say I was sorry to learn you didn't receive more encouraging news from the surgeon in Denver?"

"You may," he replied evenly, before his mouth quirked in a crooked grin that reminded Victoria so much of his son that her breath snagged in her chest. "I'm not quite ready to accept his opinion, however. I'm afraid I can be rather bullheaded at times…as Julia quite often informs me."

Catching her name, his wife threw him an amused glance. The years might have added fine lines to her face, but the legendary belle of New Orleans still turned heads whenever she entered a room.

"Whatever it is I supposedly inform you of so often," she said, "you know very well that you hear me only when you wish to."

The teasing smile that passed between the general and his wife started a little ache just under Victoria's ribs. Her own parents had a comfortable marriage, but she'd never seen them display anything close to the love shining in Julia Garrett's violet eyes.

That's what she wanted, she thought with a pang. A love more enduring than time. A passion that knew no physical bounds.

Her gaze strayed to the man lifting his youngest nephew to see above the bunting-draped rail. Pursing her lips, she studied his strong, handsome profile. Unlike his father, Sam wore civilian attire. Victoria thought his elegantly cut suit, high-necked shirt points and black bowler looked completely dashing, if a bit drab, compared to the colorful uniforms of his one-time comrades in arms.

The yearning she'd felt for so long edged everything else out and she let herself look her fill before she made her way across the reviewing stand. His jaw was taut, she noted, his eyes narrowed as he watched the regimental sergeant majors inspecting their troops.

"Do you miss all this pomp and pageantry?" she asked.

In the blink of an eye, his expression relaxed. Lifting his nephew down from the rail, he gave Victoria a cheerful grin.

"No, not at all. Marching about with a tin bucket on your head, a horsetail tickling your neck and your collar buttoned so tight around your neck you can't breathe isn't something any man would miss."

"Truly, Sam?"

"Truly. Come, we'd better take our seats. The parade's about to begin."

Victoria found the way he dismissed her questions so lightly rather annoying, but the hand he slipped under her elbow effectively ended their conversation. Hiding a frown, she allowed him to escort her to her chair.

Suddenly the piercing notes of a bugle soared through the air. With a rattle of sabers, three hundred men snapped to attention.

The bugle sounded again, and the infantry marched smartly to the edge of the parade ground. With saddles creaking and bridles jingling, elements of the Ninth and Tenth Cavalry followed. Dubbed Buffalo Soldiers by the Plains Indians, who considered them among the bravest and fiercest of their foes, the all-black cavalry units had been headquartered at Fort Russell for some years.

The colorful spectacle that commenced enthralled Victoria. She, like the rest of the viewers, was soon swept along on a wave of rousing martial music and patriotic pride.

Victoria wasn't the only one with a too-keen eye, Sam discovered when he wheeled his father into the back parlor of the Garretts' imposing, two-story town house after dinner that same evening.

When his parents had commissioned construction

of the house, his mother had purposely set the back parlor aside as a smoking room and furnished it accordingly. Humpbacked sofas upholstered in maroon velvet invited a man to sprawl at his ease. Handy humidors kept cigars moist and ready. Potted palms added a touch of greenery to the maroon wall coverings, and the sturdy marble-topped table in the center of the room was the perfect size for the general's Tuesday night poker club.

In these comfortable surroundings, father and son indulged their nightly ritual of a good Cuban cigar, which inevitably raised the subject of war. With a cloud of fragrant smoke wreathing the air, the general asked much the same question Victoria had earlier that afternoon.

"Have you had second thoughts about resigning your commission, son?"

Sam might have been able to brush aside Victoria's questions, but he could never hide the truth from his father.

"A few," he answered with complete honesty. "And those only in recent weeks."

The general nodded. "It goes hard against a soldier's grain to sit idle while his country gears up for war."

Ashamed, Sam put a tight rein on his own feelings. The frustration building within him couldn't begin to match that of his father's. If and when Congress declared war, the army would have to recall a good number of senior officers to command the expanded ranks. Rumors were already circulating that Secretary of War Alger would bring back Major General Wheeler, the fire-eating former Confederate cavalry officer whose exploits during the War Between the States had earned him the nickname Fightin' Joe. Even General Shafter, who weighed more than three hundred pounds and had to be hoisted into the saddle, had petitioned for a command. Yet Andrew Garrett, a much-decorated cavalry officer who'd proved himself time and again in the field, would never again lead troops into battle.

"Neither one of us will be idle if—when war comes," Sam reminded him with a forced grin. "Jack's already set his hands to building more corrals for the horses he wants me to help train to army standards. And Colonel Dawson has asked for your assistance in sorting through all the men who want to fill the vacancies in the Eighth Volunteer Infantry."

"Harrumph!" The general couldn't quite conceal his grimace. "Volunteers."

Sam's grin widened. "You'd better watch out," he warned, only half joking. "Senator Warren may also ask you to help train the volunteer cavalry regiment he's trying to push through Congress."

"No, he intends to ask you."

"Me?"

"Warren spoke to me about it this afternoon, after the parade. He very much wants you to accept command of one of the companies."

Carefully, Sam flicked a half-inch ash into the spittoon placed beside the sofa. "He'll have plenty of other eager volunteers to pick from."

"He wants you."

"I'll help train the recruits in any way I can, but I won't accept command."

"Because you promised your mother you'd stay home and take up the slack in the reins I can no longer handle? Or because of Victoria Parker?"

"Victoria? What the devil does she have to do with anything?"

"Your mother, your sister and your niece seem to think she has quite a bit to do with it," his father drawled. "Or at least with your present distracted frame of mind. In fact, they all feel you haven't been quite yourself since the night of Elise's birthday party, when, your niece claims, you spent some time alone with Victoria in the sewing room."

"The little brat! Has she spread that about?"

"Only among the family." His father's gaze was thoughtful above the glowing tip of his stogie. "I know no son of mine would ever play fast and loose with any woman, much less a girl like Victoria."

"No, of course I wouldn't. And she's not a girl. As the minx informed me rather pointedly, she's a woman grown."

"That sounds like Victoria." A smile tugged at his father's mouth. "What was your response to that pronouncement, if I may inquire?"

"I kissed her."

Actually, Victoria had kissed *him,* but Sam's gentlemanly instincts ran too deep to reveal that, even to his father.

"I watched her at the parade this afternoon," the general commented. "The girl's— Excuse me, the woman is in love with you."

"What?"

Startled, Sam almost let his cigar slip through slackened fingers. Through the haze of cigar smoke, the general's eyes held his.

"That kiss you gave her may not have been more than a pleasant interlude for you, son, but apparently it meant more to Victoria."

Sam shifted uneasily in his chair. He didn't need his father to tell him that. He'd felt guilty as all hell when he'd looked down into her dazed face. Her emotions had been right there for any fool to see, readily apparent in her flushed cheeks and wide, confused eyes.

"It was more than a pleasant interlude," he admitted. "She stirred a few emotions in me, too, the kind a gentleman doesn't admit to. Which is why I've been careful around her these past weeks. I wouldn't want to hurt her."

Or raise false expectations. Granted, that kiss had

kicked him square in the midsection, but it was just a kiss.

"Victoria's a good sort," he added with a shrug. "She'll be the making of some lucky man one of these days."

"You know, I've been thinking the same thing." The general's gaze lingered on his son's face for a moment before drifting to a corner of the room. "Fetch those crutches for me, will you? I think I'll give them another try."

The sound of a crash brought Julia Garrett hurrying into the back parlor a few moments later. Clucking her tongue, she helped her son lift his grim-faced father from the floor, then calmly righted the table and lamp that had gone over in his fall.

5

Sam made a conscious effort to avoid Victoria in the days that followed. He also tried to ignore the way his chest tightened each time he remembered how she'd all but melted in his arms.

It helped that overseeing his parents' various financial interests kept him occupied enough for two men. With war now all but inevitable, the military faced an exploding demand for lumber for tent poles and wagons. Urgent orders rolled in by wire from Washington and from the quartermaster at Fort Russell. Sam made several trips to the logging camp on the slopes of the distant Rockies to consult with Garrett Enterprises's head logger on the virgin timber stands to be harvested.

Between these trips, he managed the commercial properties in Cheyenne that Julia and Andrew Garrett had shrewdly invested in during the general's years in service. Whenever possible, he rode out to help Jack Sloan and the Double-S hands with the bone-jarring task of breaking the half-wild horses they brought in from the ranges.

Elise caught him right before he climbed into the saddle after one of those long, grueling days and, all unknowingly, sabotaged his determined efforts to put her friend out of his mind.

"Oh, Sam! I almost forgot. Victoria rang me up last night."

She swiped her forearm across her forehead, leaving behind a smear of sweat and dirt. Like her father, brothers and uncle, Elise had spent hour after hour at the corrals these past days. She was rather smug about the fact that she could break a horse to saddle in half the time it took most of the Double-S hands.

"Victoria found a pattern for a tea gown she thinks would particularly suit me," she explained. "Would you pick it up and bring it out with you tomorrow?"

"A new tea gown, is it?" Sam tweaked her nose. "You never seemed to care about such matters before that young lieutenant began to come calling."

"Yes, well, a girl does like to wear something other than smelly chaps once in a while." She shot him a mischievous look. "Even a girl who can ride circles around her uncle."

Unaware that something as innocuous as a gown

pattern would completely and irrevocably change his life, Sam laughed and agreed to execute the errand.

He attended to it the next afternoon, after a morning spent poring over the books with the Garrett Enterprises accountant and lunch at home with his parents.

Changing into boots, a pair of Levi Strauss pants, a sturdy blue work shirt with a button-over flap and the leather vest that protected his back whenever he parted company with the mustangs he was helping to break, he sent word to the stables to have his horse saddled. While that was being done, he made the short walk to the Parker mansion.

"I'm so sorry, Sam," Rose Parker said when he explained the reason for his visit. "Victoria's down at the *Tribune* office and I have no idea which gown pattern she intended for Elise."

With a little cluck of disapproval, she shook her head.

"I suspect the dratted girl has forgotten that she, too, has an appointment this afternoon with the seamstress. I tried to ring the office but the operator can never get me through these days. Their line is always busy."

She turned a hopeful eye on Sam. Graciously, he took the hint. "Shall I deliver the message for you?"

"Yes, please! Or better yet, deliver my daughter

to Miss Henry's shop at one o'clock sharp. Tell her I'll meet her there.''

"Yes, ma'am.''

The moment Sam opened the front door to the *Tribune*'s offices, the clack and clatter of the presses in the back room assaulted his ears. The stench of printer's ink was worse than the din. It permeated the air, so thick and heavy he felt as though he were breathing in a dark cloud. Hiding a grimace, Sam stepped inside.

None of the folks scurrying about the offices seemed to notice either the stink or the noise. A young man with a pencil stuck behind each ear stepped up to the counter.

"If you're looking for a copy of yesterday's paper, we're all sold out.''

"No, I'm looking for Miss Parker.''

"She's in her office.''

He jerked a thumb toward a series of cubbyholes partitioned off with frosted glass. Sam caught the gleam of Victoria's red-gold hair through one opaque pane. More than a bit surprised to learn she had an office of her own, he pushed through the swinging gate in the counter.

"She's very busy,'' the young man warned. "Her father wants her to finish a piece for this evening's run.''

Sam didn't bother to advise him that Miss Parker's mother had different intentions regarding her daughter. He figured Victoria could sort through her obligations on her own.

The noise of the presses masked his footsteps. Since she was bent over, writing furiously, Sam leaned a shoulder against the cubicle entrance, crossed his arms and waited patiently for her to finish her lines.

She looked different in this setting, he thought. Less like Elise's charming minx of a friend. More like a telephone operator or a bank teller or any one of the many women moving into the business world these days. A pencil pierced the little knot of hair atop her head, and she'd used black garters to secure the pushed-up sleeves of her high-necked white blouse. She had a blue-black smudge on her cheek, he noted with interest.

Suddenly, her forehead creased. Muttering a phrase he'd never expected to hear from her, she scratched over the words she'd just written. Her pencil slipped between her lips. Nibbling on the nub, she glanced up.

"Sam!" Hastily, she removed the pencil from her mouth. "Whatever are you doing here?"

"Elise charged me with an errand. I'm to pick up a pattern for a tea gown that you promised her."

"Oh!"

Sternly, Victoria repressed the ridiculous warmth that had invaded her limbs when she'd looked up and spotted him. Of course, he hadn't come to see her. She wasn't stupid. He'd done everything but cross the street to avoid her recently.

"The gown pattern is at home."

"I guessed as much, but when I stopped by your house, your mother charged me with another task. I'm to remove you from the *Tribune* immediately and escort you to Miss Henry's. Evidently, you've an appointment to be fitted for a new carriage dress."

"Oh, dear! I forgot all about that!"

A grin tipped his mouth. "So your mother suspected."

Victoria's pulse skipped. Instantly, she administered another stern rebuke. She *must* stop fizzing like a phosphate soda at the mere glimpse of Sam's smile!

"Thank you for the offer of escort, but I'm afraid I can't leave right at this moment. We've just received a wire from Washington." Excitement crept into her voice. "The Navy Board of Inquiry investigating the *Maine*'s sinking has just released its findings."

Sam straightened abruptly. "What were they, or can you say?"

"Yes, of course. The board concluded from the twisted angle of the metal that the explosion came from outside rather than inside the ship."

"Did they indicate what caused the explosion?"

"A mine, apparently, although they couldn't determine who set it or when. And to muddy the waters more, the Spanish ambassador this morning delivered the report of *their* official inquiry, which states the loss was due to an internal accident."

"Somehow I suspect no one will put much weight in their findings."

"If you read the Eastern presses, there's little doubt who set the mine. In fact, William Hearst's *Journal* has just published a sensational story in which the reporter claims to have overheard two Spanish officers bragging about how they were going to blow up the *Maine*."

"Why the devil did this reporter wait so long to come forward?"

"Evidently he was apprehended as a spy for the rebels and tossed into prison. Mr. Hearst only just secured his release."

"Rather propitious timing on Hearst's part," Sam drawled. "The navy board can't identify the culprit, but he can. I imagine he'll sell any number of papers with that story."

The same thought had occurred to Victoria, but she shrugged it aside to share the hottest bit of news.

"President McKinley is preparing a formal demand that Spain grant Cuba its independence and withdraw from the 'American' hemisphere," she confided. "Speculation is that he'll ask our minister to the Court of Madrid to deliver the ultimatum as early as tomorrow.''

Sam's mouth settled into a grim line. ''There's little likelihood they'll withdraw now after all the blood they've spilled trying to subdue the rebels.''

''I'm afraid you're right. Really, this is quite the most thrilling time! I can't remember when I've kept so busy.'' Scrunching her nose, she essayed a wry smile. ''I must say I much prefer writing about momentous happenings like these than church socials and Fourth of July picnics.''

''Yes, I can see you do.''

''Which is why I can't leave right at this very moment. Papa and Mr. Jernigan, our editor, are down at the freight depot, trying to locate a lost shipment of paper. They left me to pull all these bits of information together. You do understand, don't you?''

He gave her another grin. ''*I* do, but I can't say whether your mother will.''

Victoria hesitated. Despite the conflicting emotions Sam roused in her, the way his smile cut across his handsome face caused the most ridiculous flutter in her stomach.

''I'm almost finished with the piece,'' she said, giving in to the traitorous need that curled in her belly. ''It shouldn't take me more than another ten or fifteen minutes. Would you mind waiting?''

Faced with such a charming and direct request, Sam could hardly refuse.

"Not at all. I'll sit in the outer office."

By forcing a fierce concentration, Victoria fashioned all the fascinating bits of information into what she hoped was a coherent whole. Dashing into Ed Jernigan's office, she placed the scribbled sheets square in the center of his desk where he would see them the moment he returned.

That done, she hurried back to her own. A quick scrub with her handkerchief cleaned most of the ink from her hands. Impatiently, she rolled down the sleeves of her high-necked white blouse, tucked it more neatly inside the leather belt that cinched her waist and slapped on her wide-brimmed hat. Shrugging into her coat, she pushed through the swinging gate into the reception area.

When she spotted Sam, her pulse took another foolish skip. Really, no man should look so dashing in scuffed boots, plain denim and a worn leather vest! Unfolding his long frame, he settled a much-creased gray felt hat on his forehead and opened the door for her. Victoria tucked her hand in his arm and stepped outside.

Bright spring sunshine instantly enveloped them, along with the hustle and bustle of the streets. Always jammed with railroad workers, wranglers bringing cattle to the stockyards and miners down from the mountains, the city now brimmed with hundreds of young stalwarts who'd poured into town to volunteer for military service. Since the sinking of the *Maine,* patriotic fervor had reached an almost hysterical pitch.

Victoria had no idea that such patriotism possessed an ugly underbelly until she and Sam were mere steps from the Frontier Hotel. Suddenly, its front doors burst open. The raucous notes of "There'll Be a Hot Time in the Old Town Tonight" spilled out along with the cowboy who came hurtling through. He landed on his face in the street, not ten yards away. A jeering crowd followed him.

"We'll be having no lily-livered coward drinking alongside of us," a heavily muscled railroad worker declared in a thick brogue.

Judging from the soot that rimmed his eyes and dusted his shock of carroty-red hair, Victoria guessed he was one of the coalers who refueled the engines. He was also, she noted, as big as he was grimy.

Sauntering to the edge of the board walkway, the Irishman planted fists the size of coal buckets on his hips. "I'm thinking you'd best be takin' yerself back to yer bunkhouse, boyo."

The object of his scorn scrambled to his feet and bunched his fists. "Jest 'cause I can't see no sense in takin' a bullet fer a bunch of Cubans don't mean I'm a coward."

"The hell it don't!" came a shout from the rear of the crowd.

"If you were any kind of a man at all," the coaler sneered, "you'd be marching down to the armory to jine up like the rest of us."

"Bein' stupid don't make you a man," the angry wrangler shot back.

"Let's send him back to his bunkhouse wearing a few feathers," another agitator suggested. "Like the chickenhearted coward that he is."

"I saw a bucket of tar out back," someone volunteered. "I'll get it."

"Well, now! That sounds like a foine idea t'me." Grinning, the Irishman surged forward. "Grab him, boys, and we'll keep holt of him until they get a fire goin' under that tar. Sean, my man, go upstairs 'n' fetch a couple of goose-down pillows."

Hooting and hollering, the rowdies surged forward. Their intended victim gamely stood his ground until the sheer volume of his opponents took him down with arms and legs flailing.

By this time, the ruckus had attracted a considerable throng of bystanders. Pedestrians jammed the board walkway. Traffic stopped as carriages and riders formed a loose ring in the street. Pressed against the hotel's brick facade, Victoria could see only the crowns of their hats. Some were neat beaver top hats, while turkey feathers and rattlesnake skins adorned others.

Of all the watchers among this motley crowd, Sam was the only one to intervene. "I'd better break this up before it turns ugly," he muttered.

To Victoria's inexperienced eyes, the situation had already reached the ugly point.

"Be careful!"

Despite her anxious warning, Sam didn't demonstrate any apparent concern for his personal safety as he waded into the fray.

"All right, boys. You've had your fun. Let him up."

A few of the agitators fell back, but a good number remained piled on the hapless wrangler.

"Let him up, I said. Now!"

The whiplike command snapped heads around and peeled away several more combatants, until only the most belligerent remained. Leaving three of his friends to keep the cowboy pinned to the dirt, the redheaded railroader disengaged and swaggered up to Sam.

"And who might you be, to be throwing orders at us like that?"

From where she stood, Victoria couldn't tell if the man was drunk or just plain bellicose. He sounded both.

"The name's Garrett. Sam Garrett."

The reply raised a buzz of whispers that came to her in snatches.

"...General Garrett's boy."

"...sister's married to Black Jack Sloan, the meanest gunslinger this side of the Mississippi."

"Used to be a horse soldier hisself, but..."

Evidently the pugnacious coaler had heard a few of the same snippets as the whisperers. His lip curling, he swept Sam with a scornful glance.

"So it's Captain Sam Garrett, is it? I've heard tell about you."

Hooking his thumbs in his belt, he rocked back on his heels.

"Word down at the armory is that you got shed of your uniform jest when it was lookin' like you might have to fight 'n' get it all dirty."

There was a hiss of indrawn breath among the watchers, then utter silence. In the staggering quiet, rage sliced into Victoria. How dare the man utter such drivel! About Sam, of all people. He *had* to be drunk. Or insane.

"Maybe you're the one we should be treating to a coat of tar 'n' feathers," the brawny coaler suggested with a sneer.

"You're welcome to try."

Sam's exaggerated drawl raised a tide of red in the Irishman's cheeks.

"Well, now, I'm thinking perhaps I will!"

With no more warning than that, he launched his attack. The men who had just staggered away from the fray took that as a signal to leap back in. Total chaos erupted as one combatant after another rejoined the fight. Within mere seconds, the street was once again filled with a seething, punching, grunting mass.

Horrified, Victoria shoved her way through the onlookers. Her ears rang from their shouts of encouragement, and one overly exuberant spectator almost knocked off her hat when he thrust up his fist along with the fighters. Hanging on to her hat with one hand, she gained the edge of the walkway and searched desperately for a glimpse of Sam in the tangle of arms and flying fists. She found him finally half buried under a pile of burly railroaders. Blood poured from a gash on his cheek. One eye was already purpling.

Distraught, she turned to the two men on horseback just beside her. They were buffalo hunters, she guessed from their buckskins and the long-shanked skinning knifes strapped to their thighs. Looping their wrists over their saddle horns, they watched the fight with every evidence of enjoyment.

"Surely you don't intend to just sit there," she implored. "Don't you see those two men need help?"

"Ain't our fight, ma'am," the elder of the two replied. "'Sides," he added with a shrug, "I don't hold much sympathy for shirkers, either. Them two deserve whatever they get."

Infuriated all over again at hearing Sam described as a shirker, Victoria snapped her jaw shut. A single step brought her close enough to snatch the man's rifle from its fringed buckskin scabbard.

"Here now!"

Startled, the buffalo hunter jerked on his mount's reins. The gelding reacted to the vicious pull of the bit and danced sideways, ramming into the withers of the horse next to him. Before the two hunters could recover, Victoria had the heavy rifle up and to her shoulder.

She'd only fired a breech-loading Sharp once before, when she'd badgered her papa into taking her along on a deer hunting excursion. She'd hit the white-tailed doe he'd helped her aim at, but the sight of the animal going down, then struggling back up on her forelegs and dragging her haunches for yards before she collapsed, had instantly rid Victoria of all desire to join the ranks of skilled hunters.

She knew which end of a rifle meant business, however.

"Stop!" she shouted, her arms quivering under the gun's weight. "Stop this at once!"

None of the brawlers paid her the least attention. She doubted they could hear her over the shouts and grunts and nauseating crunch of bone against bone. Taking a deep breath, she aimed the barrel at the sky and squeezed the trigger. Her action produced instantaneous results.

The crack of rifle fire froze everyone right where they stood. And the wooden stock slammed into Victoria's collarbone with brutal force. With a mewling cry, she crumpled.

The small sound brought Sam surging to his feet.

Fists bunched, chest heaving, he caught sight of the woman lying in the street. Shock slammed into him.

His first thought was that she'd been shot, that some fool had fired off a round and hit her by mistake. With his heart in his throat, he plunged through the crowd. He reached her at the same instant a red-faced buffalo skinner swung out of his saddle.

"How was I to know she'd go for my rifle?" the man whined. "A little bit of a thing like that, trying to fire ole Bessie! The recoil knocked her right back on her bustle."

Shoving him aside, Sam dropped to his knees. Only after he spied the rifle still clutched in Victoria's hands did terror turn to relief. Almost instantly it flowed into fury. At Victoria for putting herself in the middle of a brawl. At himself for not protecting her. At the Irishman and everyone else in the damned street.

"You little idiot," he muttered, gathering the unconscious girl into his arms.

With the buffalo hunter pouring apologies, excuses and colorful oaths into his ears, Sam mounted the steps of the Frontier.

"Someone run for Doc Anderson," he snarled. "And fetch Mr. Parker from the *Tribune*."

6

Victoria experienced the oddest sensation, as though one half of her body was encased in cold, wet ice and the other burned by a fiery heat. Frowning, she struggled to open her eyes. The mere effort of lifting one lid sent pain slicing into her shoulder and neck.

"Oh!"

With a gasp, she reached for her shoulder. Or tried to. For some reason, she couldn't seem to raise her arm.

"Lie still!"

The bad-tempered growl produced exactly the opposite effect it had intended. Startled, Victoria wrenched both eyes open and immediately tried to flinch away from the ruffian leaning over her.

"Dammit, I said to lie still."

Only then did she recognize the voice behind the battered face.

"Sam? Good heavens, are you...? Oh! Oh, my!"

With another gasp, she abandoned her attempt to lift a hand to his bruised cheek. Agony rolled from her shoulder to the rest of her body in hot, red waves.

"Make another move and I swear I'll tie you to this sofa," the object of her anxious concern snarled.

It took a few moments for the black spots dancing in front of her eyes to clear and his words to sink in.

"Wh—what sofa?" she panted when she had her breath back again. "Where are we?"

"In a private parlor of the Frontier Hotel."

Victoria's dazed glance took in walls papered with pink cabbage roses. A marble-topped sideboard. A porcelain washbowl decorated with delicate violets on the floor beside the sofa where she now reclined. Her head whirling, she brought her gaze back to Sam as he repositioned what felt like a block of ice over the agonizing ache in her shoulder.

Wincing, she glanced down and discovered it *was* a block of ice, wrapped in a sopping tea towel. Well, that explained the cold.

The heat came from Sam's body, pressed hard against her other side. She was absorbing the welcome warmth when she made another discovery. She was practically bare from her neck to her waist.

Her blouse lay in a crumpled heap on the floor. Her chemise straps drooped down to her elbows, imprisoning her arms at her sides. And someone had loosened her corset strings. It gaped open at the back and sagged in front, letting her breasts swing free. The lacy frill on her lowered chemise barely covered their tips.

She knew better than to attempt to cover herself by now, though. Even the slightest movement would generate another shaft of pain. With heat scoring her cheeks, she met Sam's eyes again.

"What happened?"

"The recoil from the rifle knocked you flat on your back, at which point you fainted."

His utter disgust pierced both her embarrassment and pain.

"Well!" With a little huff, she tilted her chin. "I should think you'd show a bit more appreciation for the fact that I came to your aid."

He leaned over her, his battered face displaying not the least hint of gratitude. "One, I didn't ask for your aid. Two, I didn't need it. Between us, that wrangler and I were holding our own."

"It certainly didn't appear so to me!"

"Three," he ground out through tightly clenched teeth, "if you ever again do something as hare-brained as putting yourself in the midst of a mob and your father doesn't take a switch to your backside, I will."

Sheer indignation dropped her jaw.

* * *

Sam could see that his bullheaded ingratitude shocked her. Hell, it shocked him. But he'd be a long time getting over the vicious jolt to his spleen when he'd seen Victoria lying in a crumpled, lifeless heap.

"You're lucky," he said curtly. "As near as I can tell, your collarbone is bruised but not broken. I've sent for Doc Anderson. He'll be able to say for sure. In the meantime, we'll keep ice on your shoulder to hold down the swelling."

"It—it doesn't hurt in the least."

The lie was barely out of her mouth before tears filmed her cornflower eyes. One after another, the glistening drops rolled down her cheeks.

Hell! Sam felt guilty enough as it was. Guilty and angry and still rubbery with fear at knowing how easily she could have been hurt.

"I didn't mean to add to your hurts," he said gruffly. "I know your shoulder pains you."

"I'm not crying because of my shoulder. I'm merely so…so *incensed* at your ingratitude that…that…"

In her stuttering incoherence, she didn't notice that her chemise had slipped another inch, baring one rosy-tipped nipple.

Sam noticed, however. Suddenly, he couldn't breathe.

"Victoria—"

"You needn't try to apologize at the moment," she informed him with a sniff. "Later, perhaps, when I'm…when I'm more prepared to…"

"Victoria, sweetheart!"

His voice raw, he reached across with his free hand. He intended to tug up the lacy edge of her camisole. At that moment, he would have sworn on a dozen Bibles that was *all* he intended. But the brush of his hand against her breast stunned her into immobility, and, right under his palm, her nipple hardened to a tight, taut bud.

His gaze dropped like a stone tossed into a well. For a heartbeat, maybe two, he savored the sight and the feel of her smooth, firm flesh.

"Sam—"

Her hoarse whisper pierced the roar in his ears. He started to pull away, but she leaned forward. Or he thought she leaned forward. However it happened, her warm breast filled his hand. Against his will, against every instinct in him, he caressed its creamy softness.

"You're so beautiful."

He couldn't believe he'd uttered the words aloud. Or that she didn't faint dead away when his thumb stroked the engorged nipple.

Heat flamed across her shoulders, rushed into her cheeks. Her mouth parted. Her tongue traced a nervous trail along her lower lip. But she didn't faint, and she didn't draw away so much as an inch.

"Sam—"

This time his name came out on a moan. Or a plea. Sam still hadn't decided which when he bent his head. His mouth was only a breath from hers when the door to the parlor crashed open.

"Liebchen, ist du...? Mein Gott!"

With a smothered curse, Sam jerked upright and tried to shield Victoria from her father.

Not just from her father, he saw with a swift glance over his shoulder. From her mother. From Doc Anderson. And from an unidentified female in a straw hat decorated with a stuffed pheasant.

"Victoria?"

Rose Parker's strangled cry produced a groan from her daughter, who scrunched up in a tight ball and cowered behind Sam.

For long moments, utter silence gripped the parlor. Then Rose tipped her chin, thrust out her impressive bosom and sent Sam a signal as clear as any wigwagged across the plains by army scouts.

"Well!" she exclaimed, surging forward. "I must say I'm shocked beyond words that my daughter would allow her fiancé to tend to her in..."

"Mama!"

Uncurling from her instinctive crouch, Victoria cast an agonized glance at Sam and opened her mouth to disavow any such intimate relationship. Before she could get out a single word, Rose ruthlessly forged on.

"...in the public room of a hotel, of all places. But Sam was quite right to put ice to your shoulder. You really are quite bruised, Victoria."

Shooing him aside, she took his place on the settee.

"Do turn over, dear, and let me see the full extent of your injury."

"Mama, please..." Holding her chemise over her breasts, Victoria cringed in embarrassment. "I really don't..."

"My stars!"

Momentarily shaken out of her rigid calm by the ugly purple that now colored the whole of her daughter's right shoulder, Rose took a moment to recover. When she did, she rapped out orders like a drill sergeant.

"Deitrich, go at once and ask the hotel manager for more ice. Mrs. Jordan, continue on to Miss Henry's shop, if you please, and inform her that Victoria and I won't be able to keep our appointment this afternoon. Sam, do move. You're blocking the light. Better yet, fetch a stiff brandy."

"Do you think Victoria should drink strong spirits just yet? Doc Anderson may prescribe a—"

With a quelling look, the matron set him straight. "The brandy's for me!"

Dutifully, Sam procured a brimming snifter of brandy. A short time later, he listened with profound relief as Doc Anderson predicted that his patient would be as right as a trivet in a few days. When Rose wrapped her daughter in a cloak and prepared to depart the Frontier Hotel, Sam took the thoroughly shaken Deitrich Parker aside and asked formal permission to call on Victoria after dinner, if she was feeling up to it.

His brows waggling wildly, Deitrich looked to his wife.

Rose glared an affirmative.

A freshly bathed, shaved and pomaded Sam joined his parents at dinner and gave them an abbreviated account of the happenings outside and inside the Frontier. He also announced that he intended to ask Victoria to marry him.

"Sam!"

Delight and dismay warred on his mother's heart-shaped face. Reaching across the table, she grasped his hand.

"You know I would love to see you marry such a delightful girl, but this is so sudden. I thought— That is, Suzanne and I thought..." Shaking her head, she began again. "Are you sure Victoria's the one you wish to marry? You're not just asking her to save her embarrassment? She wouldn't want that. No woman would."

"I don't think I'll ever forget how I felt when I saw her lying in the street," Sam answered with brutal honesty. "Yes, Mother, Victoria's the one."

An image of a warm-skinned woman with glossy black hair and dark, compelling eyes flashed into his mind. Resolutely, he banished it.

"The only one," he said firmly.

Julia might have been convinced if not for the tick in the side of her son's jaw. Uncertain, she threw a look at her husband.

The general leaned back in his chair and eyed Sam thoughtfully. "You're doing the right thing by Victoria, aren't you, son?"

"Yes, sir." Their eyes met across the expanse of mahogany. "I'll make her a good husband."

Sam repeated exactly the same vow to Victoria later that evening.

She was waiting for him in the ornately furnished front sitting room when he arrived at her parents' home. Hands folded and gripped in her lap, she watched him with wide eyes. Aside from her pallor and the bulge of a bandage under the shoulder of her high-necked claret gown, she showed no sign of the afternoon's ordeal. Nor any sign that she welcomed him or the proposal they both knew he'd come to make.

"Are you all right?" he asked, depositing his

bowler on a gate-legged table crowded with tin-types, painted porcelain boxes and a glass-globed lamp.

"I'm quite recovered, thank you," she replied coolly. "No, don't sit too close to me. I smell disgustingly of horse liniment."

Ignoring her request, he claimed the seat beside her on the settee. He tried to claim her hand, as well, but she drew it back.

"Let's not make this moment more awkward than it needs to be, Sam. I'm well aware of why you've come. You and my mother think to save my reputation with a sham engagement."

Before he could refute the blunt statement, her chin tipped. China-blue eyes flashed a warning.

"I refuse to participate in such a charade," she stated flatly. "I think— No, I'm quite sure I have backbone enough to withstand whatever snickers and smirks are aimed my way."

"After this afternoon, I don't doubt you have backbone enough to withstand far more than that," Sam agreed. "And, like you, I have no intention of participating in a charade."

Surprise took some of the starch from her sails. "You don't?"

"No."

"Then why are you here?"

"To ask you to be my wife."

"But you just said— You agreed—"

"I agreed I wouldn't take part in a subterfuge. I want to marry you, Victoria."

She stared at him, speechless, for long moments.

A smile pulled at the corners of his mouth. She looked so young, so confused. So damnably innocent and sensually seductive. The hard knot Sam had carried in his chest since that scene in the Frontier Hotel loosened a fraction. Their union would work. He'd make it work.

"Why?" she asked at last.

His smile widened. "You may have noticed that I can't seem to keep my hands off you."

"As a matter of fact—" she wet her lips "—I have."

"I tried, Victoria. I told myself you were just a girl, Elise's friend. I stayed away from you these past weeks. But it seems we have only to get within striking distance of each other and the sparks fly."

It was the truth. Sam could admit that much at least without a trace of guilt. He wanted her, and he'd sensed the same leaping hunger in her. Patiently, he waited for her to acknowledge the desire neither one of them had succeeded in curbing.

Her heart throbbing as painfully as her shoulder, Victoria tried to sort through her jumbled thoughts. She'd had hours to reflect on the mortifying incident this afternoon, hours to prepare a polite rejection of the proposal Sam obviously felt compelled to present.

She hadn't lied when she said she could withstand the whispers and titillated smiles she knew would come her way when word got around about the afternoon's incident. But she hadn't expected the sincerity she now saw in his eyes. Or the desperate longing to join her life and her body with his that pulled at her very being.

Her head spun and her chest squeezed so tight it hurt, but Victoria was her father's daughter. She wanted to know—no, she *had* to know the facts before she leaped to any conclusions.

"I can't seem to keep my hands off you, either," she admitted. "But is this…this hunger enough to make a marriage, Sam?"

His smile tipped into a grin so wicked that Victoria's breath caught.

"More than enough."

Somehow, she found the strength to resist the heat curling in her belly and ask the question that hung poised like an ax blade.

"What about Mrs. Prendergast?"

His expression didn't alter. "What about her?"

"I thought— Well…I had formed the impression that you hold her in some regard."

"I do."

The quiet affirmative set the ax blade swinging.

It had sliced halfway through Victoria's heart before Sam's next words registered.

"Mary Prendergast is a friend. A very good friend. Her mother and mine were closer than any sisters when they were young. My mother considers her an adopted daughter."

She'd seen his face that night in the upstairs hall, when he'd swung the widow off her feet. The look in his eyes hadn't struck her as the least brotherly.

He must have read the doubt in her eyes before she turned her head away. Catching her chin, he brought her face gently back to his.

"I won't lie to you. I care for Mary. Very much. Everyone in my family does. And we're exceedingly proud of her accomplishments in the field of medicine."

Victoria felt hollow inside, as though she'd tried and failed some crucial test. She could never measure up to a woman as accomplished as Mary Two Feathers Prendergast. Or so she thought, until Sam smiled down at her.

"But you're the woman I want as my wife."

"Because you can't have Mary?"

"Because I desire you."

The resonating honesty in his voice reassured her, but it was the tenderness in his eyes that vanquished her.

"Now, do I get an answer to my question? Will you marry me, my darling?"

He hadn't said he loved her. Only that he desired her. A small, protesting corner of Victoria's mind recognized the difference. Yet the warm endearment overcame her lingering doubts.

He might not love her with the same passion she did him. Not at this moment, perhaps. But he would! He *would!* She'd see to that. With the utter confidence that came with youth and beauty, she vowed he'd soon forget Mary Two Feathers, forget every woman but her.

"Yes," she answered on a tremulous sigh. "Yes, I'll marry you."

"Good girl!"

It wasn't quite the response she'd imagined all those hours she'd snuggled under her covers, dreaming of the moment she brought Sam to his knees. She was feeling just a bit let down until he tipped her chin up another inch.

"Do you think we can seal the bargain without doing more damage to your shoulder?"

"I think we should at least try."

That was all the encouragement he needed. Exercising extreme care, he bent his head. Victoria hid a wince at the ache in her shoulder and tipped her head.

Once her mouth opened under his, however, the

pain disappeared and she felt only wild, singing joy. It was there, the moment their lips met. The instant, fiery heat. The greedy want. The burning need. When he raised his head, she had to fight for breath.

"I'll make you a good husband," he promised softly. "I swear it."

With a shaky laugh, she gave him fair warning. "Well, I shall probably make you a wretched wife."

"I doubt that."

"I'm entirely serious." Dragging in a breath, she enumerated her faults. "I can't play two notes in a row on the piano without causing Papa to wince. Mama says my embroidery would put a one-armed paperhanger to the blush. And Cook won't let me anywhere near his kitchen. Not since the time I became distracted by a story I was composing in my head and set a pan of hot grease afire, anyway."

Laughing, he tucked a strand of hair behind her ears. "Is that the worst I have to worry about?"

She made a clean breast of it. "I'm told I can be a bit…well…stubborn at times."

Wisely, Sam made no comment. Dipping his head, he brushed her lips again.

Longing leaped to life inside Victoria once again, so quick, so all-consuming. She felt its answer in the need that rippled through Sam, in the hardening of his muscles and the careful restraint.

He was right, she thought, her throat tight. This hunger was enough. For now. Love would come. With care, with patience, with time. He couldn't want her like this and not come to ache for her as much as she ached for him.

She couldn't know, of course, that time was the one commodity they didn't have.

7

Victoria awakened the next morning to a piercing joy and a horrendously sore collarbone. So sore, she almost submitted to her mama's stern injunction that she must remain at home and allow her bruises to heal.

"At the same time," Rose suggested, "you might compose the announcement of your engagement."

"I'll do it later. I'm going in to the *Tribune* with Papa this morning. I have another piece to compose first."

"Victoria! What could be more important than the announcement of your forthcoming marriage?"

"You'll read it in tomorrow's edition," her daughter teased, dropping a kiss on Rose's cheek. "I'll be back before lunch, I promise."

She escaped to the foyer before her mother could object further. Hiding a grimace, she struggled awk-

wardly into her coat and brushed aside her papa's
concerns when he came down the stairs a moment
later.

"Thank goodness it's not the arm I write with."

Tucking her hand in his, she tripped out into the
bright March sunlight.

The entire staff was at the paper when she and
her papa arrived. When her papa proudly announced his daughter's forthcoming nuptials, Ed
Jernigan led a round of hearty congratulations.

The celebrations were short-lived. A dozen or
more urgent dispatches had come over the wires
during the night. Leaving her papa and Ed to pore
over their contents, Victoria retreated to her desk
and plucked a freshly sharpened pencil from the
holder in her drawer. After thinking for a moment,
she began to write.

All upright and decent citizens of Cheyenne
will be dismayed to learn that certain rowdy
elements among them displayed the most unseemly lack of manners outside the Frontier
Hotel yesterday afternoon. It must be assumed
that whiskey was the reason a dozen or more
men set upon one of their companions and
took him to task for his decision not to join
those who've volunteered to join the ranks. A
near-brawl ensued, and only the timely intervention of a courageous passerby kept the poor

man from being tarred and feathered.

Apparently it had not occurred to these overzealous patriots that each citizen must follow his or her conscience. The decision to take up arms is and must always remain a private matter, not one subject to general consensus. We should honor those who choose to step forward to fill the ranks, and respect the rights of those who, for reasons of their own, cannot or will not don a uniform.

Quite proud of the piece, she submitted it to Ed Jernigan for editing. He in turn took the draft to her papa, who returned it to Victoria.

"I'm sorry, *liebchen,* but ve cannot run this as you haf written it."

"Why not?"

"You give our readers too much opinion and too little fact."

"Yes, well, it's an opinion that needs airing."

"Perhaps."

"Papa! Surely you don't condone the kind of atrocious behavior I witnessed yesterday?"

"You know I don't. But ve haf talked, you and I, about vhat sells newspapers. This von't. Not vhen so many of our readers vill soon be sending sons off to fight."

Shocked and more than a bit disillusioned, Victoria could only stare at her father.

"Rewrite the piece," Deitrich said gently. "Remove the emotion. I haf taught you the difference betveen reporting the news and shading it. You must not let Sam's situation influence how you report things vhen var comes."

With a little sniff, she snatched the draft from his hand and marched back to her desk. It was several hours before she could admit that her father was right. She'd put too much of herself into the piece. Too much of Sam.

With a little ache just under her breastbone, she took a clean sheet of paper and began again. When it was done, she gave it to Ed once more, returned to her desk and began composing the announcement of her engagement.

The bold-face paragraph announcing the engagement of Victoria Rose Parker to Samuel Garrett appeared in the March 31 edition of the Cheyenne *Tribune*. Mr. and Mrs. Deitrich Parker capped the announcement with a brilliant soiree at their home that evening.

Quite by coincidence, the Spanish Cadiz chose the same date to angrily denounce the United States's arrogant demand for Cuba's independence.

World events were quite overshadowed for Victoria when, amid popping corks and boisterous toasts, Sam presented her with a solid gold locket as a betrothal gift. The heart-shaped pendant dangled from a pin in the shape of a bow and was studded with sapphires. To match her eyes, he declared to the rapturous sighs of every female present that night.

Victoria begged a photograph from his mother and cut it to fit one side of the locket, with hers on the other. Caught up in the excitement of all prospective brides, she spent the next weeks daydreaming, attending gala dinner parties given in honor of the engaged couple and planning a trip to New York with her mama to shop for a trousseau.

Somehow she managed to squeeze those activities around hurried hours at the *Tribune,* where she and her papa and Ed Jernigan pored through the continuing avalanche of dispatches. Diplomatic tensions mounted daily as first the pope, then the ambassadors of England, Germany, France, Italy, Austria and Russia appealed to President McKinley to avoid war.

As Victoria had confided so ingenuously, and so very, very ignorantly, to Sam, it was quite the most exciting time. Not until after the president formally requested Congress to issue a declaration of war did hard, cold reality begin to set in.

She was never quite sure when she first noticed the elevated eyebrows and sideways glances aimed at Sam whenever he was asked when he would shake the mothballs from his uniform and rejoin his regiment.

Sometime after April 9, she thought, when the American consul general and other U.S. citizens departed Cuba in anticipation of imminent hostilities. Perhaps after April 10, when the U.S. high-handedly declared the island independent and American warships began a blockade of its harbors. Certainly by April 23, when Spain, driven to the wall, declared war and President McKinley responded by issuing a call for 125,000 volunteers.

Not to be outdone, Congress authorized funds for some 200,000 volunteers, including three regiments of cowboy cavalry. Wyoming's Senator Warren, North Dakota's Grigsby and the bold, brash assistant secretary of the navy, Theodore Roosevelt, who'd spent a number of years in the West and wanted badly to experience actual combat, immediately set about organizing the three regiments.

All across the country young stalwarts jammed recruiting stations. Grown to manhood during the three decades of peace following Appomattox, they'd never tasted combat, never heard cannons roar or the earsplitting din of bullets fired in fusillade. But they had absolutely no doubt that they would handily whup the thousands of well-armed, battle-tested Spanish regulars currently in Cuba.

As eager as other Americans, Wyomans poured into Cheyenne. While harried officers tried to sort through the twenty or more applicants for every billet, the city's saloons and brothels did a booming business. High spirits inevitably produced high jinks. Streetlamps got shot out. Two drunks stumbling down busy Fourth Avenue one afternoon decided to douse a glowing cigar stub by peeing on it. A half-dozen furiously squawking chickens mysteriously ended up inside the coffin of the recently deceased deacon of the Episcopalian church.

Even Victoria, who'd firmly believed women should throw off the outdated strictures of the declining century, took care not to walk the streets alone. Her mama escorted her to the shops to purchase what they'd need for their upcoming expedition to New York, and her papa accompanied her to and from the newspaper offices.

Sam provided frequent escort in the evenings. She was on his arm, strolling home from a stirring concert of Mr. Souza's rousing marches, when a short, stubby wrangler planted himself directly in front of them.

"Remember me?"

How could they have forgotten the pugnacious pacifist whose adherence to his principles caused the near riot outside the Frontier Hotel a few weeks ago?

"Yes," Sam said. "I do."

"The name's Powdry. Dan Powdry." He thrust

out his hand. "I jest wanted to thank you for steppin' in like you did."

Sam gripped the callused paw. "You're welcome."

"I coulda took 'em, you understand. Bunch of damned fools, thinking they're the only ones with sand in their craw."

"Courage takes many forms," Sam said quietly. "You displayed more than your share that day."

"I don't know 'bout that, but I do know I'm not one to forget someone what done me a good turn." He jerked a thumb toward the saloon across the street. "Can I buy you and your lady a beer?"

Bawdy shrieks of laughter almost drowned out the honky-tonk piano music coming from inside. Victoria wasn't surprised when Sam politely declined.

"Some other time, perhaps. It's late and I have to get my fiancée home."

Powdry shrugged and tipped his hat in Victoria's direction. "You got you a good man here, ma'am. No matter what them fools said."

"Yes, I think so, too."

Yet she couldn't help noticing how silent Sam became whenever the war turned up in conversation. Aching for him, Victoria snuggled close against his arm for the rest of the way home.

The good-night kiss she gave him that night was unrestrained and unabashedly hungry, as if the

sheer force of her passion could make him forget
the names he'd been called, the sideways glances,
the damned war itself.

Victoria wasn't the only one who observed
Sam's slow withdrawal. Julia Garrett, too, watched
her son turn more and more inward, though his
smile was as ready as ever, his manner as solicitous
as any mother could wish.

He was gone for days at a time attending to the
family's cattle, timber and real estate interests
spread across most of western Wyoming. When he
returned, he divided his energies between helping
Jack break and train horses for the cavalry and
squiring Victoria around town.

He never spoke about his feelings concerning the
war. Although Sam celebrated along with everyone
else when Admiral Dewey soundly defeated the
Spanish fleet in the Battle of Manila Bay on May
1, Julia noticed he had little to say concerning the
War Department's stupendous struggle to train and
equip the two hundred thousand volunteers now in
uniform.

Her husband took note of his son's reticence, as
well. Two nights after Dewey's stunning victory,
the general studied Sam across the dinner table.
There were just the three of them that night. Victoria, who'd joined them frequently in the weeks
since the engagement was announced, had gone to

cover the meeting of the Ladies' Auxiliary War Relief Committee for the *Tribune*.

Slipping a hand into the pocket of his waistcoat, Andrew fingered the telegram he'd received this afternoon. His glance drifted from his son to his wife.

Julia was a tried-and-true army wife. From the day she and Andrew had found each other again after years apart, she'd followed the drum without so much as a murmur of complaint. Packing up an entire household. Riding across snow-covered prairies and sun-baked deserts. Braving Indians and outlaws, droughts and flash floods, scorpions and fleas. Cheerfully, she'd set up housekeeping in tents, sod shanties, and once, when stranded by a ferocious snowstorm, an abandoned chicken coop.

Following her husband from one remote outpost to another was one thing. Watching her only son ride off to war was another. Andrew knew she'd felt more relief than remorse when Sam resigned his commission and came home. Even now, knowing how it ate at their son's soul to stand back while his friends and brothers in arms readied for war, Julia had cried when Andrew shared with her the contents of the telegram.

She showed no trace of tears now, though. Calm and serene, she met her husband's gaze. ''You might as well tell him and get it over with, Andrew.''

Sam glanced up from his beefsteak. "Tell me what?"

"You know I've been coordinating the revisions to the training manuals for the three regiments of cowboy cavalry," Andrew began.

"How could I not? You and Colonel Wood have been burning up the telegraph wires."

"It's been a busy time," the general admitted with a smile.

Laying aside his fork, Sam lounged back in his chair. He was glad to see the animation in his father's face. All three of the men organizing the volunteer cavalry units had relied heavily on the general's vast experience as a horse soldier to help set up the tables of organization for the new regiments. Senator Warren from Wyoming and Torrey from North Dakota had consulted with him extensively. Charged with forming the regiment from New Mexico and Oklahoma Indian Territory, Colonel Leonard Wood and his enterprising, enthusiastic friend Theodore Roosevelt had also drawn heavily on Andrew Garrett's expertise.

Proud of his father's role in the enterprise, Sam set aside his fork. "I'm still surprised Mr. Roosevelt insisted that Colonel Wood take command of the First Volunteer Cavalry instead of assuming that honor himself."

"For all his occasional bluster, Roosevelt has enough sense to realize that his years in the New

York Guard don't qualify him for command of a regiment. Leonard Wood won a Medal of Honor during the Geronimo campaign. Although he's a surgeon by profession, he's a born leader.''

"Like the man who trained him?" Julia put in.

"Yes, well…" With a roll of his shoulders, Andrew shrugged aside his years of command. "Wood is a good soldier and a brilliant organizer. Did you know he's convinced the War Department to purchase Krag-Jorgensens for his entire regiment?"

"No!"

Despite his determination to remain as detached as possible, Sam couldn't suppress a leap of excitement. So far, the army had only issued the Krag-Jorgensen rifle to regulars. The first small-caliber, smokeless powder repeating rifle, the Krag didn't give off a telltale puff of black smoke when fired— a puff that too often pinpointed troops' positions to snipers and gunners.

"How in the devil did Colonel Wood pull off that miracle?"

"I suspect you'll find out when you get to San Antonio."

Sam's eyes narrowed. "What do you mean?"

He knew as well as anyone else that Wood had chosen San Antonio as the staging and training site for his volunteer cavalry, a colorful group variously labeled the Rocky Mountain Boys, Teddy's Terrors or the Rough Riders after the shoot-'em-up cowboys in Buffalo Bill Cody's Wild West Show. Still, he wasn't prepared when his father pulled a crumpled telegram from his pocket and laid it on the table.

"Colonel Wood has filled all his company-level command billets," the general informed his son calmly. "So have the commanders of the Wyoming and Dakota regiments. But Wood desperately needs a good regimental supply officer. He's holding the job open for you. It's the best I could do at this late date, son."

Sam's chest squeezed. He felt as though he was caught in a vicious vise.

"Thank you," he said with quiet sincerity. "I know what it must have cost you to beg a place on the colonel's staff for me. But I can't— I won't—"

His mother gave a small sigh. "You can and you will. You're your father's son."

Julia had seen enough of death during the War of Rebellion to wish the blasted Cubans had never dragged the United States into their struggle for freedom. She hated the idea of Sam going off to fight and perhaps die on foreign shores, but hated even more watching him slowly wither inside.

"Your father and I have talked about this, Sam. We don't know what we would have done this past year without you here to take care of things while we consulted with doctors and surgeons."

"I'm only too happy to help! You know that."

"Of course I do. But there are no more doctors to consult and we must learn to cope as best we can. And you must do whatever you and Victoria decide is best for the two of you."

"Victoria?"

From his startled expression, it was apparent that Sam hadn't considered his fiancée to this point.

"Yes," his loving mother answered rather tartly. "Don't you think the possibility you might go off to war could be a matter of some interest to your future wife?"

"Oh. Yes, of course."

Stunned by this unexpected turn of events, Sam could barely form two coherent thoughts, much less consider Victoria's possible reaction. Although he longed to let loose with a joyous whoop, jump up from the table and rush upstairs to pack his gear, the sense of duty that had brought him home held him firmly in his chair.

"We need to discuss this more fully," he said to his parents.

"We can discuss it as much as you wish," Andrew answered with a shrug, "but unless I've misread the man my son has become, he'll board the train to San Antonio tomorrow. Now, fetch me those damned crutches, would you? I think I've almost got the hang of them."

It still ripped Sam apart inside to watch his

proud, once indomitable father struggle to move his useless legs an inch, only an inch.

He would have helped, supporting the general as he had during his previous attempts to walk, but his mother waved him off. They must learn to manage, she insisted.

After an hour of intense discussion and another spent pacing the floor, trying to sort through his jumbled thoughts, Sam still hadn't reached a decision. Mindful of his mother's strictures, he realized he'd have to inform Victoria of the possibility he might be leaving.

He caught her just as the Parkers' carriage returned her from the Grange Hall and the meeting of the Ladies' Auxiliary. Begging a few moments alone with her, he drew her into the front parlor and delivered his news.

"Your father's secured a position for you with the Rough Riders? Oh, Sam, how wonderful for you! When do you leave?"

Her enthusiasm took him aback. "Tomorrow, if I decide to take it."

"You will! You must!"

A wry smile tipped his mouth. "Are you so anxious to see me leave?"

"No, of course not." She bit her lip. "It's just that you've been so unhappy. I've seen it, Sam. You won't talk to me about it, but I've seen it."

Ashamed that he hadn't done a better job disguising his feelings, he tweaked her nose. "Well, if you're sure you won't miss me..."

"I shall miss you desperately."

Her eyes held his. Sam glimpsed a maturity in their blue depths that surprised him.

"I want only for you to be happy," she said simply. "I shall always want only that."

"I can see now I'm going to be the most fortunate of husbands."

His teasing tone covered layers of intense relief. He'd made his decision. He would rejoin the ranks, even if only as a volunteer.

"My father thinks this little fracas can't last more than six months at most. Just enough time for you and your mother to make your trip to New York and complete your trousseau. With any luck, we'll have a September wedding after all."

"With any luck, we shall."

Victoria joined Sam's parents and his sister and her family at the train depot the next morning to see him off.

The din was indescribable. Train whistles shrilled. Horses being led aboard freight cars whinnied. Porters shouted and strained to load crates of equipment. Regulars sweating in their blue wool uniforms marched in precise ranks to the troop cars. Volunteers garbed in everything from homespun to buckskin whooped and hollered and generally gave their harried sergeants a time of it.

When the whistle signaled last call to board, the regimental band struck up a rousing martial air. The tide of the music quite carried Victoria away...until Sam made his final farewells to his family, then swung her into his arms.

As his mouth came down on hers, the stark reality of the moment gripped her. This might be the last time he held her. The last time his warmth and strength enveloped her. On a swift rush of terror, she clung to him. Quite suddenly, the call to arms had lost all hint of romance or excitement.

Although she tried to hide it, her desperation must have shown in her face when Sam set her on her feet.

"No tears now," he chided. "I want to carry your bright, beautiful smile with me all the way to Cuba and back."

Swallowing, she blinked the tears from her stinging eyes and managed to curve her lips. "Sam, I—"

A hiss of steam stole her words.

"What?"

"I—"

At the screech of metal on metal, he threw a quick glance over his shoulder. "Sorry, sweetheart, I've got to climb aboard."

Planting another hard kiss on her mouth, he

jumped aboard the now rolling train. Victoria stood unmoving, a small, still island amid the sea of humanity that waved and shouted and cried unashamedly.

Fingering the gold-and-sapphire locket pinned to her lapel, she whispered what she'd tried twice without success to tell him.

"I love you, Sam."

8

Sam arrived in San Antonio on May 7 with the second contingent of the First United States Volunteer Cavalry. The men swung down from the train to wild cheers and a booming welcome by a brass band.

The press had congregated en masse at the station, anxious to weave more stories about the men they persisted in dubbing Teddy's Boys despite the fact that Colonel Wood commanded the regiment. A good number of San Antonio's citizens had also turned out. Women stood on tiptoe and men lifted children onto their shoulders to see the latest addition to the cavalry unit that was already gaining near-legendary status.

Sam had to admit the Rough Riders more than lived up to their reputations. He'd met a good number of his fellow recruits on the train ride south. The motley group included a lawyer, a Texas

Ranger, a Presbyterian minister, the mayor of Prescott, Arizona, two miners down from Montana, a full-blooded Dakota Sioux and a host of wranglers. These Westerners carried names like Rocky Mountain Bill, Rattlesnake Pete, Bronco George and Dead Shot Jim.

More First Volunteer Cavalry recruits boarded the train at junctions in Dallas and Austin, only these hailed from the East. Pressed on all sides, Mr. Roosevelt had squeezed a small number of his friends and acquaintances into the company ranks. These dandies wore straw boaters and striped jackets and included such luminaries as a Yale quarterback, ex-captains of the Harvard and Columbia rowing crews, a Princeton tennis champion and several famous polo players. A few tough New York City policemen were sprinkled among gentlemen with names like Tiffany, Knickerbocker and Kane. Like the Westerners, the Easterners were driven by the all-consuming desire to do their duty to God and country and get a taste of combat.

In addition to the eager Americans, a sprinkling of adventurous foreigners had also argued or cajoled or bamboozled their way into the Rough Riders. As Sam learned during the long train trip, the swarthy Italian reporting in as chief trumpeter had formerly served with the French Foreign Legion in both Egypt and South China. A tall, sinewy Australian had once held a commission in the New South Wales Mounted Rifles.

When this extraordinarily diverse group detrained in San Antonio, a number of them goodnaturedly agreed to demonstrate their skills to the crowd. One gave an exhibition of dazzling lasso twirling and rope-dancing. Another whipped out a buffalo-skinning knife with a razor-sharp twelve-inch blade and put it right through the center of a playing card held up by an intrepid friend. Bill Larned, twice United States tennis champion, dug his racket out of his valise and lobbed balls to squealing children.

Finally the cheering crowd allowed the new arrivals to claim their baggage. A new major with bright, shiny shoulder pips formed them into loose ranks. The long, rather undisciplined column marched on foot to the Exposition Grounds just outside the city. There they were met by their commander, Colonel Leonard Wood.

Wood strode out onto the Exposition's dusty main square and greeted the recruits with the news that they'd be issued uniforms of sorts, but half of the horses and most of their weapons had yet to appear. Evidently Mr. Roosevelt, still in Washington, was working furiously to direct supplies and equipment to the newly formed regiment. With a silent groan, Sam realized he was going to have his work cut out for him in the next few weeks.

"I don't know how long we'll remain in San Antonio," Wood warned. "Our orders are to train with all diligence and be prepared to move to a point of embarkation immediately upon notification. So you men must all apply yourself and work hard."

Narrowing his eyes against the dust and glare, he skimmed the ranks.

"Some of you come from wealth and privilege. Each of you is used to acting independently and with great courage. But now you must learn to think and act not as individuals, but as a company. We'll drill you hard, both afoot and in the saddle. You'll take your turn at kitchen and latrine duty. Promotions to fill company positions will be based solely on merit. If any man among you wishes to leave, he should do so now, because I shall begin making cavalry troops of you before sunrise tomorrow."

Not a single individual so much as blinked.

"Good," Wood said after a moment. "We'll sort you into companies now and turn you over to your sergeants. Captain Garrett, you'll come with me and meet the rest of the regimental staff, if you please."

Shouldering his canvas bag, Sam left the ranks and followed Wood to the building designated as temporary headquarters. There he was introduced to the harried adjutant and assistant adjutant, the chaplain, the bandmaster, the acting regimental surgeon, the sergeant major, the saddle sergeant and the quartermaster sergeant, who greeted Sam with profound relief.

"Heard tell you were regular army," the Denver native confided when they went to inspect the equipment that had arrived with the troop train.

"That's right."

"Well, I sure hope you know how to read these blasted tables of organization. I can't make heads nor tails of 'em."

"We'll sort them out," Sam promised, blessedly unaware that those were the last calm moments he'd enjoy for the next three weeks.

By the following dawn, Sam and the rest of the new arrivals were wearing a bastardized uniform of slouch cap, standard-issue dark blue flannel shirt, suspenders, khaki-colored canvas pants, leggings and black leather boots with spurs. Some knotted their handkerchiefs loosely around their neck, cavalry-style. Others tucked them under the back of their hats to protect their necks from sunburn while they drilled.

Although regulars would never be caught off post in the canvas pants normally worn only for stable duty, Sam soon discovered the Rough Riders paid little attention to such fine distinctions of dress. They were, however, intensely interested in their weapons.

The canny Colonel Wood had anticipated equipment shortfalls as hundreds of thousands of volunteers were mobilized. Knowing army stocks of the time-honored cavalry saber would quickly run out, he'd secured authorization for the emergency purchase of Cuban-style machetes. He'd also wrangled the prized Krag-Jorgensen carbines for his men instead of the Springfields being issued to other volunteer units. Delighted with the smokeless repeating rifles, the sharpshooters among the ranks soon organized shooting competitions and raked in considerable amounts of extra cash.

With more First Volunteer Cavalry recruits reporting to San Antonio each day, Sam and Quartermaster Sergeant Douthett worked almost around the clock locating and issuing uniform items, arms, cartidges, rations kits, two-man shelter tents, blankets, saddles, fodder bags and, finally, mounts. They fell into their cots long hours after midnight each night, only to roll out when the bugler sounded reveille at four-thirty. While the recruits drilled and performed kitchen, police and latrine duties, Sam and his cohorts bought, borrowed or traded with local merchants for everything from mustache wax to lamp oil. But whenever possible, they joined the ranks for drill. No one on QM staff intended to spend his time in Cuba issuing mustache wax!

Sam had shed a good ten pounds and burned to dark brick when his brother-in-law arrived in San Antonio a week later. Jack rode out from the train depot with one hundred and fifty prime mounts and a dozen hands from the Sloan ranch to string them along.

"Jack!"

Striding through the clouds of dust around the corrals, Sam pounded his brother-in-law on the shoulder.

"You old dog, I didn't know you intended to bring these nags down yourself."

"Actually," Sloan replied with a grin, "my primary mission is to deliver letters from your mother, your sister, your niece and your fiancée. Fulfilling my contract with the army is only a secondary charge."

Reaching into his saddle bags, he extracted a packet of letters tied with a ribbon. A delicate lilac scent rose from Victoria's. Sam tucked the envelopes into his shirt pocket to savor later.

"What's the latest from home?" he asked, eager to hear the news firsthand. "Are my parents well? How about Suzanne and those brats of yours?"

"Everyone's as well as can be expected. Elise mopes about the stables because her lieutenant shipped out last week and the general—"

Worry stabbed into Sam. "What about the general?"

"Your father's as ornery as ever," Jack drawled, having survived a number of run-ins with his father-in-law over the years. "He's also determined to master those blasted crutches. He goes down at least once or twice a day while trying, which, unfortunately, doesn't improve his temper.''

"Damn!"

"I know.'' Rolling his neck to remove the kinks, Jack surveyed the neat rows of tents. ''What're the chances a man can get a cold beer around here?''

"This is a cavalry regiment. I'd say your chances are pretty good.''

Shaking off his guilt at leaving his father crippled in body, if not in spirit, Sam escorted Jack to the officers' canteen. The one-time gunslinger needed little introduction to the men in the canteen. Most had read the lurid stories about him published by the penny presses in his more notorious days. With a wry grin, Jack verified some of the tall tales and flatly denied others. Finally he and Sam claimed two wooden chairs in a quiet corner.

"What's the word?'' Jack asked. ''Do you think you're headed for Cuba or Puerto Rico?''

"No one knows yet. There's talk that two separate expeditionary forces will be launched.''

"I hear Roosevelt is about to join you.''

"We expect him by the end of the week. We've been put on notice that we could move to Tampa at any time for embarkation, and Roosevelt's worried to death he'll miss the opportunity to train with the regiment before we ship out.''

"You're not the only ones headed for Tampa.''

Downing another long swallow of foaming beer, Jack slouched back in his chair. "Suzanne got a letter from Mary. Now that the Hospital Corps has been officially established and the first nurses recruited, Mary's decided to join the ranks."

"The devil you say!"

"She'll be in Florida when you arrive."

Sam felt a sudden jolt just under his ribs. When he leaned forward eagerly, the letters in his pocket rustled. A delicate lilac scent wafted up.

Victoria. He was engaged to Victoria.

Deliberately, he sat back and lifted his beer.

Former Assistant Secretary of the Navy Theodore Roosevelt arrived in San Antonio on May 15 to great fanfare. The bluff, colorful character had already generated so much intense public interest that reporters followed him in droves out to the training camp.

Since organizing and equipping the thousand-man regiment left Wood little time for drill and teaching tactics, he turned that responsibility over to his second-in-command. Shrewdly, Sam guessed Wood wanted the inexperienced Roosevelt to learn right along with the men.

At first the horse-savvy Rough Riders weren't quite sure what to make of the bespectacled politician with the neighing laugh and exuberance of an overgrown puppy. Roosevelt soon won their respect with his superb horsemanship and utter dedication. Sam was present the day he also won their hearts.

As he did whenever he could snatch a break from his quartermaster duties, Sam had joined the troops for mounted drill. On this occasion, Roosevelt led the three companies far out into the dusty Texas countryside, where they practiced column formations, sometimes at a trot, sometimes at full gallop. More than once Sam had to bite his tongue at the irregular line intervals and wild charges, but the consummate horsemanship of the men more than made up for their lack of discipline.

It was on the way back to San Antonio that Roosevelt himself committed a serious breach of discipline.

"I say!" Squinting through his thick, pinch-nose spectacles at a bustling inn, he instructed the bugler to sound dismount. "I'll stand the men to a mug of beer. I could use one myself!"

The regular officer in Sam winced, but he said nothing. It wasn't his place to lecture a senior officer about fraternizing with the troops.

Colonel Wood, however, had plenty to say on the subject. He heard about the stop at the inn shortly after the company returned to camp. Immediately, he called his long-time friend to his tent. As the troopers listening outside later reported, Wood delivered a blistering lecture to Roosevelt about becoming too friendly with men he might soon have to order into a murderous crossfire.

The New Yorker's cheeks glowed beet-red when he marched out of Wood's tent. When he marched back in again less than an hour later, the whole camp held its collective breath. At least a half-dozen different sources later quoted his reply.

"I wish to say, sir, that I agree with what you said. I consider myself the damnedest ass within ten miles of this camp!"

Saluting smartly, he wheeled and departed again.

After that incident, the troopers admired and re-spected Colonel Wood, but they loved Teddy. Within days, most of the regiment had purchased blue polka-dot neckerchiefs like the one Roosevelt wore. The distinctive scarf became identified with the Rough Riders almost as much as the rousing "There'll Be a Hot Time in the Old Town To-night," which the men belted out night and day.

On May 27, the U.S. Navy blockaded the port of Santiago de Cuba, trapping most of the Spanish fleet inside the big, curved bay. On May 28, the First Volunteer Cavalry received orders to report immediately to Tampa.

Unfortunately, every other unit received the same order. Rail lines became clogged overnight with hundreds of thousands of troop transports all head-ing south. The estimated twenty-four-hour trip from

San Antonio to Tampa took four hellacious days. Sam and his harried quartermaster staff raced around at each stop to procure fresh food and water for the one thousand hot, tired Rough Riders and more than twelve hundred horses and pack mules.

Roosevelt and the wealthier recruits in the regiment paid out of their own pockets for fodder for the horses and fresh meat for the men. Thankfully, crowds turned out by the hundreds at every station to cheer and wave flags. The more enterprising among them passed buckets of milk, pails of water and fat, ripe melons to help the troops relieve the raging thirst engendered by the heat and dust.

By the time the First Volunteer Cavalry finally rolled into Tampa and set up their tents on the sandy, pine-studded flats two miles north of the city, Sam felt as though he hadn't slept, bathed or eaten in a month. He and QM Sergeant Douthett spent the rest of that day computing the tally of the supplies expended during the trip, after which Sam sent the exhausted sergeant off to snatch some sleep. Changing into a clean uniform shirt, he scraped the bristles from his cheeks and rode down to the hotel where the senior officers were quartered to make his report.

Constructed in 1891 by wealthy financier Henry Plant, the Tampa Bay Hotel was a Moorish fantasy come to life. Minarets gilded with silver glowed at the corners of the massive structure. Graceful arches welcomed guests at every turn. Dozens of fountains flowed amid lush gardens.

Sam had heard that the hotel had cost an astonishing two and a half million dollars to build and boasted more than five hundred rooms, each furnished with paintings, Venetian mirrors and sculptures purchased by the Plants during their European travels. Reportedly, every room also included such modern amenities as electric lights, private baths and telephones. As he approached the fairy-tale structure, Sam could well believe the reports.

Somewhat stunned by the hotel's lavish extravagance, he tied his mount's reins to the long, white-painted hitching post and climbed the steps to the veranda. Once inside, he encountered officers in every imaginable uniform strolling about the cavernous lobby. Newsmen and foreign attachés swarmed as thick as flies. Adding to the din of lively conversation, a regimental band was giving a concert in center court, much to the delight of the ladies who'd traveled to Tampa to see their high-ranking husbands off to war.

Sam was edging his way through the crowd to the front desk when a bandy-legged civilian planted himself directly in his path.

"Captain! I been kickin' my heels in this pile of sand and fleas they call a town for two days, waiting for you to get here."

Sam took the callused paw he held out, astounded to recognize the belligerent pacifist from the Frontier Hotel.

"Powdry?"

"Yessir, it's me. Dan Powdry."

"What the devil are you doing in Tampa?"

"I come to join up with the Rough Riders. Tried to catch you boys in San Antonio, but you done left. So I rode over to Galveston, hitched a ride on a tramp steamer and been sittin' here twiddling my thumbs for two days now, waiting on you."

Which is what the regiment should have done, Sam thought wryly, instead of inching along by train for four days. Curious about the man's change of heart, he reminded him of his words the night of the brawl.

"I thought you didn't see the sense in taking a bullet for a bunch of Cubans."

"I don't! No sir, I surely don't. But when I heard you joined up, I got to thinkin'. The way I now see it, this war ain't so much about fightin' for the Cubans as it is about standin' shoulder to shoulder with men you trust and doin' your duty."

During his years of active service Sam had heard the profession of arms described in brilliant prose and stark poetry, but he'd never heard it described so simply or so accurately.

"I don't figure to be no foot soldier, though,"

Powdry warned. "I come down here to join up with you and the Rough Riders."

"I'm sorry. The regiment has no vacancies."

The cowboy's face fell like a stone. Sam had respected him for standing his ground against overwhelming odds. Now he could only admire his ingenuity in getting to Tampa with more speed and a great deal less fuss than the army. He'd be a good man to have in any unit.

"Every regiment loses men to illness or accidents. If a vacancy occurs in our company, I'll see what I can do to get you in."

"Well, I guess I kin hang around Tampa for a week or so and hope one of your boys comes down with the trots. Say, how's that pretty young thing who fired off the buffalo skinner's cannon and broke up the brawl? Your fiancée, wasn't it?"

"She's well."

"You got yourself quite a woman there, Captain. Quite a woman."

"Yes, I think so, too."

After assuring Sam that he'd be in touch, Powdry sauntered off, undaunted by the admirals and generals surrounding him on all sides. Smiling, Sam wove his way through the crowd to the front desk.

A half hour later, he'd made his report to Roosevelt. Aching with weariness, he squeezed into a brass elevator cage and took the slow, clanking ride to the lobby.

Thinking only of the cot waiting for him in his tent, Sam edged through the crowd. He had almost reached the door when he caught a glimpse of two women half obscured by a tall, potted palm. One was small and wizened, well into her seventies. The other stood with her back to him, but her proud carriage and glossy, upswept black hair stopped Sam in his tracks.

It was Mary. It could only be Mary.

His pulse suddenly erratic, he forged a path to the potted palm. "My compliments, Mrs. Prendergast."

She swung around, delight flooding her dark eyes, and held out both gloved hands.

"Sam! The word is all over Tampa that the Rough Riders have arrived! I was going to seek you out this very evening."

"Were you?"

"Yes. I was so surprised when Suzanne wrote and told me you'd rejoined the ranks. I want to hear all about it. And to offer my congratulations on your engagement."

He searched her face and found only happiness for him. With a queer little pang, Sam grinned.

"So you've heard about that, too, have you?"

"From Suzanne." She gave his hands a squeeze.

"I only spent a few moments with Victoria, but found her a most delightful young woman."

For the second time in less than an hour, Sam accepted praise on behalf of his fiancée.

"She's that and more. But what's this I hear about you?"

He skimmed a quick glance down her gray dress with its puffy, mutton-leg sleeves and trim skirt. A white band emblazoned with a red cross encircled one arm, and an army badge of an unfamiliar design was pinned to her high collar.

"Jack told me you'd contracted to serve with the army as a nurse. You're already in uniform, I see."

"Yes, I'm assigned to the field hospital north of town, but I haven't performed nursing duties as yet." She made a little face. "My commander set me to administrative tasks, which is why I'm here at the hotel this afternoon. Oh, how rude of me! You must let me introduce you to Miss Clara Barton, president of the American Red Cross."

Turning to the diminutive woman at her side, Sam bowed deeply. "Captain Garrett, at your service, ma'am. It's an honor and a privilege to meet the Angel of the Battlefield."

All his life Sam had heard stories about this extraordinary woman. During the War Between the States, she'd purchased medical supplies and ambulances with her own funds, recruited nursing volunteers and driven right to the front lines to minister to the wounded on both sides.

"My father still talks of the miracles you performed on the battlefields of his war," he told her.

"Let's hope such miracles won't be necessary in this one," she replied with a twinkle in her berry-bright eyes. The merriment faded, edged out by a long sigh. "I must admit I'm not sanguine. As Mrs. Prendergast and I were just discussing, the Army and Navy Hospital Departments are sadly underequipped for the number of sick and wounded they'll have to treat."

Sam wasn't surprised. Medical staff and equipment were in as short supply as everything else during this rapid mobilization.

"My hospital commander has appointed me to act as liaison with the Red Cross," Mary explained to Sam. "Miss Barton and I are attempting to coordinate our resources."

"Then I mustn't keep you from such important business. I merely wanted to say hello."

"Will you visit me at the hospital when you get leave? We've so much to catch up on and barely had time to talk in Cheyenne."

"Why don't you visit now?" Miss Barton suggested. "We've finished our business for today."

"So we have. Can you spare a few minutes, Sam? I should love to hear how you came to be back in uniform."

"Yes, of course."

They would just talk, he told himself. Share a few moments of friendship. Nothing more. Tucking her hand in the crook of his arm, Sam led her toward a small salon just off the lobby.

They parted an hour later with Mary promising to visit the Rough Riders' camp as soon possible to consult with their regimental surgeon about the assistance he might expect from the newly recruited corps of nurses.

"It won't be much," she cautioned. "Most of us will be assigned to the field hospitals, both here and in Cuba. The regiments will have to carry in their sick and wounded. And speaking of the sick—" Worry creased her forehead. "Warn your surgeon that we're already taking in fever patients."

Sam's gut tightened. He'd grown up on army posts. He knew how swiftly fever could ravage massed concentrations of troops like the ones gathering in and around Tampa.

"Typhoid?"

"Mostly malaria."

The kink in his stomach didn't ease. "I don't like that you're exposed to all manner of sickness and disease."

"I'm a nurse," she reminded him quietly. "Caring for the sick is my job, just as soldiering is yours."

* * *

Despite the pointed reminder, the thought of Mary working among ill and possibly contagious patients plagued Sam as he rode back to the tent city north of Tampa.

Night had dropped by then, and thousands of cook fires flickered among the scrawny pines. After several wrong turns, he finally found his way back to the Rough Riders' bivouac area. Lines of pup tents stretched straight as an arrow, with the officers' tents at one end, the company kitchens and latrine sinks at the other. Picket lines for the horses stretched down either side of the streets.

Wearily, Sam unsaddled and tended to his horse, then downed a meal of beans and boiled beef before retiring to the tent he shared with the regimental assistant adjutant. Every one of his muscles ached with fatigue, but before he dropped onto his cot, Sam pulled out the small traveling desk his mother had given him when he'd left for West Point years ago, along with instructions to write home. Often!

The letter he penned wasn't to his mother, however, but to Victoria. In it he related the more amusing details of the long train trip, the incredible confusion of trying to sort out the mountains of baggage upon arrival and his meeting with Mary.

Mosquitoes the size of California vultures buzzed about his head by the time he folded the letter into an envelope, addressed it, then blew out the lamp. Stretching out on his cot, Sam laced his hands under his head and stared up at the shadowy canvas. Deliberately, he forced his thoughts from a slender, dark-eyed widow to a girl with delft-blue eyes and hair the color of a summer sunset.

9

To allow their mounts to recover from the grueling train journey, the First Volunteer Cavalry drilled on foot for the next four days.

Military attachés from England, Germany, Russia and as far away as Japan rode out from Tampa to observe their maneuvers, as did whole platoons of reporters, photographers and sketch artists. Roosevelt's flamboyant unit had captured the world's imagination as well as that of all Americans. One such reporter was dapper Richard Harding Davis, who had attached himself to Roosevelt in San Antonio. Another was a bulldoggish young correspondent by the name of Winston Churchill, who was covering the war for a London paper.

The evening of the fourth day, the men marched back into camp after another long, hot drill and were met with devastating news. Headquarters had belatedly realized that there weren't enough ships to transport the assembled troops. Only half could go with the Expeditionary Force and most of those would be regulars. A frantic Roosevelt had pulled every political string in the book to secure places for two of the Rough Riders' three volunteer companies.

He and Wood now faced the agonizing task of deciding who would go and who would remain in Tampa. A number of the men chosen to stay behind broke down and cried like babies. Those picked to go considered themselves so lucky they didn't mutter a single complaint when told they'd have to leave their horses in Tampa and fight as dismounted cavalry.

Sam's herculean efforts as quartermaster as well as his eight years of experience won him a place with the invading forces. With so many Rough Riders being left behind, he wasn't able to work a billet for Powdry, much to the man's bitter disappointment.

Between drill and helping to reorganize and re-equip a cavalry regiment to fight on foot, Sam barely had time to breathe, let alone pen further letters to Victoria. He received several from her, however, each filled with details of the wedding preparations and a lively commentary on the momentous events as viewed from her increasingly keen perspective.

Although she often expressed the fervent desire

to join the army of reporters in Tampa and observe the mobilization firsthand, Sam dismissed that as mere girlish whimsy. So his jaw dropped in sheer astonishment when she rode into camp late on the afternoon of June 7, accompanied by Theodore Roosevelt himself.

"Captain Garrett!" the beefy New Yorker boomed. "Come and see the surprise I have brought you."

Several hundred heads turned as Roosevelt's charger pranced through sand. Disbelieving, Sam gaped at the woman riding beside him on a neat bay.

"I say!" one of the Harvard skulling captains exclaimed. "What glorious hair. It reminds me of the sun going down over the Charles River."

"Never mind her danged hair," an Arizona miner muttered. "Take a gander at them bosoms!"

Sam swung around with a fierce glare that sent both men back a hasty step. "Watch your tongue," he snarled. "You're speaking of my fiancée."

"Jesus! Sorry, Capt'n. We didn't know she was your woman."

Jaw locked tight, Sam accepted his hasty apology, performed a stiff about-face and marched forward. Roosevelt swung out of the saddle at his approach.

"My wife encountered this enterprising young woman at the Tampa Bay Hotel this afternoon," he boomed. "She was inquiring after her fiancé. Mrs. Roosevelt charged me to deliver her to you forthwith."

Lifting Victoria down, the New Yorker set her on her feet and gave one of his loud, braying laughs.

"Go ahead, man! I know you're in uniform, but you have my permission to kiss her. I think the troops will forgive a breach of army protocol this once, won't you, boys?"

Embarrassment stained Victoria's cheeks, but she gamely tipped her face to his. Sam wrapped an arm around her waist, drew her up against him and delivered a kiss that set the men to cheering.

Her blush had deepened to a fiery red when he released her, and there wasn't a doubt in any man's mind that she was, in fact, the captain's woman. He'd thrown a crude mantle of protection over her, but he knew it would be effective. Among the Rough Riders, at least.

"Show your lady around camp, why don't you?" Roosevelt suggested. "I'll authorize a night's pass so you may escort her back to the hotel and share a late supper."

"Yes, sir."

Grasping Victoria's elbow, Sam steered her toward the long row of tents.

"Well!" Red flags still flew high in her cheeks. "I had expected to surprise you, but hadn't planned on providing entertainment for the entire regiment.''

"You've surprised me, all right."

He was recovering from the shock of seeing her ride into camp. The fury that had gripped him at the trooper's crude remark would take a little longer to subside.

"What are you doing here?"

"Oh, Sam, it's quite the most exciting thing! I badgered and badgered Papa to send me to Tampa to report for the *Tribune*. He adamantly refused…"

"I should hope so!"

"…until I read Anna Benjamin's stories in *Leslie's Weekly*," she gushed on, ignoring his exclamation. "And when Kathleen Blake Watkins began sending such enthralling dispatches over the wires, I finally overcame all Papa's objections."

Sam supposed he shouldn't be surprised. Victoria had always been able to wrap her father around her little finger. Her mother was another matter, though. When he said as much, his fiancée made a little face.

"Mama took a great deal more persuading, it's true. But I simply *had* to be part of all this. And," she added on a shy note, fingering the locket pinned to the lapel of her tan traveling dress, "I wanted most desperately to be with you. I knew you would understand."

"Well, you're dead wrong."

"I beg your pardon?"

Tightening his grip on her elbow, he dragged her between two tents. Gnats swarmed around their faces as Sam gave vent to his feelings.

"How could you think I'd want you exposed to the dirt, fleas and stink of an embarkation camp? Or to the risk of disease," he added, recalling Mary's warning that fever had already broken out among the ranks.

"But— But—" Completely taken aback by his vehemence, she stammered out a protest. "Your mother accompanied the general to—"

"To various frontier posts," he cut in. "Not on campaign and certainly not to war."

The excitement that had sizzled in Victoria's veins throughout the long train journey to Tampa and boiled hot when she'd first seen Sam a few moments ago died a slow, agonizing death.

He didn't want her here. Despite that audacious kiss in front of the entire regiment, he wasn't the least happy to see her. She could only blame her hurt for the foolish argument she offered next.

"You didn't raise these objections to Mrs. Prendergast's presence in Tampa. In fact, you described her work most glowingly in your letter."

"Mary's a skilled nurse. She's needed here."

And Victoria wasn't. The blunt truth of that stung far more than she could have imagined.

"She's also wearing a uniform that affords her

the protection of the army,'' Sam pointed out with brutal candor. ''You are not.''

''I see.''

''No, you don't.''

Blowing out a long breath, Sam tried to curb his anger. She looked so hurt. And so damned vulnerable. Gentling both his grip on her arm and his voice, he tried to make her understand.

''You can't possibly comprehend how things are in a camp like this unless you've experienced them firsthand.''

''That's why I've come.'' Drawing in a deep breath, she tipped up her chin. ''Whether or not you approve of my presence in Tampa, I'm a credentialed reporter. General Shafter's adjutant signed my papers this very afternoon.''

Well, hell! Sam would have a thing or two to say to that dunderheaded idiot later.

''If you don't care to advise me on how to proceed,'' she informed him stiffly, ''I shall just ramble about Tampa on my own.''

His stomach did a quick roll at the idea of this young, vibrant woman roaming among men who swore like lumberjacks, relieved themselves at open pits and gleefully boasted about their previous night's tumble with the prostitutes who'd set up tents in convenient proximity to the bivouac areas.

''All right,'' he conceded with a marked lack of graciousness. ''I'll show you around camp and introduce you to some of the fellows. You can talk to them while I clean up. Then I'll escort you back to the hotel and we'll discuss this further over dinner.''

Regally, she inclined her head the barest fraction of an inch. "Thank you."

By the time they arrived back at the Tampa Bay Hotel, Victoria had filled almost an entire notebook and Sam had marshaled an extensive list of reasons why she would board the first train out of Tampa tomorrow morning.

The excited buzz that greeted them when they walked into the lobby drove every reason but one out of his head. If the wild rumors flying about held even a grain of truth, the order to march down to the port and board transport ships could come at any time.

His mouth grim, Sam escorted his fiancée to the elegant dining room. The large throng waiting patiently in line for a table decided them in favor of a private dinner in the room Mrs. Roosevelt had managed to secure for Victoria by outrageously flaunting her husband's name.

Placing an order for steamed duck, baked redfish and a chilled white wine, Sam escorted her to the elevator, then through a maze of thickly carpeted corridors dominated by Moorish arches and painted frescoes.

Victoria's suite was just as lavish as the rest of the hotel. Venetian mirrors, Dutch paintings and statues carved from gleaming marble crowded together to cover every inch of wall space in the sitting room. The bedroom beyond, Sam saw, was draped from floor to ceiling in apple-green damask silk, with a crystal chandelier spilling a shower of electric light over the entire room.

The rooms were magnificent. So was the girl—woman!—who faced him across a lace-draped table. Steeling himself against the pull of her lush beauty, Sam removed his slouch hat, tossed it on the table and cut right to the point.

"You heard the rumors downstairs. We might receive orders to march down to Port Tampa at any moment. I would like to see you safely on board a train for home before that happens."

Unpinning her hat, she dropped it onto the table beside his. Limp copper curls clung to her neck and temples.

"At this point, they're only rumors. I understand your concerns for my welfare, Sam. I really do. But I should very much like to stay another day, perhaps two."

Encouraged by her conciliatory manner, Sam rounded the table, lifted his hand and brushed the reddish tendrils back from her sweat-dampened temples.

"In fact," she murmured, blushing a bit at his touch, "I was thinking that I could—"

"You could what?"

Lord, she was beautiful. So soft and dewy and lushly feminine. One touch of her creamy skin tightened his belly and sent desire spearing into his groin. Fighting a sudden, knifing need to sweep her up and carry her into the next room, he wrapped the curl around his fingers.

They'd spend their wedding night in a hotel every bit as lavish as this one, he vowed. He'd lay her on a four-poster covered in patterned damask and slip the buttons on her dress free of their loops. Loosen her corset strings. Free the firm, high breasts he'd caressed that night in the Frontier and...

"I was thinking I could go on to Cuba," she finished on a breathless note.

"No."

The hard, flat negative elicited a sigh. "I suspected you wouldn't like the idea. Neither did General Shafter's adjutant when I broached it this afternoon."

"I should think not!"

"I understand why you might object. Truly, I do." Laying her palms on his chest, she gave him a soft, cajoling smile. "But I spoke to a number of reporters here at the hotel, including Mr. Richard Harding Davis. Perhaps you've heard of him?"

"Mr. Davis and I became acquainted in San Antonio."

"Oh, Sam, then you must understand how his stirring stories about the Rough Riders could inspire me with a wish to join the ranks of war correspondents. When I spoke to him this afternoon, Mr. Davis told me that General Shafter has invited him and several other journalists to sail with him on the *New York*. Only think! If I could—"

"Dammit, Victoria, you will *not* join the ranks of combat correspondents. You will *not* board the *New York*. And you will most definitely *not* sail to Cuba."

Any one of the men Sam had commanded during his years as a regular officer would have quailed under such a lashing. Even the redoubtable, fiercely independent Rough Riders had learned to respect his knowledge and judgment. To his surprise and profound irritation, Victoria abandoned all attempts at cajolery and lashed right back.

"May I remind you that we are not yet married. Nor, sir, am I one of your troopers. You have no right to bark orders at me, and I am not in any way constrained to obey them."

"That locket pinned to your blouse says otherwise."

"Indeed? Then perhaps you would be wise to remember that it can be *un*pinned."

"You think so?"

His reply was soft, slow and dangerous. She must have sensed that she'd stumbled into quicksand. Her tongue flicked along her lower lip, and the palms she'd laid against his chest flattened in an attempt to hold him in check.

"Sam—"

Her breathy protest barely registered in Sam's whirling thoughts. He'd put aside his secret, unspoken desires and asked Victoria Parker to be his wife. He'd proposed with the most honorable of intentions, and she'd accepted his offer of marriage. Less than an hour ago, he'd marked her as his in front of the entire regiment. There was no way in hell he'd allow her to follow the troops to Cuba. Whether she liked it or not, he'd sworn to protect her.

She was his.

Victoria read his thoughts as plainly as if they'd been printed in four-inch type on the front page of the *Tribune*. Hers were every bit as chaotic.

For so long she'd loved this man with all the passion of her girlish heart. She'd pulled him into his sister's sewing room on the pretext of seeking his advice, then practically attacked him. She'd bared her breasts to him at the Frontier Hotel, if only by accident. She'd moaned at his touch. Ached for his kiss. Followed him all the way to Tampa and submitted to a primitive, possessive kiss in front of hundreds of strangers that branded her as surely as the brand on the Double-S horses.

Maybe, she thought on a wave of pulsing heat, it was time to match deed to word. Prove that she *was* his in the most basic, elemental way.

"Sam," she whispered again, her voice low and ragged. "I've missed you so."

When he swooped down to cover her mouth with his, Victoria could have sobbed with relief, with joy, with fierce, unrelenting need. Her leaping senses registered the tang of healthy male sweat, the taste of raw hunger, the feel of muscles corded to steel under a thin layer of blue flannel.

Afterward, Victoria could never quite remember how they moved from the sitting room to the bedroom. Nor could she recall how she reached a state of naked, trembling eagerness so swiftly and so efficiently. All she would remember from that hot June night was the feel of Sam's strong body pressing hers into the bed and her raw, dizzying passion.

It came on her so quickly, like one of the summer storms that raced across Wyoming's plains and pummeled the prairie grasses to the ground. One moment she was trembling in an agony of embarrassment and uncertainty. The very next it seemed, she was gasping and arching her back and crying out at the rasp of Sam's tongue and teeth against her nipple.

She'd never imagined, had never *dreamed* she could feel such heat and such indescribable sensations. Fire seemed to streak from her breast to her belly. Her whole body went taut, and her fingers fisted in his hair. Yet when he kneed her thighs apart and slid a finger into her most private of places, Victoria bucked like a wild mare.

"What are you doing?" Frantically, she tried to dislodge his hand.

"Easy, darling. Easy. I'm just making sure you're ready for me."

"You shouldn't— I can't—"

In an agony of embarrassment, she writhed on the satiny bedcover. She couldn't believe he was touching her there, couldn't imagine how his fingers could generate such wild, pulsing pleasure.

Gritting his teeth, Sam stroked her hot, slick flesh. Like every randy young soldier, he'd contributed a good portion of his pay to the whores who serviced the troops at every Eastern military bastion and Western outpost. He'd also dropped more than a few dollars at Cheyenne's bustling bawdy houses.

He'd never bedded a virgin before, however, and was finding the experience almost more nerve-racking than it was pleasurable. He ached for Victoria so badly he couldn't straighten the lower half of his body, but the thought of penetrating the shield his probing finger had just encountered raised a cold sweat.

For all his nervousness, though, he had no intention of stopping now. He wanted her too badly. Had to take what she'd offered him for so long. Covering her mouth with his, he pressed his thumb against the hard nub at the juncture of her thighs and began to slide his finger in and out of her tight, narrow channel.

Eyes wide, she endured his touch with flaming cheeks. Suddenly, she arched her back.

"Oh! Oh, my!"

With a strangled cry, she threw her head back on the green-damask duvet. Her young body went taut. Hot, wet liquid gushed onto his hand. Shudders racked her as she cried his name once more.

"Sam!"

His blood pounding, he pried her legs farther apart and positioned himself between her thighs. One swift thrust ripped through her maidenhead.

Her eyes flew open. Surprise glazed their blue depths for a second, maybe two, before giving way to a look of shocked reproach.

"You hurt me!"

"Victoria. Sweetheart." Feeling like the vilest wretch alive, Sam held himself rigidly still inside her. "The pain will ease."

Or so he'd been told!

"Let me slide my arm under your hips and lift them a bit so you can move with me."

She lay stiff as a tent pole in his arms. Torn be-

tween fear of hurting her again and his own raging
need, he began a slow, careful mating dance.

To his profound relief, the reproach gradually
faded from her face. After a moment, she caught
his rhythm. Tentatively, her hips canted. Timor-
ously, she wrapped her arms around his neck. When
he drew his shaft out and slowly slid in again, she
received him with little more than a flinch.

And when he picked up the pace, his breath coming hard and fast, she soon began to flex her muscles. All of them.

With a grunt, Sam went stiff from his neck down.
He barely pulled out in time to turn aside and spill
himself onto her hip. With another inarticulate
sound, he buried his face in the fragrant mass of
her hair.

"Sam?"

Victoria shifted under his crushing weight, uncertain and confused. The most incredible pleasure
still pinwheeled through her mind and her limbs felt
as though they were weighted with lead. If not for
the warm liquid trickling down her hip and dripping
onto the green damask, she might never have stirred
at all.

"Sam? I'm— I'm rather wet. Is that how it's
supposed to, er, end?"

He dragged up his head. A wry smile danced in
his brown eyes.

"No, sweetheart, it's not. But until you're ready to begin breeding, that's how it will have to end."

"Breeding! Good heavens!" She wiggled in alarm. "We can't make a baby yet. We have to be married first."

"Exactly."

Threading his fingers through her sweat-sheened hair, he stilled her with a swift, hard kiss.

"We will be married, Victoria. As soon as I return to Cheyenne, where you'll be waiting for me."

"But I—"

"Will you give me your promise that you won't go roaming about Tampa unescorted?"

Like most males of his times, Sam honestly believed in the right of men to order their womenfolk's lives. He hadn't imagined that he'd have to exercise such rights over Victoria this soon or this forcefully, but she needed to understand from the start that she wouldn't get around him as easily as she did her parents.

When she didn't answer, he shifted. The press of his groin against her soft belly added crude but unmistakable emphasis to the rights he now exercised over her.

"Victoria?"

"All right, I promise."

"And you'll board the train for home as soon as I can procure you a ticket?"

"Is that what you want, Sam? Truly?"

"That's what I want."

He softened the blow with another kiss, longer this time, and sweeter. She clung to him, returning the kiss with a passion that roused Sam to hardness once more.

He took her again, tutoring her soft, lovely body, awed by its passionate response.

At the peak of their pleasure, a sharp pounding on the door elicited a moan from Victoria and a curse from Sam. He ignored it. When the hammerer refused to go away, he muttered another oath and dragged on his pants. Thinking it was a waiter with the dinner they'd ordered, he pulled out a wad of bills and yanked open the door.

To his astonishment, Quartermaster Sergeant Douthett stood in the hall, quivering with excitement.

"The colonel sent me to fetch you, sir! You have to return to camp at once. We just got word we're to pack up and be at Port Tampa by daybreak to board our transport."

10

With Sergeant Douthett's urgent message hammering in his head, Sam yanked on his uniform, issued another brusque order to Victoria to get on a train for home the very next day if possible and planted a hard kiss on her mouth. He left her sitting in the middle of the bed with the green coverlet clutched to her breasts and her hair tumbling about her shoulders.

With Sergeant Douthett at his heels, he charged down four flights of stairs and plunged into the lobby. It was already mobbed with staff officers, newsmen and foreign observers, all scurrying to gather their gear and make the exodus to Port Tampa, some nine miles south. Sam joined the flow and had almost made it out the door before being waylaid by Dan Powdry.

"Captain! I just heard the news. You got to get me into the regiment!"

"I'm sorry. We don't have an empty billet and I've no time now to work one."

"Well, dangnabit!"

Sam turned away, then swung back again. "Will you do me a favor?"

Swallowing his disappointment, the cowboy nodded. "Just name it. I still owe you for standing with me against them railroaders."

"My fiancée, Miss Parker, arrived in Tampa this afternoon. She's staying here at the hotel. Will you see that she gets on a train for home, tomorrow morning if possible?"

"Sure, I kin do that."

Relieved that he'd tied up that loose end, Sam tipped two fingers to his slouch hat. "Thanks."

"Good luck," Powdry called after him. "And keep yer head down!"

Sam and Sergeant Douthett arrived back at camp to find it a scene of indescribable turmoil. The war planners knew the number of men and amount of baggage that would have to be transported to the port. They should have issued orders to allow for sequential, orderly movement. Instead, the entire operation turned into a mad scramble.

The First Volunteer Cavalry had been ordered to a specific track at midnight. After a frantic rush, they arrived at the track, but the train didn't. While the men sat about on the ground, Wood and Roosevelt and the other officers tried in vain to find someone in authority who could confirm when the train would come.

At three-thirty in the morning, a much-harassed major general ordered them to march to a different track. No transport appeared there, either. Finally, the redoubtable Roosevelt commandeered a coal train coming up from the south and argued vociferously with the engineer until he agreed to back up nine miles to the port. The Rough Riders arrived at the quay covered in coal dust, but with all their baggage.

The confusion at the dock was worse than at the rail yard. The ship transports, anchored in midstream, were being brought one by one to the dock, but no one seemed to have the least idea which regiments were to board which ships. As train after train arrived quayside, a free-for-all ensued. Once again Roosevelt proved his mettle.

Somehow, he secured a promise from the dockmaster for the next ship. Leaving Sam and a heavily armed escort to guard the baggage, he ran at full speed back to the regiment and brought the First Volunteer Cavalry up just in time to take possession of the ship before the Second Regulars and the Seventy-first arrived. The Seventy-first went away grumbling, but four companies of the Second managed to wrangle berths with the Rough Riders.

By dawn, the men were tired and hungry, but cheerfully went to work loading baggage, food and ammunition. Sam sweated in the hot sun as he and the ship's captain worked together to fill the holds. Although the troops of the First Volunteer Cavalry would fight on foot, their officers required mounts to survey the battle scene, carry messages and lead the forays. Accordingly, Sam got the horses aboard a second ship and left them in charge of Roosevelt's groom, one of the famed Buffalo Soldiers from the Ninth Colored Cavalry.

When the transports finally pulled away from the quay and anchored in midstream, the men were jammed together both below and above decks. Sam had to step carefully over bodies to reach the fore-cabin, where he reported to Roosevelt.

"Everything's aboard, sir."

"Including the artillery guns?"

"Yes, sir."

"Bully!"

"I stored extra rations in the hold to supplement the travel rations the men carry in their packs. Several drums of water, too."

"Let's hope the voyage is swift," Roosevelt commented, polishing his spectacles. "If we have to eat that damned rot the army calls beef, we'll arrive in Cuba with every man sick as a dingo."

Sam could only hope so, too. Instead of the traditional canned corned beef, some fool had decided to can fresh, unsalted beef. The stuff was stringy and tasteless and spoiled quickly. Most of the men tossed it aside. Those who could force it down too often retched it back up.

Yet as he stepped over the hot, tired troops and found a spot for his bedroll alongside those of the other regimental staff officers, he didn't hear a single Rough Rider complain. To a man, they were excited and eager to be on their way at last.

A little before noon, Victoria drove down to Port Tampa in a hired carriage, escorted by a vigorously protesting Dan Powdry.

"The captain said you was to catch a train home this morning," the wrangler repeated for at least the tenth time since he'd pounded on her door earlier.

"Yes, I know," she replied as she edged the carriage in among those holding the tearful, anxious ladies who'd come to see their men off. "Unfortunately, every train has been commandeered to transport troops. It could be days before I'm able to leave Tampa."

Or so she hoped!

She'd spent hours after Sam dashed out last night writing up her notes from the previous afternoon's visit to the Rough Riders' camp. Early this morning, she'd stood in a long line at the hotel's telegraph office with other eager reporters and wired her first dispatches back to the *Tribune* as a credentialed correspondent. The thrill of that moment still sang in her veins.

"It'll be days before anyone leaves Tampa," Powdry muttered, eyeing the thousands of men and mountains of baggage piling up on the dock.

"I think so, too," Victoria said happily.

Scribbling furiously, she filled page after page with the sights and sounds of an army embarking for war. She didn't see the Rough Riders in the mass of humanity on the dock, didn't know if they'd already loaded or not. One of the wives observing the process said she thought they had.

With the sun beating down unmercifully, Victoria moved from carriage to carriage to record the women's reactions to the stirring sight. She was sure it was a perspective that none of the male reporters would think to capture.

Several rather intrepid wives and daughters hired a fishing boat to take them out to where the loaded transports sat at anchor. They were determined to locate their husbands' ships for a last farewell. When they invited Victoria to join them, Powdry registered an alarmed protest.

"Here, miss! You ain't going out among the troop transports, are you? The captain would have my scalp if I let you do something so dangerous."

Reluctantly, Victoria declined the offer. Not because she was worried Sam might spot her, she informed her self-appointed guardian. Only because she needed to write up the afternoon's stories and dispatch them before the telegraph office shut down for the night.

Victoria and Powdry returned to the docks early the next morning. Troop loading continued all that day and into the night. As the hours dragged on, Victoria coaxed stories from the most unlikely sources using a combination of winsome charm and dogged persistence.

She needed both to discover why the naval battleships that had gathered to escort the troop convoy suddenly steamed out of port late on the afternoon of June 11. Apparently, naval intelligence had received reports of Spanish warships just off the coast of the Carolinas. That meant the troop transports would have to sit at anchor in Tampa Bay several more days while the battleships prowled the coast.

After the mad scramble to get aboard, the men crammed like sardines on the troop ships now resorted to gambling, fishing, jumping into the sea to cool off, then joining in with rousing choruses during the evening concerts the regimental bands performed aboard ships. Local merchants did a booming business by loading barrels of beer and various edibles onto boats and making the circuit of the transports. So, Victoria discovered, did a number of rather enterprising prostitutes. She decided not to include that interesting bit of information in the dispatches she cabled back to the *Tribune*.

Instead she filed stories describing the doughty spirits of the men left behind to form the second wave. The tremendous logistics involved in resupplying a troop convoy. The support necessary for an invading forces—particularly from medical personnel.

Mary Prendergast supplied the details for that story.

After a diligent search, Victoria located her aboard the army hospital ship *Relief.* The hastily converted passenger ship had just steamed into port and was still tied at the quay, taking on supplies and medical personnel.

Equipped with wards, operating rooms and one of the astounding new X ray machines, the hospital ship was attracting considerable attention from newsmen, photographers and sketch artists. As Victoria understood it, personnel from various field hospitals as far away as Georgia and Alabama would deploy with the ship, then disembark in Cuba to set up their tents within close proximity to the battlefields.

When she learned that personnel from the Seventh Corps hospital north of Tampa had just boarded the *Relief,* she left Powdry in charge of the hired carriage, flashed her credentials and her most beguiling smile at the sentry manning the gangplank, and secured permission for a quick visit. A matron with a starched cap pinned atop her iron-gray curls, a red cross on her armband and a pristine apron covering her gray gown directed Victoria belowdecks. She found Mary with a contingent of nurses from the Seventh Corps field hospital taking a tour of the wardroom that stretched from bow to stern.

"Only look at the bunks!" one of the nurses exclaimed as Victoria stepped into a scrubbed and tiled bay. "They're stacked three high. And made up with rubber sheets! How I wish we had some of those to take with us when we set up our field hospital in Cuba. Think of all the hours we wouldn't have to spend boiling linens."

"We'll be lucky if we have bandages enough for the wounded, let alone rubber sheets," Mary murmured.

Victoria swallowed a sudden lump in her throat. Until now, the massive troop embarkation had evoked stirring sentiments and an almost buoyant, holiday air. The long racks of empty bunks waiting to be filled gave another perspective entirely. She stood quietly beside the bulkhead until one of the nurses noticed her.

"May we help you?"

"I'd like to speak to Mrs. Prendergast when she's free."

At the sound of her name, Mary turned. Sheer surprise blanked her face.

"It's Victoria Parker, Mrs. Prendergast. We met last February, at Elise Sloan's birthday party."

"Yes, of course." With a little shake of her head, the widow detached herself from the group. "I'm sorry I didn't recognize you immediately. I was just so surprised to see you. Whatever are you doing here?"

"In Tampa, or aboard ship?" Victoria returned with a smile.

"Either. Both. Good heavens, have you volunteered for the nursing corps?"

"Unfortunately, I have neither the training nor the skill to qualify. No, I'm here as a reporter for the Cheyenne *Tribune*. I've been credentialed," she added with a note of shy pride.

"Well, for heaven's sake! I can't imagine why Sam didn't tell me you were coming to Tampa."

Resolutely, Victoria ignored a tiny pinprick of jealousy at the easy familiarity between Sam and this woman. "Most likely because he wasn't aware of my plans until after I arrived."

"Wasn't he?" Laughter sprang into the widow's dark eyes. "Oh, my."

A defensive note crept into Victoria's voice. "Yes, well, you're probably thinking it was foolish of me not to wire him ahead of time."

"On the contrary, I find myself admiring your intelligence and foresight. Why don't we go above deck and see if we can catch a breeze?" Laughter still sparkling in her eyes, she led the way. "I can't wait to hear what Sam had to say when you arrived. I'd guess it was along the lines of not wanting you to be exposed to all manner of discomforts and rough, crude troops."

"How did you know?"

"Because he said the same to me."

As she followed the slender, dark-haired widow up the narrow stairs, the jealousy Victoria had experienced a few moments ago blossomed into hurt. And anger.

Really, she shouldn't care that Sam had voiced the same concern for Mary's welfare as he had for hers. Or that he'd administered the same lecture.

She shouldn't care, but she did.

Obviously, Mary hadn't paid the least attention to Sam's strictures. But then Mary was a nurse, as he had so bluntly pointed out. She was needed here. Victoria, on the other hand, wasn't. She'd come merely to write about the war, not participate in it.

Resentment simmered as she came topside and stepped out into the blinding sunshine. It irritated her now to remember how meekly she'd accepted Sam's strictures, how quickly she'd acceded to his demand that she return home. It irritated her even more to recall how submissively she'd surrendered her body as well as her will.

Not that she remained submissive for long. Heat singed her cheeks as she remembered how she'd progressed from timid virgin to near wanton within the space of mere hours. Even then, even after proving herself a woman in every sense of the word, she'd been prepared to pack her bag and head home like a good little girl. And would have, if Sam hadn't had to rush back to his company.

"Shall we sit here?"

With a stiff nod, Victoria joined Mary on a hatch cover shaded by the ship's forward funnel.

"Now, tell me all about your time here in Tampa," the widow begged with a smile. "I'd imagine it's been rather exciting."

"Yes, it has."

In more ways than Victoria would ever admit, least of all to this woman.

"But I didn't seek you out to talk about myself. I should like to do a story about the nursing corps. If you have a few moments to spare, perhaps you could tell me about some of the other women in your unit and what you expect to encounter when you arrive in Cuba."

Mary's smile faded. A question came into her eyes.

"Are you sure you want to know? The citizens of Cheyenne may not wish to read the gruesome details of how a field hospital operates during and after a battle."

For the first time, Victoria faced the challenge of balancing accuracy with compassion. Too much detail, and she'd strike terror into the hearts of women who'd sent husbands and sons off to war. Too little, and she'd write a story with no soul.

"Tell me whatever you wish and I'll include what I consider appropriate for my readers."

"Fair enough."

When Victoria descended the gangplank some hours later, she carried with her another filled notebook and profound respect for the women who'd volunteered for such grim service. She also carried a letter of introduction from Mary to Miss Clara Barton, who was overseeing the outfitting of the ship she'd chartered in the name of the American Red Cross.

Victoria searched out Miss Barton the very next day. Already she'd heard stories about the amazing woman who'd recruited her own corps of Red Cross volunteers, purchased tons of supplies and equipment—including four horseless carriage ambulances—and chartered the *Star of Texas* to convey them all to Cuba.

Miss Barton proved even more amazing in person than in rumor. When Victoria asked permission to do a story about her, however, the gray-haired dynamo shook her head.

"I would rather you write about my volunteers. They're quite a fascinating group, you know, and run the gamut from wealthy socialites to a one-time vaudeville dancer.''

The twinkle in her eyes told Victoria that Miss Barton knew exactly what she was doing. She'd reeled the reporter in with that fascinating tidbit.

''They lack the formal medical training to qualify for the army's nursing corps, but more than make up for that shortfall in courage and determination to serve. Come, let me introduce you to a few.''

To Victoria's mind, no one summed up that self-lessness better than Callie May Morgan. She interviewed the tall, big-boned New Orleans native down in the bowels of the *Texas*. Swiping her sweat-streaked forehead with a beefy forearm, the laundress slapped a wet sheet on a washboard.

''I don't know why Miss Barton sent you to speak with me, miss. I never been to school. I got no particular skills. All I ever done is scrub floors in a flophouse and have babies.''

''You're married?'' Surprised, Victoria blinked away the salty sting of sweat.

''No, ma'm, me 'n' my Jake never got around to standin' before a preacher. Didn't see the need, not when God looked down on us every day.''

''Is your Jake in the army? Are you following him to Cuba?''

''Jake took sick with the yellow fever some years back and passed on.'' Patiently, she bent over the washboard. "Same fever claimed my little ones, too. All four of them."

"I'm so sorry!"

"The Good Lord gives and the Good Lord takes," she said with stoic acceptance. "No, ma'm, I joined up with Miss Clara because I'm an immune."

"I beg your pardon?"

"I had a touch of Yellow Jack, too, but it didn't take me like it did Jake 'n' my little ones. So they classified me as immune. When Miss Clara put out the call for volunteers, I decided to go along to Cuba to help take care of our soldier boys. Word is, they're more likely to catch a fever in them jungles than a bullet."

Since both Mary and Miss Barton had voiced the same opinion, Victoria didn't argue the point.

"So here I am," Callie May said, her muscular arms bulging as she wrung out the wet sheet. "God done gave me a gift and it would go against His will not to use it."

Her simple faith and obvious dedication humbled Victoria. She wrote furiously, trying to capture the essence of the woman. The laundress paused to watch her pencil fly across the green-ruled lines.

"Looks like He gave you a gift, too."

"What? Yes, I suppose He did. Words come easy to me."

"Easy or not, you're doing His work."

Startled, Victoria demurred. "I don't know if I'd describe my stories in quite those terms."

"I would, miss. Not many women would have the gumption to come down here to Tampa and write about all this. No, miss, you're doing what God planned for you to do, just like the rest of us."

Her quiet words lingered in Victoria's mind long after she'd left the *Texas*.

Afterward, she would always marvel at the simple events that seemed to bring about the greatest changes in one's life.

If Mary hadn't written that note of introduction…

If Miss Barton hadn't sent her down to interview Callie May…

If Dan Powdry hadn't growled irritably that the captain wasn't going to like his woman diddling about Tampa so long and thoroughly set up Victoria's back…

If any one of those inconsequential events had not occurred, she might not have found herself aboard the *Star of Texas,* bound for Cuba a mere two days after the troop transports had steamed out of port.

11

"It's so green," Callie May Morgan murmured.
"Like the Garden of Eden."

Propping her elbows on the ship's rail, the laundress stared at the tropical island some hundred yards away. Beside her, Victoria gripped the teak rail with hands gone white at the knuckles. Like Callie May, her glance was riveted on the green-blanketed mountains rising above the port of Siboney.

"Wonder what my Jake would say if he knew I'd left New Orleans," Callie May mused. "I can't hardly believe I come so far from home."

Nor could Victoria. The evidence was right there, before her eyes, yet she had to force herself to accept that she was indeed here. In Cuba. Accompanying an invading army. With only one small valise, a purse filled with banknotes pinned securely to her petticoat, her gold locket tucked away for safety and her notebook clutched in a sweaty fist.

It had all happened so fast. She'd actually begun packing her trunk for the trip back to Cheyenne when Miss Barton sent word the *Star of Texas* was loaded and would steam out of port within the next few hours. If Miss Parker had indeed been serious when she expressed a desire to accompany the Red Cross volunteers to Cuba and record their story, she'd best get down to Port Tampa immediately.

Victoria had paced the floor of her sitting room in an agony of indecision. Sam had insisted she go home. Common sense told her that was the best course. The only course. Yet Callie May Morgan's words kept tugging at her mind. She had a gift. A God-given gift. According to her papa's cables, her stories had already boosted the *Tribune*'s circulation significantly.

Trembling with a combination of excitement and nervous bravado, she finally threw a few things into a carpetbag, deposited her leather-bound trunk with the concierge, composed a hurried cable to her papa and rushed down to the port before she could change her mind. She'd departed Tampa so quickly she'd left behind her faithful watchdog, Dan Powdry.

Now she stood at the ship's rail, a mere hundred yards or so off shore, so sick with trepidation at what she'd encounter when her feet touched dry land again that she could barely put pencil to notepaper.

Gulping, Victoria dropped her gaze to the longboats bobbing on the waves. There were hundreds and hundreds of them, all ferrying men and supplies ashore. The convoy that included the *Star of Texas* had dropped anchor in this palm-fringed bay just after dawn. Six thousand men were now struggling ashore, laden with weapons and heavy backpacks.

These six thousand followed on the heels of the first wave of U.S. troops, which had landed two days ago at Daiquirí, some seven miles to the east. That wave had established a beachhead, captured this port of Siboney and trekked into the hills where they defeated the Spanish at Las Guásimas in the first battle of the war. Signalmen using colorful flags had wigwagged the news from ship to ship just minutes after the first anchor dropped at Siboney.

Her stomach churning, Victoria once again lifted her anxious gaze to the mountains ringing the seaside town. Sam was up there in that dense green jungle. The Rough Riders had participated in the Battle of Las Guásimas. Casualties were reportedly light, with only sixteen Americans killed and fifty-two wounded, but the mere thought that Sam might be among them made Victoria feel ill.

The queasy feeling stayed with her all that long, hot morning. Not until almost noon did Miss Barton receive permission to go ashore. Hiring a mule, the indomitable woman made an arduous five-mile trek into the jungle to meet with General Shafter at his field headquarters. Shafter confirmed that casualties from Las Guásimas were, indeed, light and that his medical staff at Siboney appeared to have matters well in hand.

"He suggested we set up operations at Daiquirí," Miss Barton informed her volunteers when she returned to the ship. "I'm to consult with the commander there as to facilities."

Drawing Victoria aside, she shared news of a more personal sort. "While in town, I met a reporter who was with the First Volunteer Cavalry at Las Guásimas. He says he knows you. A Mr. Richard Harding Davis."

"I met him in Tampa," she confirmed, her heart thumping. "Did he say whether or not the First had suffered casualties?"

Gravely, Miss Barton nodded. "Eight men killed and thirty-four wounded."

"Eight of the sixteen American dead are Rough Riders?" Victoria gasped.

"So Mr. Davis indicated. Captain Garrett wasn't among them," she hastened to add.

"Thank God!"

"But he was among the wounded. Davis says he took a Mauser bullet."

Victoria's stomach dropped clear to her boots. The deck reeled under her. Clucking, Miss Barton reached out a steadying hand.

"Wounds made by Mausers are usually either immediately fatal or rather trivial. If the bullet hits no vital organ, it often goes right through, perforating bone and muscle cleanly. The entry and exit wounds soon scab over and heal quite nicely. According to Mr. Davis, the captain refused to leave the battlefield until the fight was over. You must take heart from that, my dear. "

Victoria barely heard one word in three. Her one thought, her only thought, was to get to Sam.

"I must go ashore."

"Yes, of course you must. Mr. Davis said he'd escort you to the hospital. You're to search him out at the cable office in Siboney. Once you're ashore, though, I must warn you that you'll be on your own. You're not one of my volunteers. I can't guarantee your safety."

Her warning fell on deaf ears. Victoria was already running for her valise. Mere minutes later she stumbled down a long set of folding metal stairs. With the *Star of Texas* riding the swells, she took a deep breath and leaped into the bobbing ship's boat.

Siboney. The name was so musical, hinting at gaily painted stucco buildings, trickling tile fountains and tall palms rustling in the breeze. As Victoria stepped onto a rickety wooden quay, her first glimpse of the town proved anything but gay or musical.

The first wave of the Expeditionary Army had launched a heavy bombardment to drive out its garrison of Spanish troops. Many of Siboney's buildings now gaped open to the broiling sun. Craters pockmocked the pale-yellow-and-ochre walls. Red-clay roof tiles had tumbled into the street, creating piles of debris. An artillery shell had shattered the fountain in the center of the main square.

The residents who'd fled the bombardment were only now straggling back. The men were grim-faced, the women tearful as they surveyed what was left of their homes. They edged past long lines of U.S. troops whose ranks had swelled with the addition of hundreds of Cuban rebels, all marching out to join up with the force that had landed at Daiquirí two days before.

Victoria registered only vague details of the grim scene as she made for the cable office at one end of the plaza. There she found a jam of reporters offering outrageous bribes to get their dispatches sent, each one grumbling about the one-hundred-word limit General Shafter had imposed to keep reporters from clogging the telegraph lines. Richard Harding Davis wasn't among them. One of the correspondents suggested she try the taverna next door.

When Victoria spotted the three men hunched around a table, their heads wreathed in a cloud of cigar smoke, she almost didn't recognize Davis. He looked nothing like the dapper adventurer in tropical white linens and cork pith helmet she'd met in Tampa. Several days of scraggly growth stubbled his chin and cheeks, and his once pristine linen suit was now mud brown. A leather cross belt supported his binoculars, notebooks and canteen, giving him the appearance of a *bandido*.

"Miss Parker. There you are!"

Setting down his jigger of rum, he rose and introduced his companions. "Do you know Freddie Remington and Steve Crane?"

At any other time, Victoria would have been thrilled to meet the world-renowned author of *The Red Badge of Courage* and an artist of Frederick Remington's international stature. But at that moment, the best she could manage was a distracted nod.

"How do you do. Mr. Davis, Miss Barton said you were with the First Volunteer Cavalry during the battle at Las Guásimas and spoke with my fiancé afterward."

"Right. Captain Garrett, isn't it?"

"Yes. Is his…? Is his injury serious?"

"Not to hear him describe it. 'Damned nuisance,' I believe his words were. Colonel Roosevelt was forced to issue him a direct order before he'd take himself to the field hospital."

Giddy with relief, Victoria barely refrained from flinging her arms around his neck. "Would you be so kind as to direct me to the hospital?"

"I'll do better than that," he said gallantly. "I'll escort you there myself. Freddie, old man, will you loan the lady your mule?"

"Of course."

With a shrill whistle, Davis summoned the Cuban the reporters had hired to protect their property.

"We have to keep the animals under armed guard," he confided to Victoria as she climbed somewhat awkwardly into a wooden saddle. "Transport is more precious than gold right now."

She soon discovered why. Once outside the town, the road narrowed to a dirt lane hedged on both sides by an impenetrable jungle of banana trees, spiky palmettos and all manner of vegetation she'd never seen before. In several spots the path plunged down slopes so steep the mules tucked their hind legs under them and skittered down on their haunches. At the bottom of the ravines, they'd plow through muddy streams and start up again.

As uncomfortable and precarious as the mule ride was, navigating the dirt track was even more of a chore for the troops who slogged through the mud. Sliding and slipping, the soldiers panted up and down the steep slopes.

Davis, who'd spent the better part of the past two years in Cuba, cheerfully identified the unit insignia of the troops they passed. Victoria closed her ears to their muttered curses and acknowledged with a nod their apologies when they noticed a lady among them. Sweat and mud soon stained her tan traveling suit, and she lost all pretensions to neatness when dark clouds suddenly rolled over the mountains and dumped their contents in a thick, torrential deluge.

The storm passed within minutes, leaving Victoria as wet and odorous as her mule. She had just lifted a hand to swat at the gnats that reappeared after the deluge when the brush rustled and a scaly creature the size of a small dog scuttled right between her mule's legs.

Braying, the animal humped and hopped and stomped at the spidery crustacean. Victoria grabbed the pommel with both hands and managed to keep from being tossed into the mud. Stunned, she watched the creature disappear into the brush on the other side of the track.

"What on *earth* was that?"

"Don't know the exact name for them," Davis replied. "We call them land crabs."

"Do…? Do they bite?"

"Not anything bigger than themselves, I'm told. But the blasted things feed at night and have caused more than one trigger-happy sentry to discharge his weapon. Then the nervous soldier walking the post next to him thinks it's an attack and, before you know it, we've got a whole fusillade going. Hard for a fellow to sleep, I can tell you.''

''I would imagine,'' Victoria said faintly.

''They make for decent eating, though, should you find yourself stranded in the mountains without rations. A solid whack with a stone will crack their shells.''

Sincerely hoping she never found herself in such dire circumstances, she nodded.

The journey to the field hospital seemed to last forever, but in fact they had covered less than a mile and a half when they reached a cleared cane field on a hillside above Siboney. The temporary hospital had been situated there to catch the breezes, Davis explained, but elements of it would move with the army when it pushed on to Santiago.

Victoria barely heard him. The sight of stretchers lying outside the long rows of tents held her horrified gaze. At least a hundred men lay sweating in the steamy heat while they awaited medical attention.

''I thought the battle casualties were light!''

''They were. Most of these fellows are down with fever. Doesn't take long in the tropics. Shafter will be lucky if he takes Santiago before he loses half his army.''

Swinging down from his saddle, he offered a hand to Victoria.

"Let's see if we can find Teddy's Terrors. Did you hear Roosevelt now has command of the regiment?"

"No, I didn't," Victoria murmured, stricken by the difference between her hazy mental image of the field conditions Mary had described and the stark reality of this camp.

"Brigadier General Young, Second Brigade commander, also went down with fever, so Wood has moved up to his command. Roosevelt in turn was promoted to take over the regiment from Wood."

At that moment, Victoria couldn't have cared less who commanded what. She'd spotted several men wearing brown canvas pants and familiar, blue polka-dot neckerchiefs. Her heart thumping, she lifted her skirts and rushed down the cane-strewn path between the tents.

"Are you men with the First Volunteer Cavalry?"

"Yes, ma'am."

"Can you tell me where I might find Captain Garrett?"

A tall, lanky trooper tanned to the color of saddle leather hooked a thumb toward a Shelby tent a little farther down the row. "He's in there."

"Thank you."

When she went to brush by the man, his curious

gaze swept her from the tip of her sodden hat to her muddy boots.

"Hey! Aren't you the captain's lady? The one who came out to our bivouac area in Tampa?"

"I, er, yes."

"Well, I'll be danged!"

Davis saw the astonished looks the men gave Victoria as she hurried past. A frown settled over his handsome, square-jawed face.

"I say. Garrett does know you took ship to Cuba, doesn't he?"

"No."

"Hmm. Perhaps I'd better wait for you outside."

"Perhaps you had."

He dropped back, leaving Victoria to duck inside the opening of the Shelby tent. After the bright glare outside, the gloom inside blinded her. Desperately, she tried not to gag at the stench of vomit and urine while she waited for her eyes to adjust.

Taking shallow, pinched breaths, she gradually made out two rows of cots tucked under the sloping canvas sides. Slop buckets were set beside each cot, some filled with scummy water, others with bloody bandages.

It took a moment for her to spot the orderly bent over one of the cots, and a moment more to see the tall, broad-shouldered officer standing at the rear of the tent. He wore a thick bandage under his half-buttoned shirt and was in deep conversation with a slender, dark-haired nurse in a soiled white apron.

As Victoria watched, her heart in her throat, Sam lifted his unbandaged arm and cupped Mary's cheek. The gesture was gentle and infinitely tender. Victoria stood frozen, unable to breathe, unable to speak, while Sam bent his head and brushed the woman's mouth with his.

In that moment, Victoria's hopes and dreams splintered into a thousand, knife-edged shards. Without a word, she backed out of the tent.

Blinded once again by the sun, she stumbled down the cane-lined path. Pain lanced into her with every step.

"I say! Miss Parker." Richard Davis caught her elbow. "Are you all right?"

"I— I—"

Struggling for breath, she lifted her chin. She wouldn't cry. She *wouldn't!* Not now. Not here, in front of all these strangers.

"I'm quite all right."

Frowning, Davis glanced over his shoulder. "Did you find Captain Garrett?"

"I found him."

The strangled reply raised instant alarm on the journalist's face. "Good Lord! Was his wound more serious than we thought? Is he in distress?"

"He—" She had to fight to speak around the

lump lodged in her throat. "He seems to be doing quite well. If you don't mind, I should like to return to Siboney now."

He cast another curious glance over his shoulder. A dozen questions burned in his eyes, but he asked only one.

"If you're sure?"

"Quite sure," she whispered.

The sun blazed red and low above the sea when they reached town again. Victoria was too heartsick to appreciate its molten beauty, too numb to lift her gaze from the small slice of the world framed between her mule's ears.

"Are you staying in town?" the solicitous Davis asked when they reached the taverna in the main plaza.

She hadn't thought beyond getting away from the hospital, hadn't considered anything except the need to put the sight of Sam and Mary far behind her. Aching and weary to the point of near collapse, she hooked her leg over the pommel and all but dropped out of the saddle. Her arms felt like lead when she reached up for her valise.

"Here, let me."

Davis got it down for her and stood patiently while she summoned what she hoped was a smile. She couldn't bear the thought of anyone, particularly this dashing, worldly correspondent, seeing her hurt spill into tears.

"I'm not staying in town," she said in answer to his question. "I'll get one of the longboats to take me back out to the *Star of Texas*."

"I'll walk you down to the quay, then."

"No!"

She had to get away, had to have time for the searing pain to dull before she faced another living soul. Almost snatching her valise from his hand, she fought to keep the tremor from her voice.

"I've already taken up your whole afternoon and I'm—I'm sure you have dispatches to write before the cable office closes. It's only a short walk to the dock."

"Really, I wish you'd let me—"

"Goodbye, Mr. Davis. And thank you. Thank you so much."

She left him standing outside the taverna and made her way across the square. Heat, exhaustion and the ache that went right down to her soul had her staggering long before she reached the rickety wooden dock.

Only after she'd stepped onto the planks did she lift her head and narrow her eyes against the glare of the setting sun. Her glance skipped from one anchored ship to another, searching for the *Star of Texas*. It took her several minutes and a rather frantic inquiry of the sailors bringing in a longboat to ascertain that the ship had steamed out of port almost an hour ago. For Daiquirí, they thought, but they weren't sure.

Her valise slipped from her numb fingers. In a state of utter desolation, Victoria sank down on top of it, wrapped her arms around her waist and stared out at the bloodred bay.

12

Victoria sat on the Siboney dock until mosquitoes and curious looks from sailors still ferrying troops and baggage ashore drove her back to the main plaza.

Shielded by darkness, her valise clutched tight in her hands, she stood beside the rubble of the fountain and surveyed the brightly lit taverna across the plaza. Richard Harding Davis and his companions were still there. Rum bottles littered their table. Clouds of cigar smoke kept the mosquitoes at bay.

The thin, sallow Stephen Crane appeared to be relating a long tale, lifting a hand every so often to dash his black hair back from his forehead. Remington, the artist, sprawled at his ease. Davis looked more like a *bandito* than ever with his leather cross belt and the beard stubbling his chin.

They formed a tight brotherhood, Victoria thought dully. As close as that of the troops they had journeyed to war with. It took her a moment to remember that she, too, was now a member of the fraternity. With great effort, she squared her shoulders, hefted her carpetbag and crossed to the taverna. Remington saw her first and nudged Davis, who scrambled to his feet.

"Miss Parker! I say, have you changed your mind about going back out to the ship?"

"It appears my mind was changed for me. The *Star of Texas* has left Siboney." She swiped her tongue along her lower lip. "I wonder if I might impose upon you once again to procure me a hotel room. I'm afraid I don't speak Spanish."

"I'd be happy to, but there's not a hotel room to be had. The army has commandeered every building of any size with a roof over it."

"I see."

"Look, Crane here rented us a room in a house that wasn't damaged too badly during the barrage. We have it just for a few days, as we plan to rejoin the troops for the push to Santiago, but we're so busy exchanging notes and cribbing our stories we probably won't sleep at all tonight. You're welcome to bed down there, isn't she, Stephen?"

"What? Oh, yes, of course." The novelist flashed her a charming smile. "You're a member of the press, after all. We must look out for one another."

Victoria had long passed the point of pride. With

a grateful nod, she accepted their offer. "Thank you."

"I'll take you there straight away and introduce you to the people who own the house, shall I?" Easing her bag out of her hand, Davis smiled. "I can fix you up with a few essentials, too. Unless you thought to pack mosquito netting, a pith helmet and a bar or two of soap in here."

"I'm afraid it's filled mostly with my notebooks."

Crane gave a shout of laughter. "You are most *definitely* a member of the press."

Less than an hour later, Victoria stripped down to her chemise and drawers and used a damp cloth to clean away her layers of mud before she crawled under a tent of netting. Straw rustled as she stretched out on the mattress and waited for the tears.

None came. Eyes dry and burning with fatigue, she stared up at rough-hewn ceiling beams painted silvery gray by the moonlight filtering through the shutters. Sometime between her agonized flight from the hospital tent and the long moments she sat on her valise and gazed out over the bay, she seemed to have lost the capacity to cry.

But not to hurt.

Dear God above, not to hurt!

Like a wild beast released from its chains, the

pain leaped and clawed through her again. Moaning, she clenched her fists. Still the tears didn't come. Only the bitter, bitter truth.

Here, in the suffocating darkness, she forced herself to face it. She'd known all along that Sam didn't love her. Not with the passion she felt for him, anyway. He held her in affection. He cared for her in his careless, casual way. And he lusted for her. Their hours together at the Tampa Bay Hotel had left no doubt of that in her mind.

But he didn't love her.

He loved Mary.

Squeezing her eyes shut, Victoria tried to block the image of a tent filled with cots. A bandaged soldier. A nurse in a soiled white apron. A gentle, tender kiss.

When Sam pounded on the door of the house the next morning, Victoria was in the kitchen, picking at a breakfast of fried plantains and black beans wrapped in a flat bread.

Although artillery shells had destroyed a good part of the home, the kitchen had survived intact, as had the garden outside its windows. A riot of red and orange bougainvillea climbed the garden walls. Tall, glossy-leafed banana trees waved their fronds in the sun. Victoria was just thinking dully that she should record the exotic scene in her notebook when the hard hammering sounded at the front door.

She heard a swift exchange in Spanish, then the rapid thud of boots. Drawing in a deep, shuddering breath, she turned her gaze toward the kitchen door.

"Hello, Sam."

The calm greeting stopped him cold. His eyes narrowing, he raked her with a hard look.

He looked terrible, Victoria thought dispassionately. Beneath the brim of his slouch hat, his face was haggard. The beginnings of a bristly beard shadowed his cheeks and chin. Sweat darkened the armpits and collar of his blue flannel shirt, which showed rusty stains on its left shoulder. From the Mauser bullet, she realized with a swift clenching of her stomach.

"I've been looking all over this damned town for you," he said, a muscle ticking in the side of his jaw.

Crossing the uneven tiles, he stopped in front of her. In another time, another place, the savage fury in his eyes might have frightened her.

"All right, Victoria. Let's start with an explanation of why I had to learn from one of the troopers that you're in Cuba. While you're at it, you can also explain why you came up to the field hospital yesterday afternoon and left without seeking me out."

"Does it really matter how you learned about my

presence in Cuba? And as for yesterday afternoon..."

During the long hours before dawn, she'd considered and rejected a dozen or more excuses for
her precipitous flight from the hospital. Finally,
she'd decided on the truth.

"I did seek you out. I found you in one of the
tents."

"Did you?" The fury in his face didn't abate.
"Strange. I don't recall seeing you."

"You were rather occupied at the time. With
Mrs. Prendergast."

He didn't move a muscle.

"I saw you kiss her," she said in a voice carefully devoid of all nuance. "Rather than announce
my presence and embarrass us all, I turned and
left."

His reply was a long time coming. "That kiss
had nothing to do with you and me."

Astonishingly, she managed a smile. "I wonder
how many men have uttered those same inane
words down through the centuries."

The muscle in the side of his jaw jumped again.
Once. Twice. In a detached corner of her mind, Victoria was proud of her calm as she gestured to the
blue-painted wooden chair opposite her.

"Do sit down, Sam. If we must discuss this sordid little tangle, let's at least do so in a civilized

manner. Would you care for some coffee? It's quite bitter, but I believe there's some left in the—"

"I don't want any coffee!" Yanking off his slouch hat, he dropped into the chair. "I can see how you might have formed the impression this is a—a tangle, but I assure you there's nothing sordid about it."

Her careful calm slipped a bit. "I suppose that depends on where you're standing when you view it," she snapped. "From where I stood, it looked very much like—"

"Listen to me, Victoria! Mary had just spent long hours caring for one of our men. He took seven bullets. Seven. The surgeon removed most of his organs in an attempt to save him before giving up. The doctor didn't have time to stitch the poor bastard together before moving on to the next patient. Mary stayed with him as much as she could, holding his hand, keeping the flies from his gaping wounds. After my wound was dressed, I sat with her. Neither of us expected the man to take so long to die."

"Sam..."

"Even a nurse needs comforting after something like that."

Once more, Mary's noble profession defeated Victoria. Her throat aching, she nodded.

"Yes, I can see she would. And I can see how you would need to comfort her."

It was time to lay matters out into the hot, bright sun.

"It's all right, Sam. I know you love her. I've known since the night of Elise's birthday party, but I was too vain to admit it."

And too stupidly, childishly confident that a gown with a plunging neckline would dazzle this man so much he'd become blind to every woman but her.

Suddenly, she felt as though she'd aged a thousand years since that snowy February night. So much had happened, so little was now familiar, she might have traveled to a distant planet. One filled with steamy jungles and the anguish of a broken heart instead of happy, girlish dreams and wide, windswept plains.

"I've never denied that I have a deep regard for Mary." He held her eyes, his own unwavering. "I told you as much the evening we became engaged."

"Yes, you did."

"That regard doesn't in the least alter or affect what I feel for you."

At last they'd come to it, Victoria thought with a wrenching pain. The conversation they should have had before he'd offered and she'd so joyously agreed to marriage.

"What *do* you feel for me?"

The question put a match to the fuse of anger

that still simmered in Sam's veins. It wasn't as violent as the fury that had gripped him when several troopers swore they'd spoken to Victoria yesterday afternoon. Or as savage as the rage that consumed him as he searched all over Siboney for her, torn between fear for her safety and the urgent need to return to his regiment. Or as fierce and hot as his resentment that she'd think he would dishonor the pledge he'd made to her.

He'd kissed Mary to comfort her. Only to comfort her. The brief brush of his lips on hers had stirred nothing like the near primitive lust Victoria's kisses roused in him. For some inexplicable reason, acknowledgment of that fact set Sam's anger to boiling again. Abandoning his chair, he rounded the table.

"I told you back in Cheyenne what I felt for you."

She rose to meet him, looking completely unlike the Victoria he knew in a soiled white blouse and muddied skirt, with her hair pinned up haphazardly and bluish circles under her eyes. But the angle of her chin was all hers.

"I need you to spell it out again. In plain words."

"In plain words," he growled, "I'm feeling the overpowering urge to toss you over my shoulder, haul you down to the dock and pay the first ship captain I encounter an exorbitant sum to lock you in the hold and keep you there until his ship steams out of port.''

A gritty determination came into her eyes. "Oh, no! You're not going to use bluster or threats to evade my question. I need to know the emotions I rouse in you. Tell me, Sam. Honestly.''

''Honestly?''

He curled his hand around her throat and raised her chin another notch.

''Anger. Admiration. Exasperation. Occasionally amusement. And always, *always*, desire. I want you, Victoria. Even when I tried my damnedest not to, I wanted you.''

She opened her mouth, gulped back whatever she was going to say. Sam felt her muscles ripple under his palm, felt as well the tension in the cords and tendons.

''When we became engaged," she said at last, forming each word carefully, ''wanting was enough. I was so certain it would lead to—to something deeper. A week ago, when I gave myself to you, I thought the hunger that drove us both would be enough. But it isn't. I'm sorry, Sam, but it's not nearly enough.''

He smothered a vicious oath. He'd laid his need for her bare, admitted she stripped him of any claims to restraint where she was concerned, and it wasn't enough?

Well, he couldn't give her anything more. Not at

the moment, anyway. His shoulder hurt like hell and his company was regrouping to move on to Santiago. He was damned if he'd start spouting flowery phrases of love and devotion.

"This isn't the time or the place for this discussion," he bit out. "I have to rejoin my regiment. The word to advance on Santiago could come at any time. I have to get you aboard a ship immediately."

Victoria moved away from his touch. With a little shake of her head, she refused his services.

"I'm not leaving."

"The hell you're not. I wasn't joking about tossing you over my shoulder. I will if I have to. I'm not going back to my regiment with my fiancée alone and unprotected in a war zone."

"You don't seem to understand, Sam."

Slipping a hand into her skirt pocket, she drew out a folded handkerchief. Carefully, she opened the folds. Just as carefully, she offered him back the sapphire-studded pin he'd given her as an engagement gift.

"I'm no longer your fiancée. I'm releasing you from your promise to marry me."

He took a step toward her, fire in his eyes. Victoria stood her ground for the simple reason that the table blocked her path of retreat.

"There's something you don't seem to understand. I took not only your pledge, but your virginity. You gave yourself to me in the most elemental sense of the word and I'm not relinquishing my claim on you.''

Victoria's fist closed around the locket. She'd agonized over this decision for most of the night. In her heart of hearts, she'd expected Sam to register a vigorous protest. But not once had it occurred to her that he would flatly refuse to acknowledge her right to terminate their engagement!

''May I remind you we're about to enter the twentieth century?'' she said, struggling to maintain her composure. ''A woman might have been held to betrothal against her will five hundred years ago. One hundred, even. But not today. We're no longer chattles to be passed from father to husband. Nor,'' she added on a sharper note when he appeared completely unimpressed with her speech, ''am I a section of land or—or a muddy stretch of creek that you can simply stake a claim to.''

For the first time, she caught a glimpse of the old Sam in this hard, angry man. The grim cast to his jaw softened, and what looked suspiciously like amusement flickered in his brown eyes for a second or two.

''I've never thought of you as a muddy stretch of creek, but I must say you come closer to fitting that description today than I would have thought possible.''

''Oh, Sam!'' With a sigh, Victoria searched for a way to make him understand. ''Perhaps my dirty skirts and untidy hair should tell you something.

I'm a different woman from the one you knew in Cheyenne.''

"That's the first thing you've said this morning I agree with!''

"I've set out on a journey I didn't quite plan but now must see through. For my sense of self-respect, if for no other reason.''

Gripping the locket in a tight fist, she tried to put into words the confused impulses that had driven her aboard the *Star of Texas.*

"I'm a journalist. My credentials give me the same status as correspondents like Richard Harding Davis and Anna Benjamin. I'm present at one of the turning points of history and I want to record it. I don't need your approval or permission for that. No, please! Let me finish!''

Crossing his arms, he waited with obvious impatience for her to get on with it.

"I know I'm not essential to the war effort like you or—or Mrs. Prendergast. Nor am I as brave as Mr. Davis. I have no desire to march on Santiago with the army and dodge bullets, as he did during the battle of Las Guásimas. But I can contribute in my own small way. By describing Cuba to the people back home, so they know what their sons and husbands are going through. By telling them about the heat and the mosquitoes. The incredible beauty of the mountains. Those—those scaly, spiderlike creatures.''

"Encountered a land crab, did you?'' Sam's brow hooked. "If nothing else, that should be enough to send you down to the docks straight-away.''

Victoria decided not to mention that it had. Or that she'd spent untold minutes on the quay feeling more lost and desolate than she'd ever imagined she could.

Nor had she ever imagined that she'd have the inner fortitude to offer the only compromise she knew Sam would accept.

''I appreciate your need to protect me. You'd feel the same concern for any woman, whether she was your fiancée or not.''

''Not quite the same,'' he drawled sarcastically, but at least he was listening.

''If it will ease your worries about my being in Cuba, I'll go up to the hospital and beg a bed. As a journalist,'' she added, swallowing the bitter pill of her pride. ''I know I'm not qualified to assist the nurses in their duties, but I can follow up on the story I wrote about them in Tampa and perhaps garner them a little of the credit they deserve.''

''You can't have any idea what conditions are like in a field hospit—''

He caught himself, remembering she'd observed those conditions firsthand yesterday. What she'd seen there hung between them now, as thick and dark as the clouds that dropped over the mountains and deluged the island yesterday afternoon.

Victoria would be a long time forgiving him for that kiss, he knew. If she ever forgave him. And Sam couldn't take the time now to convince her she should. Wincing at the discomfort his wound caused, he reached out and curled his hands around her upper arms.

"Listen to me, Victoria. Most of those men at the hospital are down with fever. You'll be in as much danger from them as you would be from Spanish bullets."

"Mr. Davis said the only fever that's struck so far is malaria. He very kindly gave me a supply of quinine tablets."

"Did he?"

"He also gave me his spare cork helmet, some mosquito netting and a rubber ground sheet. Mr. Davis understands why I want to stay in Cuba, Sam. He's been most helpful."

"Too damned helpful, if you ask me. I'll have a word or two to say to Richard when I see him."

"You may have all the words with him you wish. Now, I'd best pack my things if you intend to see me to the hospital before you rejoin your company."

His hands tightened on her arms, holding her in place. "You're determined on this?"

"Yes."

"I'll agree on two conditions," he said after a long, tense moment. "First, you must promise to evacuate with the nurses should it become necessary."

"No."

"Dammit, Victoria!"

"I won't make any more promises I may not

want to, or be able to keep. But I'm not a fool. And I don't have any particular wish to die. I'll take every possible precaution.''

"Will you at least agree to keep up the pretense of our engagement for the time being?" he ground out. "Let my name and rank afford you some measure of protection?"

They'd come full circle, Victoria thought. From a sham engagement to shield her reputation to a continued pretense to protect her person. The irony of it drew a long, ragged sigh.

As she'd stated only a moment ago, however, she didn't completely lack for sense. She was a woman alone in a country at war. Wearily, she nodded.

"Yes, Sam, I'll agree to the pretense."

When he left her at the hospital tents set up amid the stubble of the sugarcane field some hours later, Victoria carried only her valise and wore the protective sun helmet Richard Harding Davis had given her.

She also wore Sam's standard issue U.S. Army service revolver strapped around her hips.

13

Mary Prendergast accepted Victoria's presence in Cuba more readily than Sam had. She would, of course. She was braving considerable hardship herself to perform what she considered her duty.

After a short, private colloquy with Sam and a hasty consultation with the surgeon in charge, she escorted Victoria to one of the Shelby tents set aside as nurses' quarters.

"You must know the situation here. Sam said you came up to the hospital yesterday."

"Yes, I did."

Lifting the tent flap, she held it up. The air inside was suffocatingly hot and smelled strongly of mildew. Rows of cots marched down either side of the tent. Mosquito netting was gathered above each, ready to drop downward with a tug of a string. Small wooden boxes sat at the foot of each cot and

held, Victoria guessed, the nurses' personal be-
longings.

"Take the third cot," Mary instructed. "The
nurse who occupied it is down with the fever. We
moved her to a ward tent so we could care for her
round the clock."

Dipping a towel in a bucket of water, she waited
while the younger woman dropped her valise onto
the designated cot and removed her cork helmet.

"Here, drape this cloth over the back of your
neck. Your face is quite red."

With a murmur of thanks, Victoria sank down
beside her carpetbag. The water soaking the cloth
was tepid at best, but provided welcome relief. The
dizzying spots caused by the heat and the mule ride
up to the hospital faded.

Sliding her hands into the front pockets of her
soiled white apron, Mary regarded the newcomer.
"When we spoke a few moments ago, Sam told me
you witnessed the kiss he gave me in the hospital
tent."

Victoria rubbed the cloth over her neck and made
no response. What was there to say?

"It meant nothing, you know. He was only trying
to comfort me after a rather brutal day and night."

"So he informed me."

"Did you believe him?"

With a sigh, Victoria dropped her hands to her
lap. A few months ago, the girl she'd been might

well have shied away from such a painful question. The woman she'd since become wouldn't allow such evasions.

"Yes, I believed him." Feeling unutterably weary, she laid her heart bare for the second time that day. "I also believe he holds you in a deeper regard than perhaps either of you have acknowledged."

"I can see how you might think so," Mary said slowly. With a rustle of her skirts, she sank onto the nearest cot. "I won't lie to you. Before I went East, there *was* something between Sam and me. A spark, a tug of attraction, if you will. I felt it every time I visited his parents' house. Then cholera claimed my mother and most of my tribe and I took the loss so keenly I had to go away to heal. And to learn. I was determined to learn all I could about the sicknesses the white men had brought on us. That's when I met John."

She fell silent, reliving her memories.

"John Prendergast was gruff and short-tempered," she said after a moment. "And quite the most annoying man I'd ever had to deal with. I must have packed my bags and marched out of his house a dozen times the first year I spent under his tutelage."

He must have been annoying indeed, Victoria thought, if he'd driven this seemingly indomitable woman out of his house.

"The dratted man never made the least effort to stop me," Mary continued, "but I always went back. Always. I never really understood why until after we married. It wasn't the passion that drew me, although it was quite intense with a man like John, I assure you. Nor even our shared interest in medicine."

Her gaze drifted to a hazy corner of the tent.

"It was sensing that I'd found an eagle," she murmured, more to herself than to Victoria. "One who would soar on the winds with me."

Slowly, she brought her glance back. "Eagles mate for life, you know. Although I had John for only a few years, he was my mate. He will always be my mate. Just, I suspect, as Sam would always be yours if you'd but let him."

"I have no desire to mate for life with a man who longs for another woman."

Silenced, Mary stared at her.

"I can see that you would not," she admitted after a moment. "No woman would."

"You, at least, understand that." Despite her every attempt to keep it out, a note of bitterness crept into Victoria's voice. "Sam seems to be having some difficulty."

The older woman hesitated, then chose her words with obvious care. "Sam might long for me in some distant corner of his mind, but you're the woman

he wants to spend his life with. He asked you to
marry him, after all.''

Only because circumstances obliged him to.

The brutal truth would remain forever carved into
her heart, but pride kept Victoria silent.

''Well,'' Mary said with a shake of her head,
''I'm hardly the one you'd want advice from on
this matter.''

That, at least, they could agree on.

''I'll get back to work and leave you to settle
in.'' Rising, she smoothed her sweat-dampened hair
under her limp linen cap. ''I'm on duty until—
Well, until I'm not. Meals are whenever you can
catch them at the kitchen tent. If you want anything,
come find me.''

She started for the entrance, then swung back.
''Oh, and I would recommend you leave that revolver here. Hopefully, you won't need it. You
might also want to shed your corset and your petticoats. The corset will give you a prickly rash in
this heat, and we've found our skirts catch on the
cane rubble and appear to provide the most irre-
sistible attraction to beetles and earworms.''

With that bit of practical advice, she ducked out
and disappeared into the blinding sunshine. When
the flap dropped down again, Victoria's shoulders
slumped. Between her wrenching meeting with Sam
earlier, this interview with Mary and the torpid heat,
she felt drained of all energy.

She allowed herself a moment to indulge in a fierce longing for Cheyenne's clean, biting winds and crab-free streets. But only a moment. She and she alone had made the momentous decision to travel to Cuba, and the equally momentous decision to stay. She refused to give way to doubts or panicky second thoughts.

Resolutely, she scrubbed her face with the damp cloth and pushed off the cot. Moments later, she'd shed several layers of fabric, steel and bone. Rolling the discarded garments into a tight ball, she bent to stuff them into her carpetbag.

A small square of neatly wrapped handkerchief tucked just inside the bag gave her pause. Setting aside her undergarments, she lifted out the handkerchief and slowly peeled back the folds. In the diffused light, a rim of sapphires glowed along the edge of the gold, heart-shaped case.

Swallowing, Victoria pried open the locket's lid. Sam stared out at her from the photograph she'd begged from his mother. She stroked the grainy portrait with her fingertip, then sighed and snapped the lid shut. Replacing the locket in the bag, she pulled out her notebook.

With Sam's service revolver tucked in the valise beside the locket, Victoria settled her borrowed cork helmet on her head once again and went out to record her impressions of the war as seen through the eyes of those who tended the wounded.

* * *

It didn't take her long to discover why correspondents in Cuba not only reported on events, but plunged right into them. Why Harry Scoval of the *World* had hired a boat just moments after the *Maine* exploded and rushed out to help. Why Frederick Somerford of the *Herald* had spent the months prior to the invasion with the rebels and sent cables advising Washington of their will to fight. Why Richard Harding Davis had gone into the jungle with the Rough Riders and used his glasses to spot enemy troop emplacements while bullets ripped through the leaves above his head.

It was impossible to merely observe.

Impossible to remain detached.

Victoria's stomach heaved each time she entered a hospital tent to record her impressions of the medical staff at their tasks, but she soon grew used to the stench of vomit and human excrement. She couldn't, however, grow used to standing idly by while the nurses and male hospital orderlies sweated and strained and worked themselves to the point of exhaustion.

She'd been in camp less than two hours before she slid her notebook in her pocket and approached a haggard nurse who was sitting on an upturned bucket, bathing the face of a malaria patient.

"I could do that while you tend to the others."

The woman didn't hesitate. Relinquishing her bucket, she passed Victoria the damp cloth.

"He's had a heavy dose of quinine. If his fever doesn't break within an hour, come fetch me."

It was, the reporter-turned-medical-attendant soon decided, one of the longest hours of her life. Burning with fever, the trooper tossed and flailed his arms. One caught Victoria square in the chest and almost knocked her off the bucket. Sweating almost as much as her patient, she dunked the cloth in tepid water and drew it over his face, his arms, his chest.

He wasn't much more than a boy. Close to her own age. When he cried out for his mother in his delirium, Victoria answered as calmly as she could and counted the minutes until the estimated hour had passed. Her heart wrenching at his pitiful condition, she went in search of the nurse as instructed.

By the time dusk began to purple the sky, she'd bathed a half dozen more troopers. She'd also emptied slop buckets, changed soiled sheets and scraped a razor over a number of bristling cheeks. Mary found her sitting on another bucket, writing a letter for a man too ill to pen it himself.

"Have you eaten today?"

Victoria looked at her blankly. "I don't remember."

"I'm on my way to the kitchen tent. Come with

me. You'll be of no use to anyone if you faint away from heat and hunger," she added to forestall protest. A smile softened her face. "And from what I've heard, you've been of great use."

Meals, she informed Victoria as they walked to the kitchen tent, consisted of beans, beans and more beans, supplemented by indigestible army rations and the ever-abundant local plantains. The mess tent was like an oven, so the two women took their tin plates to a fallen log beside the creek that provided the camp with fresh drinking water.

To Victoria's amazement, several of the nurses were sitting in the rock-strewn creek fully clothed, splashing away their sweat and grime and gore.

"The women bathe in the evening," Mary explained. "The men in the morning. We keep our clothes on both to preserve our modesty and to wash them. As hot as it is, they dry right on our backs."

"How practical."

"You should take a plunge after you eat. You'll sleep better."

Despite her unorthodox bath, Victoria barely slept at all that night. She spent the first hours in the tent composing the dispatch she didn't have time to write during the day. It took every bit of her skill to compress the wrenching sights and sounds and emotions she'd experienced that day into a hundred sparse words.

The rest of the night she spent jerking in and out of sleep. Patients required care twenty-four hours a day, and the constant coming and going of nurses jarred her awake every time she dozed off.

"You'll soon grow used to it," the exhausted woman stretching out on the cot next to hers murmured before she dropped into instant sleep.

The next afternoon Victoria begged a place on a supply train going down to the docks and made the arduous mule ride into Siboney to send her dispatch. As before, she found the cable office jammed with journalists. Many, she discovered, offered outright bribes to the harried telegraph operators in hopes they'd relax the hundred-word limit.

"Damned nuisance," a veteran correspondent ahead of her in line complained bitterly to the man behind him. "If the War Department hadn't issued credentials to every man jack who got it into his head to grab a pencil and traipse down to Cuba, the real members of the press among us could get our stories through."

Naturally, his comment elicited a round of hisses and boos. Victoria said nothing, but endured a good number of stares and sidelong glances before she got her turn at the window.

Escaping the crowded office, she walked next door to the taverna where she'd met Davis, Crane and Remington the day before. None of those distinguished correspondents were present, but the ones that were filled the air with excited talk of the imminent advance on Santiago.

She returned to the hospital to find it, too, buzzing with rumors.

"Fightin' Joe Wheeler and old man Shafter ain't about to sit 'n' stew," a feverish sergeant predicted confidently. "Our boys will take Santiago, you watch my words, and damned soon now that they're all ashore and in position."

Sam echoed the trooper's prediction when he appeared in camp that evening and found Victoria at her evening meal, such as it was. She heard him inquiring for her and clutched her spoon in a tight grip. A moment later he approached the fallen log where Victoria and two other nurses were seated.

Tipping his hat, he gave them all a polite greeting. "Ladies."

"Good evening, Captain," the younger responded. "Can we help you?"

"No, I've just come to have a word with Miss Parker."

"Oh, of course." The two nurses rose. "We'll leave you alone, then, shall we?"

Obligingly, they deposited their plates and spoons in the bucket of water standing ready beside one of the cook fires. As they moved away, Sam raked Victoria with a hard glance. She resisted the urge to smooth her wrinkled skirts.

"You look like the devil."

"Thank you."

She could have said the same of him. If he'd snatched any more sleep than she had last night, Victoria would be very much surprised. And the way he favored his right shoulder told its own story.

"Does your wound pain you?"

She'd learned enough about bullet wounds in the past twenty-four hours to appreciate the truth of Miss Barton's observation. Mauser bullets quite often went in and right out again, then scabbed over quickly. But as one patient had sardonically advised, the hole it left behind burned like hell on fire.

Sam shrugged aside the query. "I'm all right. You're taking your quinine pills, aren't you?"

"Yes."

"It's important to guard against foot rot in this climate. Have you a change of stockings?"

"Yes."

"And under linens? I might be able to purchase some in Siboney if you—"

"I have everything I require at the moment, thank you."

Biting back the reminder that neither she nor her under linens were his concern, Victoria set aside her plate.

"Did you find Mary? She was in the surgical tent the last time I saw her."

His face tightened. "I didn't trek through five miles of jungle to visit with Mary. I came to check on my men…and on you."

"As you can see, I'm faring quite well. Shall I walk with you to the Rough Riders' tent? I believe Private Holbrook is recovering well, but Trumpeter Sergeant O'Rourke took a turn for the worse last night."

"Victoria—"

He checked her with a hand on her elbow. Annoyed at the way her skin leaped at his touch, she tipped him a cool look.

"Yes?"

"We got word this afternoon." Under the brim of his gray slouch hat, his eyes held hers. "We're moving forward at first light tomorrow."

"Oh!"

It was one thing to stand on a train platform or a boat dock crammed with cheering crowds and send the man you loved off to war. It was another matter altogether to stand amid the tents that sheltered the victims of that war, to see the carnage bullets and cannon shells wrought on human flesh, and know he was going back into battle.

A lump lodged in Victoria's throat and refused to budge no matter how hard she swallowed.

"Be careful."

"I will. Like you, I have no particular wish to die."

If nothing else, the hours she'd spent at the field hospital had taught her that a wish to live was small protection against a bullet or cannon.

"Don't worry," Sam said, trying to ease her fear. "Our men showed their pluck at Las Guásimas. Now that the rest of the expeditionary force is ashore and in position, we should take Santiago easily."

"I hope so!"

"I'll send word to you when I can." His touch gentle, he cupped her cheek. "We'll sort matters out between us when this is over, sweetheart."

For the third night in a row, Victoria spent long stretches of darkness staring up at the gauzy netting that protected her from the insects buzzing around it.

Sam was going into battle.

Heat and dread of the coming dawn pressed down on her chest like an anvil. Every breath she drew in felt as heavy as lead, every thought brought her back to tomorrow.

Sam was going into battle.

The refrain echoed over and over in her mind until the reedy trill of a harmonica pierced her thoughts. It took only a few notes to identify Stephen Foster's long-time favorite, "My Old Kentucky Home." Tucking a hand under her head, Victoria listened to the haunting notes.

After the first verse, a solitary singer picked up the words. One voice after another gradually joined in. The chorus became an aching tribute to soldiers everywhere, and to the families they'd left behind.

Weep no more, my lady,
Oh, weep no more today.
We will sing one song
For the old Kentucky home,
For the old Kentucky home far away.

When the last verse died away, silence gripped the entire hospital. It was as if everyone at Siboney was thinking of the battle to come, and of the troops who would never see their homes again.

Just when Victoria thought she couldn't hold back her tears, a soaring tenor broke the stillness. Lively and irreverent, he belted out the rousing song Sam's regiment had adopted as its own. Once again a chorus of male voices joined in. Everyone, it seemed, was ready and eager for a hot time in the old town tonight!

The singers' unquenchable spirit eased the burning behind Victoria's lids. Slowly, her eyes closed. But she didn't fall asleep until after the last stanza was sung and someone shouted out that they'd better shut up or they'd bring the whole damned Spanish army down on their heads.

The boom of cannons jerked her awake just after dawn.

14

Nancy of Sam's years on active duty or months of service with the First Volunteer Cavalry had prepared him for the battle that commenced on July 1.

Although the day dawned clear and cloudless, the damned jungle made it impossible to spot the enemy. The Spanish were in position atop the line of ridges that stood between Santiago and the Expeditionary Force. Occupying abandoned sugarcane factories, blockhouses and trenches dug into the hills, they had the advantage of an unobstructed view of the jungles below. Those struggling through the dense green undergrowth couldn't see the man in front of him, much less the enemy above.

The battle plan called for the infantry division to launch the major offensive up the ridge at El Caney, several miles to the right. An artillery battery and the cavalry division would provide a diversion by attacking the hills above the San Juan River. Since only the officers had been allowed to bring their mounts on the jam-packed troop transports, the cavalry would fight on foot.

Unfortunately, the artillery was ordered into position directly behind Wood's brigade. As soon as the cannons at El Caney began to boom, the battery behind the cavalry division opened fire. The Spanish guns on the ridges above answered with a devastating shower of shrapnel.

With metal and death raining down all around them, Wood and Roosevelt leaped onto their horses and rushed to lead the men to safer positions. Wood's horse took a piece of shrapnel and went down, as did a good number of troops. One shell exploded right in the middle of the Cuban rebels, killing and wounding dozens. Another landed just yards away from Sam's company. Deadly metal fragments sliced through the leaves, beheading the captain at the head of the troop.

As the next senior ranking officer, Sam instantly assumed command. "Move out! Follow the colonel!"

He'd no sooner shouted the command than another shell detonated. Sam dropped like a stone, then picked himself up to find that one of the New Mexicans in his company had lost his left leg below the knee. Sweat pouring down his face, Sam shoved his borrowed service pistol into its holster and dragged the man to a giant palm, where he propped him against the trunk. The trooper's belt made a crude but effective tourniquet.

"Thanks, Captain." His face gray, he shouted hoarsely over the din of the artillery barrage. "I'll just sit here in the shade until the orderlies come."

"They'll be here soon. I'll send someone back to look for you when I can."

Sam sprinted through the brush, bent double to avoid the bullets singing overheard. By the time he and his men rejoined the regiment, it was spread all to hell and back. Burrowing in where they could, the men waited for the artillery barrage to cease.

It continued for more than half an hour, after which Wood reformed his Second Brigade with the Rough Riders' regiment in front. Shouting an order to Roosevelt, Wood instructed them to follow the First Brigade, which was to move down the trail to the ford of the San Juan River.

The sunken, muddy trail ran between two hills covered in dense jungle. Fortified blockhouses crowned the hill to the right. Ruins of buildings that once must have been a sugar-refining station topped the more distant one to the left. Both were occupied by companies of Spanish, who fired continual volleys at the advancing troops.

They were in the thick of it now. Bullets ripped through the leaves with a peculiar whizzing sound. The heat was so intense the men began to drop with it, too. Sam left his canteen beside a trooper from Oklahoma Territory who crumpled in a heap, cursing as he went down for fear he'd miss the fight.

The San Juan River provided some relief. With bullets singing all around them, the men dug into the muddy banks and waited for the order to charge the hills.

It didn't come.

Sam ranged back and forth to inspect the condition and placement of his men, keeping his head low—unlike the commander of Arizona's A Troop, Bucky O'Neill. The former sheriff and mayor of Prescott, Arizona, famous throughout the West for his battles against Apaches and road agents alike, strolled up and down in front of his lines, smoking a cigarette.

"Get down, Captain!" one of the men pleaded. "You're going to get hit."

O'Neill laughed and blew a cloud of smoke.

A few minutes later, he and Sam went to consult with another officer concerning the placement of their troops. As they turned to head back to their companies, O'Neill took a bullet through the mouth. It came out the back of his head. He was dead before he hit the ground.

Still no order came to charge.

Losing men like O'Neill and dozens more hit Roosevelt almost as hard as the enforced inaction. He sent messengers to both General Wood and

General Shafter, requesting permission to advance. Just when the colonel was ready to take action on his own authority, General Shafter's aide rode through a storm of bullets with the welcome order to charge the hills.

With a flagrant disregard for his own safety, Roosevelt spurred his mount up and down the line to relay the order. The Rough Riders surged to their feet. They were ready, more than ready, to engage the enemy. Whooping and cheering, they plunged into the jungle and ran right through the troops deployed ahead of them. Utter confusion reigned for a few moments as regimental lines merged. Then the First Regulars-White and the famed Buffalo Soldiers of the Ninth Regulars-Colored jumped up and raced alongside the First Volunteers.

Sweat poured down Sam's face. Smoke stung his eyes. Spiky leaves slapped at his face and neck as he struggled up the steep hill. Finally, he and his troop broke out of the jungle.

The rifle fire that had been lethal before became murderous. Roosevelt's horse stumbled and went down. Jumping out of the saddle, the colonel panted alongside his men. The blue-spotted neckerchief tucked under the back of his hat flapped like a signal flag. The regimental standard bearer followed hard on his heels, streaming blood from two wounds and waving the colors madly.

Sam fixed his sights on a huge, overturned black

kettle lying outside the ruins atop the hill. His throat raw from smoke and thirst, he echoed the roar pouring out of a thousand troops.

"Remember the *Maine,* boys! Remember the *Maine!*"

The first casualties started to trickle in to the field hospital at Siboney just after nine in the morning. By noon the trickle had become a steady stream. By three, litters were jammed end to end and the walking wounded slumped wherever they could find space. The surgeons and nurses sorted through the casualties with ruthless efficiency, identifying those who required immediate attention and leaving the rest to the care of the orderlies.

Victoria would never have imagined men could sustain such horrible injuries and still breathe. Or that they'd take their pain with such stoicism. Only those with the most ghastly, gaping wounds moaned. A few were out of their heads and screamed and writhed on their litters. But as Victoria sweated alongside the orderlies and offered what aid she could to those men the nurses and surgeons indicated must wait their turn, an astounding number declined her services.

"See to Benji, ma'am," an Illinois infantryman begged, holding a bloody bandage over the mangled side of his face with one hand while gesturing with the other to the soldier he'd carried in over his shoulder. "He's worse off than me."

Every time Victoria spotted a man wearing a polka-dot neckerchief, or khaki trousers instead of regulation blue, her heart would stop. There seemed to be so many Rough Riders among the wounded! Far more in proportion to the other regiments. Each man she asked could say only that Captain Garrett was alive last time he saw him. One reported that he'd taken control of his company after the commander was killed.

As the long, agonizing afternoon slipped toward dusk, Victoria pieced the bits together to form a hazy picture. The infantry had conducted a frontal assault of the fortified Spanish emplacements in the hills above Santiago. The cavalry had flanked the infantry. The talk was all of El Caney. El Pozo. San Juan Hill. Some place called Kettle Hill. Of heavy concentrations of Spanish troops. Of digging into the crests or jumping into captured trenches or lying flat on their bellies to return fire.

Night dropped. In the distance, cannons continued to boom. Every nurse and doctor and orderly labored on, working by lamplight, by firelight, by torches made of bundled cane stalks. Patients whose uniforms had been soaked in sweat and blood now shivered in the wet, dewy night.

The next day brought more wounded back to Siboney.

So did the next.

Late on July 3, two bits of news electrified the entire camp. Wild cheers erupted. Victoria dashed outside one of the tents, her face and hair dripping with sweat, and grabbed the arm of a man waving his crutch in the air.

"What's happened?"

"The Spanish fleet tried to break through the blockade of Santiago harbor," he exclaimed, hopping gleefully on his one good leg. "Our boys done sent every last one of their ships to the bottom of the bay."

Shortly after that came the news that a cease-fire had been declared and a delegation had gone in under a flag of truce to demand Santiago's surrender.

"It's all over now but the shouting," the young artillery man Victoria was giving water to predicted with a grin. "Sure glad I got my licks in at El Pozo."

Since he was lying on bare ground, with the stump of his right hand wrapped in bloody bandages, she could only marvel at his insouciance.

The gunner's prediction proved overly optimistic.

Negotiations for Santiago's surrender dragged on for more than a week. During the prolonged negotiations, the troops of both sides faced each other from the trenches that scarred the hills around the city. The shaky cease-fire broke down repeatedly, resulting in fierce skirmishes and repeated artillery barrages.

Casualties continued to mount, and word came that the regimental surgeons at the staging hospitals right behind the lines were running desperately short of supplies and help. Many of their orderlies had gone down from either wounds or heat prostration.

Although short of supplies and near dropping with exhaustion themselves, the staff at the Siboney field hospital immediately organized a relief expedition. Two of the surgeons, six orderlies and four nurses would go forward with the heavily laden mules. At the same time, they learned, Miss Barton was sending in supplies of food and medicines from the Red Cross base she'd established at Daiquirí.

Victoria caught up with Mary just as she was gathering a satchel of precious medicines. The widow had traded her linen nurse's cap for a slouch hat, borrowed, Victoria guessed, from one of the dead troopers. She'd also discarded her skirts in favor of a pair of trousers held up by suspenders. Her black hair hung in a thick braid down her back. To Victoria's startled eyes, she looked far more like the full-blood Arapaho she was than the cultured widow of a Philadelphia physician.

''You can't go with us,'' the nurse said with a

quick shake of her head. "The colonel won't allow it."

"I know. I'm not asking to go. But if you should see Sam, will you give him a message for me?"

"Of course." Her dark eyes flicked over Victoria's face. "What is it?"

A hundred thoughts tumbled through her head. A dozen urgent cautions trembled on her tongue. But she decided Sam didn't need the burden of her fears.

"Tell him I heard he was given command of his company. And that I'm proud of him."

Mary didn't encounter Sam during her trip to the forward staging hospitals. He was with his men on the front line and exercising all his leadership skills to minimize their wretched conditions.

Like the rest of the Expeditionary Force, the Rough Riders slept on blankets on the ground at night, or simply scooped a hole in the mud if they'd lost their blankets. With no wagons to bring forward extra baggage or supplies, they had only the clothes they wore on their backs. The tough canvas trousers held up well enough, but shirts soon became frayed and socks shredded inside boots.

Since the Cowboy Cavalry boasted a number of sharpshooters among their ranks, they managed to augment their field rations of salted pork and hardtack with a bit of fresh guinea hen or quail. Huddled together in small groups, they'd fry the meat while the hardtack soaked, then pound a handful of coffee beans with the butts of their revolvers and toss them shells and all, into tin cups.

Although it went against his grain, Sam was forced to harden his heart and order his men to limit the rations they shared with the thousands of refugees who'd streamed out of Santiago in anticipation of heavy bombardment and street-to-street fighting. Half-starved, the refugees now wandered behind the American lines begging for food.

"It's just a bit of hardtack," one of the troopers muttered as he gave the last of his rations to a thin, big-eyed child.

Since Sam himself had already emptied his ration kit, he could hardly discipline the man.

Summer storms severely aggravated the problem of resupply. It rained every day, great drenching downpours that turned the trenches to quagmires and made the rivers impassible. It also contributed to the spread of disease and illness that decimated the ranks. During those long days of negotiations, the army lost ten times the number of men to sickness than they had to bullets.

Like the other commanders, Sam snatched a few hours whenever he could to go to the hospital and check on his men. Unlike the other commanders, his gut twisted with worry whenever he thought of the two very different, very determined women he knew at Siboney.

And he thought of them often in the long stretches of quiet between skirmishes and firefights. During the day, when he'd sink down beside one of his troops in the trenches for a brief rest. At night, lying on his blanket with his arm bent under his head and his unseeing gaze on the stars hanging brilliant in the onyx sky.

Mary had known what she'd face in Cuba. She'd trained in medicine, had worked alongside her husband during the yellow fever epidemic that ravaged Philadelphia.

But Victoria…

Sam felt his insides twist again.

Victoria, who'd teased and enticed him with her girlish charms and woman's body. Victoria, who'd jumped aboard ship and arrived in Cuba with only her blasted notebooks and her stubborn courage. Victoria, who toiled alongside the hospital orderlies in a place others might consider hell on earth, yet crafted stories that celebrated the honor, dignity and dedication of those she worked with.

Staring up at the stars, Sam was forced to concede that the woman at Siboney wasn't the same woman he'd asked to marry him, a point she'd emphasized when she'd broken their engagement. Or attempted to break it. Sam still hadn't relinquished his claim. He wouldn't, until she was home safe again.

And then only if she insisted.

He didn't quite understand this bone-deep reluctance to let her go. It went beyond desire, struck at something more fundamental than lust. He wasn't sure when it had taken root, or how it had grown to such proportions.

He'd dreamed of Mary for so long. Had quietly ached for her for so many years. Sam knew he would always hold her in a small corner of his heart, but Victoria—this Victoria he hardly recognized—had somehow taken possession of the rest.

Although the days and nights had long since blurred into one another, Victoria would never forget the afternoon the surgeon in command at Siboney established a contagion ward away from the main body of tents.

"It's yellow fever," he confirmed to the staff he gathered in the mess tent. "Only twelve cases so far, but more will soon show up now that it's started. I'm asking for volunteers to act as nurses, orderlies, cooks and burial detail."

Before anyone could move or speak, he held up both hands and issued a warning.

"Remember, those of you who go in will have to stay in. And I can only accept immunes for this duty."

That restriction severely limited his pool. Ignoring the strenuous objections of those who wished to volunteer despite no previous exposure to the infectious disease, the colonel made his choices. Mary was among them. Because of her experience, he put her in charge of the detail.

Victoria recorded the gripping moment they entered the contagion area in a tersely worded dispatch she put on the wires the following afternoon. It concluded with a simple observation:

> One can only admire the bravery and fortitude of these extraordinary men and women. They have dedicated themselves to a higher ideal. They are heroes, every one.

Not until July 16, the day after the general commanding the Spanish forces in Cuba agreed to terms of surrender, did more help arrive at the Siboney hospital. By then fever patients outnumbered the wounded by ten to one, and more than half of the medical personnel who'd volunteered to care for those in the contagion area were down themselves.

The commander couldn't afford to lose any more of his trained staff and put out a desperate call for help to the regimental commanders. An entire company of the Twenty-fourth Infantry-Colored answered the call.

They arrived at Siboney late in the afternoon.

The hospital commander greeted them with tears of gratitude in his eyes. A reporter from *Leslie's Weekly* accompanied the infantry and later quoted the surgeon when he noted that there was more real heroism in marching into a fever-stricken hospital camp and staying there day and night than there was in charging up any hill. The same correspondent would later inform his readers that only twenty-four of the sixty-five men who volunteered to work in the contagion area escaped illness. Thirty-one of them eventually died.

By then, however, Victoria had left Siboney. Sam came for her the same evening the Twenty-fourth arrived, offering an inducement for her to leave.

"The formal surrender takes place tomorrow in Santiago. I've wrangled a pass for you to go into the city and observe the ceremony."

As he must have known it would, the bait proved impossible to resist. Victoria had heard such passes were scarcer than dry boots. When she'd gone down to the town to file her dispatches, the correspondents jamming the cable office could talk of little else. Evidently Harry Scoval's articles in the *World* criticizing the grossly overweight General Shafter's handling of the Santiago campaign had enraged the commander. As a result, his already strained relations with the press had snapped completely. Informing Scoval that he would "god-

damned never'' be allowed into the city as long as
Shafter had anything to say about it, the general
approved only a handful of passes to selected newsmen. Victoria couldn't imagine how Sam had
snagged one.

"His aide owed me a favor," he explained with
a shrug. "Will you come?"

Torn, she agreed to leave. She owed it to her
readers to be present at the historic occasion.

Victoria rode out of Siboney on a bony-spined
mule, twenty pounds lighter and a thousand years
older than when she'd arrived mere weeks before.
Her tattered, mildewed clothes had been replaced
by a gray skirt and white blouse bequeathed to her
by a nurse who'd shipped home, too ill to continue
her duties. Richard Harding Davis's spare pith helmet shaded her eyes from the broiling sun, and her
soiled valise carried notebooks crammed with stories of the nurses she'd come to admire and respect
beyond words.

Both she and Sam twisted in the saddle to take
a last look at the hospital camp. Neither spoke of
it, but the knowledge that they were leaving Mary
behind in the contagion area hung like a stone
around both their necks.

15

Victoria spent the night of July 16 at a tumble-down sugarcane plantation on the outskirts of Santiago. About twenty correspondents had commandeered the ruins, which they'd irreverently dubbed the Santiago Pressmen's Club.

"Richard Harding Davis is here," Sam said as he lifted her from the saddle and set her down in a courtyard strewn with rubble. "He's promised to help you secure a good spot to observe the ceremonies tomorrow."

"They should prove interesting," she murmured through her weariness.

Sam had used the ride from the hospital to fill her in on what he knew of the highly charged politics surrounding the ceremony. Not only had General Shafter alienated the entire press corps by limiting their attendance, the irascible commander had also neglected to issue passes to any officers of the navy, whose warships had sunk the entire Spanish fleet within sight of the city. Nor did Shafter invite General Calixto Garcia, leader of the Cuban Army of Liberation. The freedom fighters who'd battled so long and so fiercely weren't included in the celebration of their first major victory after ten years of war.

That Sam could secure a pass for Victoria in the midst of all this political turmoil was nothing short of a miracle.

"I knew you wouldn't want to miss the ceremony," he said with a shrug.

"No, I wouldn't." Cocking her head, she studied him in the light of the full tropical moon. "You know, I believe you're finally coming to accept my status as a credentialed correspondent."

His drooping hat brim shaded his face, but she caught the glint of white teeth as he smiled down at her.

"You've earned your spurs, Victoria. I had to learn how to separate the woman from the journalist before I could admit it."

It was a step, she thought on a quiet thrill of pride. A major step. Perhaps one day soon Sam might take the next and learn that the woman *couldn't* be separated from the journalist. Victoria was only beginning to realize that herself.

"What about you?" she asked as he hoisted her

valise down from the saddle. "Will the Rough Riders be present at the ceremony?"

"Those who can still march will. We'll enter Santiago with the Second Brigade. Not that we'll look much like a victorious army entering a conquered city," he added, rasping a hand over his whiskered cheek. "My men are even scruffier than I am."

She had to admit he looked more like a street beggar than a United States Army officer. After weeks of slogging through dense jungle, sleeping in the mud, subsisting on army rations and dodging bullets, Sam had lost considerably more weight than she had. His face was gaunt beneath its scratchy beard, and his tattered uniform hung on his spare frame like rags on a scarecrow. With a jolt, Victoria realized she might not have recognized him if she'd passed him on the street in Cheyenne.

He'd changed as much as she, she thought. Outwardly, at least. They could have been two strangers staring at each other in the moonlight. Wanting—needing—to find the old Sam under this lean, leather-tough warrior, she picked her way through the rubble to the farmhouse.

"Do you have to return to your unit right away?"

"I can steal a few hours."

"Good. We haven't had a chance to just sit and talk since Tampa."

"Funny," he murmured as they stepped through the open doorway. "I don't recall we did all that much talking in Tampa."

The memory of just what they *had* done in Tampa sent a sudden, slicing spear of heat into Victoria's belly. Thoroughly shaken by its intensity, she stepped inside.

"Miss Parker!"

While Victoria struggled to recover her composure, Richard Harding Davis detached himself from the group of correspondents clustered around a wooden table. Most of them looked every bit as ragged and tattered as the army they'd marched with. There were one or two exceptions, most notably the woman in a clean, simply tailored suit of lightweight cotton.

"I don't know who you've met," Davis said, drawing Victoria and Sam toward the group. "You remember Stephen Crane, don't you?"

"Yes, of course."

"This is George Clarke Musgrave, with the London *Times*. William Paley, who's here taking movies for Vitascope. A. W. Layman, Associated Press. Harry Scoval, from the *New York World*, and his wife, Frances. She's just arrived from Key West."

Victoria nodded to each in turn, feeling more than a bit intimidated. She'd read many of Layman's dispatches. Harry Scoval, who'd already become a legend for his coverage of the Cuban situation, was now gaining almost as much notoriety for his continuing skirmishes with General Shafter. Rather awed to be in the presence of such distinguished journalists, she blinked in surprise when Davis included her among their ranks.

"This is Victoria Parker," he announced. "She writes for the Cheyenne *Tribune*."

"So you're the one!"

With a smile, Frances Scoval rose and shook Victoria's hand. "I've read your stories about the army nurses and the Red Cross volunteers. They make one quite proud of our American women."

Both flattered and curious, Victoria returned her friendly shake. "However did you find copies of *Tribune?* We're rather a small paper compared to most."

"I saw your pieces in the *World.* AP has picked them up. Didn't you know?"

"No!"

The Associated Press stringer confirmed the astonishing news. "They've appeared in any number of papers across the country," Layman told her. "Evidently the *Tribune*'s owner made them available to the AP network. Make sure he pays you syndication fees when you get back."

"Yes," Victoria murmured, dazed by the knowledge that her readership apparently extended far beyond Cheyenne. "I'll certainly speak to Papa about that."

That won a round of hearty laughter. When it died down, Davis introduced Sam to the group.

"Join us for a drink," he said, gesturing to the others that they scoot their chairs over to make room. "Frances, divine angel that she is, brought us several bottles of cognac from Key West. We're toasting the surrender and debating how best to get around Shafter's ridiculous edict limiting our attendance."

"I don't intend to get around it," the thin, intense Scoval announced with a scowl. "I shall simply ignore it."

"Of course, you shall, dear," his wife said, patting his hand. "And then you'll write a blistering piece about how the general maligned the press corps, offended our Cuban allies and insulted the navy, and we shall be banned not just from Santiago, but from the whole of Cuba."

The prospect didn't appear to concern her husband. "We're leaving tomorrow, anyway," he said with a shrug. "With the rainy season coming in a few weeks, the army won't be able to march on Havana until December at the earliest. The fun's over in Cuba for the time being."

Victoria would hardly classify the Santiago campaign as fun, but she'd learned that women tended to view such matters differently from men.

"The *World* has directed the captain of the *Seneca* to take us to Puerto Rico," Scoval informed his companions. "Word is General Miles will land with his expeditionary force any day now."

"I'm for the Philippines," the moviemaker announced. "The fighting's still pretty fierce there. I hear the troops who didn't make it to Cuba are being transported to San Francisco for embarkation. With luck, I'll get there in time to ship out with them."

"What about you, Miss Parker?" Frances Scoval asked. "Will you stay in Cuba or follow the sound of drums to the next battle?"

"I don't know. I haven't really thought about it."

"Well, if you decide to push on to Puerto Rico, I'm sure Mr. Pulitzer would have no objection to letting you come aboard the *Seneca*."

"Only if she gives him exclusive rights to her stories," her husband drawled, generating another round of laughter.

Victoria joined in the laughter, but she couldn't help but notice the way Sam had gone stiff beside her.

Quite suddenly, their on-again, off-again engagement seemed to have taken on an added dimension of uncertainty. When she'd made the painful decision to end it, Victoria had assumed she'd go home after Cuba and wait for her heart to heal.

Yielding to Sam's insistence, she'd agreed to

keep up the pretense as long as she was on the island—to give her the protection of his name and rank. At Siboney, he'd cupped her cheek and promised quietly that they would sort matters out, but by then she was too weary to think beyond the next hour, let alone the next week.

Now…

Now a whole new vista of possibilities shimmered in the hazy future. She didn't have to return home with an aching heart. She didn't have to go back to writing amusing little anecdotes about Fourth of July picnics. As Sam said just moments ago, she'd earned her spurs. Dare she go to Puerto Rico? Or halfway around the world to the Philippines? Did she want to?

Her thoughts churning, Victoria listened with half an ear to the animated discussion by the journalists who'd so casually accepted her as a peer.

Beside her, Sam swallowed a string of silent curses. Like the rest of the troops, he had heard rumors that the Puerto Rico campaign would kick off any day now. Had known, too, that veteran correspondents like Davis and Scoval and the others would jump right into the thick of it, as they had in Cuba. But never for a moment had Sam imagined that Victoria would consider joining their ranks.

He slanted her a glance, searching for a glimpse of the girl he'd proposed to in her parents' front parlor that chilly night in March. Her hair was still as bright as a copper penny, if darkened a bit with sweat. She still looked out at the world with clear blue eyes. But heat and weariness had put dark circles around those eyes, and her tanned skin now stretched taut over her cheekbones. Her borrowed clothes hung on her loosely, all but obscuring what remained of her lush curves.

The girl had aroused him despite his every determination to the contrary. The woman fascinated him, yet she drew farther and farther away from him with each passing hour. With a slow tightening of his gut, he was forced to admit she now had more in common with this group of war-hardened correspondents than she did with him.

Frances Scoval's cognac had disappeared and the fragrant Cuban cigars were down to stumps when Sam pushed back his chair.

"I'd better get back to my men."

Regret flickered across Victoria's face. Shoving back her chair, she walked with him to the door. "We didn't get a chance to talk."

"No, we didn't."

"Perhaps we'll find time after the ceremonies tomorrow. Will you and your troops be quartered in town?"

"We don't know yet. Stay close to Davis. I'll find you and let you know."

* * *

Like Harry Scoval, scores of uninvited correspondents simply ignored General Shafter's edict and strolled into the city on the morning of July 17, 1898. Apparently the guards at the checkpoints hadn't been advised to keep them out. Victoria and Richard Harding Davis didn't have to produce their precious passes. Their credentials alone gained them access to the city.

Threading through the maze of barbed wire and sandbag barriers the Spanish had erected in anticipation of a long siege, they made their way down narrow streets to the governor's palace. The long, low stucco building rambled along one side of the main plaza. A towering cathedral dominated the opposite side, its spires spearing straight into the cloudless blue sky.

Since Frances Scoval had already gone aboard the *Seneca* to prepare for its imminent departure, her husband joined Victoria, Davis and a group of others in the shade of the cathedral. Elbow to elbow with throngs of Cuban residents and foreign observers, they waited while the conquering army entered Santiago.

Even to Victoria's eager eyes, their entrance appeared to be more of a scramble than a parade. The troops tried valiantly to keep ranks, but the city's defenses necessitated circuitous routes down winding side streets. As a result, the various regiments arrived at the plaza in a distinctly haphazard fashion. Once there, they formed into massed ranks and assumed parade rest. Stretching up on tiptoe, Victoria searched for the Rough Riders. Their khakis weren't hard to find among the blue of the regulars.

Sam stood at the head of his company, tall and proud despite the ravages to his uniform. Roosevelt had ridden in on his charger, which had miraculously survived the assault on Kettle Hill. His eyeglasses clouding in the steamy heat, the colonel took his position at the head of the regiment.

"Damn," Harry Scoval muttered. "I can't see a bloody thing. Here, give me a boost, Richard."

"Keep out of sight," Davis hissed as Scoval scurried up a tree and climbed onto the roof of the building adjacent to the cathedral. "If General Shafter spots you, he'll likely order one of his men to shoot you."

Victoria dismissed the warning as mere hyperbole, but soon realized Davis hadn't exaggerated.

"Here!" one of the staff officers shouted, spotting the correspondent on the roof. "Get down at once!"

His shout attracted the general's attention. With a bellow, Shafter ordered the major to damn well throw the bastard down off the roof. Wide-eyed, Victoria watched Scoval hastily drop to the ground and melt into the crowd.

"How like Harry," Davis said dryly. "He makes almost as much news as he reports."

Thankfully, a stenorian command rolled across the plaza at that moment and diverted both the general and his harried staff officer.

A-tennnnnnn-shun!

Backs snapped straight. Thousands of heels clicked together. Rifles slapped onto shoulders.

Preeeee-sent, arms!

The officers whipped up their swords. With a crack that rifled through the air like gunfire, the enlisted men slapped their palms against wooden stocks, unshouldered their weapons and stiff-armed them forward. The band broke into the opening bars of "Hail, Columbia." Slowly, the Marine Guard hoisted the Stars and Stripes over the palace.

With shivers of sheer excitement darting up and down her spine, Victoria scribbled furiously in her notebook. She couldn't believe she was here, witnessing this historic moment, capturing the sights and sounds and searing, steamy magnificence of it for the *Tribune*'s readers.

At that moment, she felt as though she'd not only earned her spurs, she was truly wearing them.

After the formal ceremony concluded, the commanders gave the order to break ranks. The troops mingled about in the plaza, savoring their victory. Victoria wove her way through the crowd in search of Sam and the First Volunteer Cavalry. She wanted to record their sentiments on this momentous occasion.

She was halfway across the plaza when war suddenly, and without warning, broke out once more.

Apparently hoping to bury the hatchet amid the joyousness of the moment, Harry Scoval approached Shafter. The general was in no mood to bury anything. Bellowing with rage, he unleashed a barrage of uncomplimentary remarks about journalists in general and Scoval in particular. As angry now as Shafter, the reporter shot back that he had no right to use such language to someone who'd come under fire alongside his troops.

"Shame on you, sir!" he snapped at the general. "Shame on you!"

To everyone's complete astonishment, the three-hundred-pound Shafter hauled back and swung at the *World* correspondent. To the general's complete astonishment, the correspondent returned the punch. Mere seconds later, Scoval was on his back on the cobbles, surrounded by two dozen U.S. Marines with fixed bayonets pointed at his throat.

Slack-jawed with amazement, Victoria almost dropped her pencil and notebook.

"I'd better fetch Frances," Davis muttered. "She's going to have the devil of a time getting Harry out of this one."

Only after Scoval had been marched off under guard did Victoria recover from her astonishment enough to jot down a hasty note. How odd, she wrote. How very, very odd. The only instance of hand-to-hand combat she had personally observed during the war with Spain occurred between the conquering hero and a member of the press.

She was still musing over the irony of it when Sam found her and passed on a bit of news that disconcerted her almost as much as the unseemly brawl. Slipping a hand under her elbow, he guided her through the throng to a quiet spot in the shade of the cathedral.

"Although it's not for public knowledge just yet, General Wood's to be appointed military governor of Santiago. He's asked Captain Max Luna from the New Mexico contingent to act as his interpreter. He wants me to serve on his staff as provost marshal."

"Does that mean you'll leave the Rough Riders?"

"I'll be detached from them, yes."

"I see," Victoria murmured, although she really didn't. It hadn't occurred to her that Sam might stay behind when the main body of the army moved on.

"How long do you think you'll remain in Santiago?"

"I don't know. Until the war's over, anyway, and a Cuban government takes over administration of the island."

"But that could take months."

"Or years," he said with a wry grimace.

The lingering excitement of witnessing the Stars and Stripes rise above the governor's palace fizzled and died on the spot. Belatedly, Victoria realized that fighting constituted only part of winning the war. After the battles came the task of governing captured territories. And Sam, apparently, had been tapped to help with that task.

"Have you decided where you'll go from here?" he asked quietly. "I'll admit I don't care for the idea of you going off to Puerto Rico or the Philippines."

To be honest, Victoria didn't particularly care for it, either. Not if Sam wouldn't be there.

"I don't know where I'll go," she admitted. "Home, probably. I really haven't planned that far ahead."

"I was thinking…" he said slowly. "Perhaps you could stay in Santiago for a few weeks, until the rainy season sets in."

"Stay here?"

"You said you wanted to write more about Miss Barton and her volunteers. You might also find any number of stories in the occupation and administration of a conquered province."

"Well, I— I—"

"I'll have a house in town," he said while she struggled to gather her whirling thoughts. "Nothing grand, I imagine, but surely more comfortable than the quarters you've occupied up to now. You could stay there, make it your temporary headquarters while you write your stories. And we could get to know each other.''

Her breath caught. Smiling at her wide-eyed surprise, he brushed his gloved hand down her cheek.

''I realize now you were right. I barely knew the girl I asked to marry me back in Cheyenne. The woman she's become is even more of a mystery. Shall we start again, Victoria? Get to know each other? Will you spend the next few weeks with me?''

''Yes,'' she got out when she could breathe again. ''I believe I will.''

16

On the day following Santiago's formal surrender, the Spanish government forwarded a message to President McKinley asking for a suspension of hostilities and the start of negotiations to end the war. The U.S. ground forces in Cuba went into bivouac in the hills around Santiago while their commanders waited for a decision as to where and how they would next be deployed.

As Sam had predicted, General Leonard Wood was officially named military governor of Santiago. The former commander of the Rough Riders wasted no time setting up operations in the Spanish governor's palace and assembling his staff. Their job, as he explained in his clipped, humorless way, was to restore order to the town and surrounding countryside, while ensuring that citizens still loyal to Spain didn't rise up against their new masters.

Sam and Captain Maximillian Luna of the New

Mexico Rough Rider contingent were assigned quarters just off the main plaza on Calle San Giorgio. Formerly occupied by a Spanish general and his family, the low, rambling house boasted a courtyard filled with a riot of flowers, creaking wooden ceiling beams in every room and a staff that included a cook, a housekeeper, two maids and a stable boy.

"They don't speak a word of English," Sam warned as he carried in Victoria's mud-stained valise. "But Max has explained to the housekeeper that you're promised to me, and Señora Garcia's agreed to act as a duenna of sorts."

"So we're to continue the pretense of an engagement, then?"

He glanced down at her. "Unless you find it irksome."

"No, not irksome."

Just...strange. As though they existed in some in-between land. Everyone from the Rough Riders to Richard Harding Davis and her acquaintances among the press assumed Victoria belonged part and parcel to Sam. Only the two of them knew that the truth was something else again. At this point, however, neither one of them could say exactly what that truth was.

Leading the way down a long, tiled hallway, Sam showed her to a spacious bedroom dominated by a four-poster bed draped with mosquito netting. An ornately carved mahogany clothespress stood against one wall, while the other was taken up by a dressing table topped by a wavy mirror. Green shutters filtered the light, while thick adobe walls stuccoed in pale cream kept out most of the heat.

"I think you'll be comfortable here," Sam said, depositing her valise beside the clothespress.

"I should think so, indeed!"

Enchanted, she peered around. A forgotten hat cockade and an ivory hair comb lying on the floor under the dressing table gave evidence of the previous occupants' hasty departure. A twinge of guilt at displacing the Spanish general and his family from their home attacked her momentarily. But only momentarily. The Cuban people had suffered too long and the Americans had fought too hard for the victors to as yet feel sympathy for the defeated Spanish.

Besides, she'd just discovered that the wooden screen in the corner shielded a tin tub.

"Sam! A hip bath!" Her eyes sparking, she spun around. "I can't remember the last time I soaped down in something other than a cold stream, wearing all my clothes."

Sam started to reply that she could now soap down wearing nothing at all, but the very vivid image of Victoria doing just that gave him a sudden jab square to his middle. Luckily, she was too delighted with the prospect of a real bath to notice his swift, in-drawn breath.

"I'll send Señora Garcia to you on my way out."

"Are you going back to the palace?"

"Yes, I'm afraid I must. General Wood has already declared that administering a conquered city is more of a challenge than commanding a regiment composed of cowboys and Fifth Avenue swells. Every man, woman and child in Santiago seems to have a petition or grievance that requires his—or his staff's—personal attention."

"Oh, dear."

"I've exchanged some American dollars for Spanish," he told her, digging a roll of colorful bills out of his pocket. "Fresh vegetables and meat are still hard to come by, but we expect supply ships by tomorrow or the next day. In the meantime, Señora Garcia can help you purchase whatever you might need in the way of personal items at the local market."

Whatever she might need? Good heavens, what *didn't* she need? Victoria's mind immediately began spinning out a long list.

"I recommend you take her or one of the others with you if you decide to roam about," Sam cautioned. "There are parts of town it's best you don't stray into just yet."

"I understand." Tucking the thick roll of notes into her skirt pocket, she made a mental note to reimburse him later from the funds she'd brought with her.

"So I'll see you when I see you, then?"

"I'll try to join you for dinner tonight." A rueful smile entered his eyes. "I still plan to use this time together in Santiago to our advantage. I only hope General Wood cooperates."

"I hope so, too," she murmured as he strode down the tiled hall.

Victoria spent two hours that afternoon with Señora Garcia at the local market, which had sprung to life again in the main plaza.

As Sam had warned, there was little food available. Not surprising given the disruption caused during the past decade by the forcible relocation of hundreds of thousands of peasants from their farms. A few green, stringy plantains cost dearly, and black beans went for a shameful price. Señora Garcia haggled ferociously for what the seller swore was a plucked quail, but looked suspiciously like pigeon to Victoria.

In contrast, clothing and personal items abandoned by the Spanish who'd fled the city had already flooded the market. Victoria purchased embroidered linens of the softest cambric, a rustling taffeta underskirt and a ruby-red dinner gown that clashed horribly with her hair but was so beautiful she couldn't resist it. With vigorous gestures and enthusiastic nods, Señora Garcia insisted Victoria also acquire a tall comb and exquisite black lace mantilla.

The roll Sam had given her was considerably slimmer when the two women returned to the house on Calle San Giorgio. The heat and walk from the market took more of a toll on Victoria than she'd anticipated. With black spots dancing before her eyes, she used pantomime and hand signals to express her fervent desire for a bath.

The long, sybaritic soak was heaven. With her legs draped over the front edge of the tub and her head resting against its high, sloping back, Victoria lolled in blissful abandon while her skin wrinkled to a prunelike consistency. She felt very much herself again after washing her hair, brushing it dry and dressing in her new finery for dinner.

Dinner had to be put back twice before Sam and Maximillian Luna returned to the house. Scion of a distinguished Spanish family that had settled great tracts of land around Santa Fe, Captain Luna exhibited all the grace and sophistication of his heritage. His dark eyes gleamed as he took in Victoria's gown and the black lace mantilla draped over her clean, shining hair.

"So this is the intrepid Miss Parker I've heard so much about." Bowing, he brought her hand to his lips with Old World charm. "May I say you're every bit as beautiful as you are adventurous?"

"You may indeed, sir."

Smiling, Victoria couldn't help but marvel at how strange it felt to dress in silks and engage in polite banter once again. The hospital at Siboney might have been a thousand miles away instead of a mere eight.

Another twinge of guilt attacked her at the thought, much fiercer than her brief bout of sympathy for the previous occupants of this house. Here she was, clean, cool and about to sit down at a real table to dinner, while Mary still labored in the contagion ward.

"Have you had word from Siboney?" she asked Sam when they'd settled in at the table. "Is Mary well?"

"She was the last I heard." His jaw took on a grim cast. "But the number of yellow fever cases is mounting. The Red Cross intends to help by taking some of the spillover from Siboney. They're setting up a temporary hospital here in Santiago."

"Miss Barton's here?" Victoria asked, her eyes brightening.

"She arrived this morning. She's taken over the boathouse down by the harbor as a hospital."

"She and her volunteers will soon have their hands full," Max Luna put in. "General Wood expects the worst once the rains come down in earnest. Although," he added with a grimace, "I don't see how they can get much worse than they are now. I've never missed Santa Fe's dry, blistering heat as much as I have this past month.''

"You'll miss it more in a few weeks," Sam warned. "I understand it pours all day, every day, from August through October.''

"At least we have a roof over our heads. The poor troops steam like lobsters in their tents.''

"When they're not swimming in mud.''

Shaking his head at the plight of his men, Sam told Victoria that General Shafter had already petitioned Secretary of War Alger for permission to redeploy the army to higher, drier ground.

"Or better yet, take them back to the States until we see whether or not the peace negotiations bring an end to the war. Alger will have to decide where to move them, and soon.''

His brown eyes met hers across the table. She read the message in them with a little skip of breath. She, too, would have to decide where she'd go from here. And soon.

As if reading her mind, Sam confirmed that the other journalists were already deserting Cuba. Richard Harding Davis had taken ship that morning. Scoval would leave as soon as his wife could convince Shafter to release him.

"Stephen Crane leaves tomorrow. He came by the palace and said to tell you he'd be happy to carry dispatches back to Key West for you.''

"Crane interviewed Colonel Roosevelt this afternoon," Max put in. "I can imagine the dispatch he'll file when he gets back to Key West."

Inevitably, the talk turned to the experiences the two officers had shared under Roosevelt's command. They regaled Victoria with accounts of the more farcical aspects of the Santiago campaign, which she solemnly swore not to include in her dispatches. Although fascinated, she was drooping with fatigue when Sam escorted her to her room.

"I can't imagine why I'm so tired," she said, unsuccessfully hiding a yawn.

"The past weeks are catching up with you."

With a little wave of her hand, she indicated her new finery. "And here I thought to sparkle for you tonight."

"You can sparkle tomorrow night. Max has to interpret for General Wood at a banquet he's giving for the local dignitaries."

That caught her attention. "So Captain Luna won't be joining us?"

"No, it will be just the two of us." Smiling, he dropped a kiss on her mouth. "Sleep well."

With the prospect of a night alone with Sam hovering in her mind, Victoria sat down at the dressing table and forced herself to record her impressions of a city under military occupation. Freed of the hundred-word restriction, she let the adjectives flow.

* * *

The next morning, she stuffed the pages in an envelope and took them down to the harbor to search out Stephen Crane. She found him just about to board ship. The journalist's hand shook when he accepted her pages. Alarmed, Victoria noted that his normally pale face was ashen and dewed with sweat.

"Are you all right?"

"It's this damned malaria. I'm afraid I'm coming down with another bout of it. I had the devil of a time convincing the captain it's not yellow fever, I can tell you. The bastard— Pardon me. The wretch almost refused to take me aboard."

Tucking her envelope into his pocket, he made for the gangplank. "I'll put these on the wires for you as soon as I reach Key West."

"Thank you."

That task taken care of, Victoria made her way along the quay. The tall royal palms lining the harbor rustled gently in the breeze. Out in the bay, the remains of the Spanish fleet sunk while trying to escape Santiago gave grim evidence of the battle waged for the city. The navy would be some time clearing the wreckage, she guessed.

The large wooden structure Miss Barton had appropriated for the Red Cross was, for reasons Victoria had yet to discover, known locally as the English Boat Club. It was built out over the water on stilts and connected to the shore by a wooden bridge. Surrounded entirely by a veranda, the large, airy structure had shutters instead of walls to let in the sea breezes.

Already, the overflow from Siboney had filled the makeshift hospital to capacity. General Wood had supplied it with cots, sheets, blankets, clean pajamas and mosquito netting, Miss Barton informed Victoria, but they had no trained nurses and only the services of General Wood's staff surgeon to assist them. Even Callie May Morgan had been promoted from laundress to medical attendant. Cradling the sick in her big, muscular arms, she fed and changed and bathed them with damp cloths when the fever gripped them.

As she had at Siboney, Victoria offered her services. To her surprise, Miss Barton declined them.

"I'm not saying we couldn't use another pair of hands," she admitted, "but you're doing far more good for these patients with your writing than you could ever do in wards."

"Whatever do you mean?"

"Oh, my dear! The Red Cross has been besieged with volunteers who've read your stirring stories, particularly your piece about Callie May. I received a cable just this morning that another ship carrying immunes will dock in Santiago tomorrow."

Her dark eyes twinkling in her sparrow's face, she patted Victoria's hand.

"Keep writing, Miss Parker. That's the most vital service you can render our gallant men in uniform.''

When Victoria related the extraordinary conversation to Sam later that evening, he agreed. They were alone, as he'd promised. Candles flickered in their holders, bathing the table in a small circle of light. Lingering over rich, flavorful coffee after a late supper, she expressed her admiration for Miss Barton and her volunteers.

''They profess to be quite ordinary,'' she murmured, stirring her coffee with her spoon. ''Yet they've performed the most extraordinary deeds.''

''So have you,'' Sam pointed out. ''With your efforts at Siboney. And with your stories bringing readers' attention to their service.''

''That's what Miss Barton implied.'' Frowning, she shook her head. ''Yet I can't include myself in the same category as the Red Cross volunteers or dedicated nurses like Mary and the others. I simply can't. I came to Cuba for my own selfish reasons. They came to serve. They're truly heroines.''

''You occupy a category all your own, Victoria. And whatever your reasons for coming to Cuba, it took a great deal of courage for you to board that ship.''

Her frown gave way to a grin. ''That's not what you said when you found me in Siboney that first day. My ears still burn when I recall the less-than-flattering things you had to say about me then.''

Matching her grin, Sam shoved back his chair and came around the table to take her hand and draw her out of hers. His thumb traced a lazy path along her lower lip.

''As *I* recall, we both said a great many foolish things that afternoon.''

The long, tiring day dissolved. All thoughts of Miss Barton and her volunteers fled. The stroke of his thumb began a slow, sweet song in Victoria's blood.

''Sam...''

For the life of her, she couldn't have said whether her breathless whisper was an invitation or a plea. Whatever it was, he responded. Dipping his head, he covered her mouth with his. Victoria leaned into his embrace with an eagerness born of desire and delight.

They fit together differently than before, she realized with a sudden clenching of her stomach. The pounds they'd both shed brought them closer. Chest to chest. Hip to hip. So intimate. So right.

Under her palms, his muscles were hard and ridged, each sinew as taut as strung rope. Through her taffeta underskirt, she could feel him swell behind the flap of his trousers. Spasms of need, of desire, of pure feminine delight rippled through her belly.

"Dammit!"

Abruptly, Sam put some distance between them. Chagrin showed plainly on his face.

"I didn't mean to do that."

"I did!" The retort slipped out, honest and quick and colored with the need Victoria didn't try to hide. "I thought… I thought this time was for us to get to know each other?"

"It is. But I swore I'd do things right this time." He took another step back, dragged a hand through his hair. "No letting my lust get the better of me. No getting caught with my hands all over you. No tumbling you helter-skelter into bed, as much as I ache to do exactly that right now."

"Oh. Well."

She could hardly argue that there was nothing she wanted more at this moment than for Sam to tumble her helter-skelter into bed. She was the one who'd insisted that passion wasn't enough, after all.

She'd been so hurt that day in Siboney. So angry and stung by pride. She'd all but thrown the gold-and-sapphire locket in Sam's face, convinced she couldn't share him or his love with another woman.

How long ago that seemed! How much they'd both changed since then. Pride now left a bitter taste in her mouth. After a long moment of rather strained silence, she heaved a huge sigh.

"I think I understand now how it feels to be hoist by one's own petard."

He gave a bark of laughter, shattering the tension that gripped them both. "Give me a minute to get the beast under control and we'll try again."

"Can you?" she asked with a curious glance at the bulge in his pants. "Get it under control, I mean?"

"I can try. Shall we take a walk along the harbor while I wrestle with my baser self?"

Unsure at this point whether or not she wanted him to win the battle, Victoria nodded.

The moon was just beginning to lose its roundness. Hanging low above the hills surrounding the city, it painted the buildings spilling down to the bay a pale gold. A breeze off the water whispered through the tall palms lining the harbor and kept the mosquitoes away.

"By day Santiago is small and quaint," Victoria observed as they walked along the stone quay. "By night, it's rather magical."

"The city certainly shows two faces to the world," Sam agreed, his glance straying past the brightly lit boathouse hospital to the charred skeletons of the Spanish fleet. "Even those hulks take on a different aspect in moonlight."

Biting her lip, Victoria surveyed the ghostly remains. "Were very many of those aboard killed?"

"I understand most managed to dive into the water before their ships went down. Several of Admiral Schley's sailors climbed into longboats and darted in under fire to rescue them.''

"I heard that one of our men crawled through a mile of trenches under fire, too, to bring aid to a wounded Spanish drummer boy.''

"A regular from the Ninth Infantry,'' Sam confirmed. "He'll likely get a medal for it, if his commander doesn't court-martial him for putting his life at risk like that.''

"How strange war is,'' Victoria mused. "Men do their best to blow each other up, then risk their lives to save each other.''

"It's the nature of the beast.''

"Speaking of beasts…'' She slanted him a sideways look. "Is yours under control yet?''

"As much as it will ever be. Ready to return to the house?''

To Victoria's secret chagrin, Sam kept himself under rigid control. They sat and talked long into the night, and the chaste kiss he gave her at the door to her bedroom could have been bestowed on a nun.

Victoria crawled under the mosquito netting, sure she would toss and turn all night. She dropped into sleep almost before her head hit the pillow.

17

"It's the heat," Victoria complained to Señora
Garcia the next afternoon when she dragged herself
back to the house after another visit to the Red
Cross hospital.

The air was thicker than ever, and she almost
welcomed the dark thunderclouds piling up above
the mountains in hopes the daily downpour would
provide some relief.

"*Muy,* er, hot," she said, waving a hand in front
of her face.

"*Sí,*" the woman agreed sympathetically, going
off in a torrent of Spanish. Victoria didn't understand a word until she heard the magic phrase *siesta.*

"A siesta! That's what I need. A bath and then
a siesta."

With so little time left before she had to start
thinking about leaving Cuba, Victoria was deter-

mined to slough off this uncharacteristic lassitude. She had stories yet to write…and precious hours to spend with Sam.

They'd linger late over coffee again, she thought as she sank into the cool water Señora Garcia had perfumed with flower petals. Perhaps take another walk along the harbor. And this time, she vowed with a drowsy smile, he wouldn't leave her at her bedroom door with a mere peck on the lips.

He might be determined to do things "right" this time. But Victoria was fast coming to the conclusion that there was no right or wrong when it came to her feelings for Captain Samuel Garrett.

Sam left the governor's palace just after four. On a mission of some delicacy for General Wood, he walked the few blocks to Calle San Giorgio. Halfway there, the skies opened and caught him in a torrential downpour. He'd left his India rubber poncho at the headquarters and was soaked to the skin by the time he arrived at the house.

Gathering from one of the maids that Victoria was in her room, he squished down the tiled hall and rapped gently on her door. The rain beating down on the roof drowned out his knock. He tried again, louder this time, then opened the door a crack.

"Victoria? I'm sorry to disturb you but General Wood has asked—"

He stopped, grinning at the view through the slice of open door. She was sprawled in the tub. Her arms and legs dangled over the sides. Her head was turned away from him, but the steady rise and fall of her breasts told him she was sound asleep.

Sam waged a short, fierce debate with himself. A gentleman would close the door and quietly retreat. So would a man who'd sworn to keep his lust on a tight rein. If he hadn't been afraid that Victoria would slide down and drown, he might have done just that. Or if his gaze hadn't fixed on those rose-tipped breasts.

Lord, she was beautiful. Trimmer than before, but every bit as sensual. It had damned near killed him to break off their kiss and put some distance between them last night. With a feeling that he was about to hurt even worse, he crossed the room and lifted her gently from the tub.

"Sam?" She lolled against his chest, blinking groggily. "Wh...? What are you doing?"

"Saving you from drowning."

He carried her to the bed and settled her atop the covers. A pile of folded underlinens sat waiting at the foot. Shaking out a petticoat, Sam covered her with the soft cotton.

"I'm sorry," she mumbled, drawing the skirt up over her breasts, unaware that the movement bared the red-gold curls at the juncture of her thighs. "I got your uniform all wet."

"The rains did that."

"Is that what I hear? The rain on the roof?"

"That's what you hear."

Exercising a heroic act of control, he kept his glance from straying and brushed her wet, tangled hair back from her face.

"Strange. I thought for a moment it was your heart hammering."

It probably was, Sam thought. His blood pumped so hard and fast right now it almost deafened him.

"Or mine," she murmured. "Maybe it's mine. Do you hear it pounding?"

"No, I—"

"Then feel it."

When she took one of his hands and slipped it under the bunched cotton, every muscle in his body stiffened.

"Victoria—"

"Do you feel it?"

She had to know what she was doing! She wasn't groggy now, dammit.

"Do you feel it, Sam?"

"Yes."

"Then perhaps you should lock the door."

"What?"

"You don't want Señora Garcia to walk in on us, do you?"

It took him a moment to remember just who the hell Señora Garcia was. He'd just managed to summon a mental image of her when Victoria wiped it right out of his head again.

"I've been thinking about this matter of lust."

"I've been doing some thinking about it, too," he confessed hoarsely.

At night, with her lying only yards away. At dawn, when he rose and left her sleeping. And now! Right now! He couldn't think about anything *except* crushing her wet, naked body against him.

"I was wrong that afternoon in Siboney," she said softly, lifting her free hand to trace the line of his jaw. "I thought we could separate this...this hunger that consumes us from nobler, purer sentiments."

Just as he had separated his longing for Mary from his desire for her, she thought with a little pang.

"I've discovered I can't distinguish between my feelings," she whispered. "What's more, I don't want to. And I don't want to waste these last days before the rains come."

Abandoning the petticoat, she wrapped her arms around his neck and drew herself up until her mouth brushed his.

"Lock the door, Sam."

After bolting the door, Sam peeled off his uniform and dropped it on the floor. Victoria helped. And hindered. She tugged at his belt buckle and pushed at the buttons along with him, but stopped to play over each stretch of exposed flesh. Nerves jumped under his skin everywhere her fingers strayed. Little pinpricks of fire burned every spot her lips touched.

When he finally rid himself of the last of his clothes and joined her on the bed, the puckered scar on his shoulder put a hitch in her breath. Gently, she fingered the wound.

"Does it pain you?"

"Not anymore."

And not anywhere near as much as other parts of him did right now. Sam ached for her so fiercely he had to grit his teeth and fight to keep his touch gentle as he skimmed his palms down the slopes and valleys of her body.

She felt as soft and warm as the rain to his touch. Her skin was so smooth, all slick and sweet-smelling from her bath. Bending, he followed the path of his slow, stroking hands with his mouth.

"Oh, Sam…"

Raising her arms over her head, she arched her back and gave him freer access to her breasts. He teased the tips with his teeth and tongue until they hardened to stiff, red peaks.

This was so different from the first time, Victoria thought on a wave of sensual delight. She'd been so ignorant back in Tampa. So embarrassed when Sam reached down to explore the moist secrets between her legs. There was no trace of that shy, startled virgin in the way she opened for him now. Or in the heat that enveloped her as he pressed and probed and gently, so gently, rolled the heel of his hand against her mound.

This time, she didn't buck or try to twist away. This time, she closed her eyes and surrendered breathlessly to the spinning sensations. Head back, body taut, she spread her legs wide and welcomed his touch.

Sam was sure the effort of holding back would grind his teeth down to stubs. The flushed, sensual woman stretched out beside him enflamed every one of his senses. His mind screamed with the need to plunge into her, but she was so glorious, so generous, that he could only marvel at the change in her.

In them both.

Despite his every intention to the contrary, he'd hungered for Victoria's young, ripe body. In Tampa, he'd let that hunger and the primitive need to assert his claim over her push him into taking her maidenhead. Yet the urgent craving that had driven him then didn't begin to compare with the all-consuming desire now gripping him.

He didn't just hunger for Victoria's body. Staking his claim was the furthest thing from his mind at the moment. She wasn't a girl needing his protection. She'd more than proved her strength and courage. Sam had come to respect her as much as he wanted her.

And Lord, did he want her! All of her. Under him. Wrapped around him. In his bed. In his heart.

Entwining his fingers in hers, he brought her hands down beside her head, braced himself on his elbows and eased atop her. His shaft probed the heat between her legs.

Her whole body went stiff for a moment, then anticipation clenched her belly. The rippling muscles drew a low grunt from Sam, but still he managed to hold back.

"Victoria," he said hoarsely. "Sweetheart."

Her eyes opened. Lips parted, her breath coming swift and shallow, she stared up at him.

"At Siboney," he ground out. "You asked what I felt for you."

"I remember. You supplied a long string of emotions." Swiping her tongue along her lower lip, she managed a shaky laugh. "If I remember rightly, anger topped the list."

"Yes, well, it did at the time."

"Are you saying you want to change the order of your list?"

"No." His fingers tightened around hers. "I want to add to it."

The look in his eyes shot an arrow of excitement through Victoria's belly. Shivering, she invited him to add as many emotions as he wished.

"I don't have your way with words," he warned.

"Just do your best."

"All right. I admire you."

"That's— That's very gratifying."

But not exactly what she'd hoped to hear.

"I respect you."

"I respect you, too."

He dropped a hard kiss on her mouth. The movement canted his hips and brought the tip of his shaft into her moist channel.

"You humble me."

With a little gasp, Victoria writhed under him. "You don't feel particularly humble to me!"

"What I'm trying to say in my clumsy way is that I love you."

Her knuckles were white where her fingers had locked around his. His hard, heavy weight pressed her into the mattress. She couldn't move, could barely think beyond the need to take him into her body.

"Oh, Sam, I love you, too." Her words tumbled out in a breathless rush. "I've always loved you, even when I was hurt and angry and too proud to accept the gift you offered me. I understand now that it's possible to hold more than one love in your heart."

"You're wrong." His grip tightened to a bruising hold. "It's not possible. I'm not sure how or when it happened, but there's no room in my heart or my head or anyplace else for anyone but you, Victoria.''

She stared up at him, stunned. Her mouth opened, closed again. Finally, she let out a little gasp.

''And you think you don't have a way with words?''

A grin slashed across his face. Contorting his body, he bent to cover her mouth and drove home with a slow, sure thrust.

It took her only a move or two to catch the rhythm this time. So deliberate. So tantalizing. Her hips moved with his. She used her teeth and tongue and lips with ever-increasing skill. And when she peaked, groaning out her pleasure from far back in her throat, she almost regretted that he pulled out and spilled his seed on her belly.

Afterward, she sprawled facedown in a tangle of damp sheets. The incredible heights of pleasure Sam had taken her to left Victoria limp and too boneless to move, even when Señora Garcia rapped hesitantly on the door.

Sam called out to her in the few words of Spanish he'd managed to pick up. Mumbling apologies, she beat a hasty retreat.

''So much for observing the proprieties,'' he said wryly as he reached for his pants.

''That was your idea, not mine,'' Victoria reminded him, stretching lazily. "Do you suppose you could talk her into serving us supper in bed? I don't think I have the strength to dress."

"Hmm. We'll have to offer General Wood some other excuse than that for declining his invitation to dinner."

"We're invited to dinner?"

"Yes."

"With General Wood?"

"Yes."

"Sam! Not tonight?"

He shot a grin over his shoulder. "Didn't you wonder why I'd returned to the house so early in the day?"

"I might have," she retorted, recovering, "if I hadn't become somewhat distracted."

"Never mind. I'll make your apologies. General Wood will be disappointed, as he particularly wished to speak to you, but we can always—"

"For pity's sake! You might have said so sooner!"

His eyes glinted. "I might have, if I hadn't become so distracted."

Curiosity had her scrambling up, the tangled bed linens tucked around her breasts. "What does General Wood want to speak to me about?"

Sam hesitated. "It might be better if you hear it from him."

Curiosity surged into quick, sharp interest. "Don't let me walk into the palace unprepared."

"Are you going, then?"

"Yes, of course! But only if you give me some clue as to what's behind this invitation to dinner."

"I believe he wants your opinion about a letter Colonel Roosevelt intends to send to Secretary of War Alger."

Victoria's jaw dropped. "*My* opinion?"

"As a member of the press corps. Shall I ask Señora Garcia to help you dress? We don't have much time."

Dazed, she could only nod.

A little less than an hour later, Sam escorted her into a small salon off the main hall of the governor's palace.

Victoria wore the black lace mantilla draped over a high comb to cover her still-damp hair. Her red silk gown swished against the hardwood floors. The sapphire-studded gold locket Sam had given her was pinned to the silk. A smile warmed her heart each time she remembered his rather gruff hope that this time she'd keep the damned thing on.

The lean, ascetic Wood waited for them in the salon. So, Victoria saw, did his boisterous former second-in-command. Colonel Roosevelt gave her a toothy grin, his eyes merry behind his spectacles.

General Wood greeted her with the courtesy that

had made him the favored physician to President McKinley and his wife. "It's a pleasure to meet you, Miss Parker. I've heard a great deal about you."

"As I have you, sir."

"I understand you made the acquaintance of Colonel Roosevelt and his wife in Tampa."

"Yes." Smiling, Victoria offered the bluff New Yorker her hand. "May I congratulate you on your promotion, Colonel? From what I've heard of the battle of Las Guásimas, it was quite well deserved."

Heat and poor rations had taken their toll on the colonel, just as they had on the rest of the Expeditionary Force. He, too, had lost weight, and his skin had burned to dark terra-cotta. But nothing, apparently, could diminish his exuberant spirits. With one of his neighing laughs, Roosevelt dismissed his first trial under fire as a trifling affair.

"Las Guásimas got us bloodied, but Kettle Hill, now, *that* was a battle, eh, Sam?"

"Yes, sir, it was."

"Would you like a glass of sherry?" Wood inquired. "It's a particularly fine blend. From an Andalusian bodega, I'm told." A smile flitted across his face. "One of the spoils of war."

At Victoria's nod, he tucked her hand in his arm and escorted her to a massive sideboard. The ornate piece was encrusted with gilt. Additional gold trimmed the coat of arms carved into its headboard.

"We're dining informally tonight," he told her as she sipped the golden, almond-flavored wine from a Venetian goblet. "Just the four of us, if that's all right with you?"

"Yes, certainly."

"I'm hoping that what we talk about during dinner won't go farther than this room. I'm also hoping you'll give us your opinion on a rather sensitive political matter."

"As to the former, you have my assurances I won't speak of it to anyone, sir. As to the latter—" She gave a little shake of her head. "I find it hard to imagine that the heroes of San Juan and Kettle Hill would want my opinion on anything, much less a sensitive political matter."

"Let's wait until the first course is served, shall we? Then I'll explain our predicament."

Their predicament, Victoria discovered over a dish of roast suckling pig stuffed with plantains, was that the number of yellow fever cases among the troops had been wildly exaggerated in various military reports sent back to the States. As a result, fear of the dreaded yellow jack now ran rampant within the War Department.

"So much so," Wood told her, "that Secretary Alger has cabled General Shafter with instructions to divide our forces into two armies—sick and well. The well are to stay in encampments around Santiago until it's decided where they go next. The sick we're to send to Siboney.''

''Including those with nothing more than a bothersome boil or infected blister,'' Roosevelt put in indignantly.

''Dear heavens! The hospital can't care for every trooper with a minor indisposition.''

''Exactly.'' The former army-surgeon-turned-field commander leaned forward, his face grave. ''Nor can we keep the troops in the field much longer. Even if the number of yellow fever cases holds steady, malaria and dysentery are decimating the ranks.''

''I know,'' Victoria said with some feeling. ''I was at the Red Cross hospital yesterday. The boathouse is filled to overflowing. But I really don't see how I can help.''

''In three specific ways.'' Holding up his hand, General Wood ticked off each item.

''One, you can report the real numbers of fever cases in your dispatches. The weeks you spent at Siboney give you the credibility to know and report the difference between malarial and yellow fever.''

She could certainly do that. Victoria was only sorry that she hadn't laid more emphasis on the numbers before now.

''Two, you can talk to those members of the

press still in Santiago and encourage them to do the same.''

''Wouldn't such encouragement be better received coming from you? Or from General Shafter? Your rank and years of experience give you both a much better grasp of the problem than I have.''

Another of his rare smiles flickered across Wood's face. ''General Shafter has discovered that journalists form as tight a band of brothers as soldiers. The incident in the plaza during the surrender ceremony has, shall we say, cooled relations between the military and the press. We'll pass the word through official channels, of course, but would greatly appreciate anything you can do to assist us in this matter.''

''I'll do my best. And the third item on your list?''

Wood and his former deputy exchanged glances.

''Colonel Roosevelt has decided to write a letter to Secretary Alger protesting the order to keep our men—both sick and well—in Cuba during the wet months,'' the general said slowly. ''It's not a military communication, but a private correspondence from one man of considerable political influence to another. We should like your opinion on the best way to make that private letter public, without causing the colonel to violate the military chain of command.''

Victoria didn't hesitate. ''Leave it lying on a table where a member of the press can sneak a peak at it.''

"Bully!" Roosevelt gave a loud, horselike laugh. "That's exactly what we thought, too.''

18

As it turned out, the senior officers in Cuba decided Roosevelt should address his letter to General Shafter rather than Secretary of War Alger.

They all gathered at the governor's palace on the last day of July to help Roosevelt draft the missive. In it, he voiced their collective concern that the flower of American manhood was being left to rot in the hills around Santiago. Moved by his willingness to risk both his command and his political career, every man present decided to sign a formal petition to Alger as well.

Both documents were left on a table, where an unsuspecting Associated Press reporter noticed them.

"It happened just as you thought it would," Sam told Victoria with a grin. "After he read the contents, the man couldn't wait to rush down to the cable office."

"You watch," she predicted confidently. "The gist of those letters will appear in tomorrow's edition of every major newspaper from New York to San Francisco."

She was right. The letters made the front pages of the *San Francisco Examiner*, the Denver *Ledger*, the *Daily Oklahoman*, the *Detroit News* and at least four of the New York dailies. Publishers clogged cable wires demanding more details from their correspondents in Cuba. At the same time, alarmed citizens deluged the Secretary of War with telegrams urging him to bring their boys home.

On August 3, a mere three days later, Alger cabled General Shafter to prepare his army to depart Cuba.

Given the near-hysterical fear of yellow fever, the order included two specific caveats. One, those troops well enough to travel would be brought back to remote bases and kept isolated until it was shown they weren't infectious. Two, those already infected with the dreaded disease would remain in Cuba until they recovered—or died.

Late on the afternoon the order came in, Sam searched out Victoria to tell her the news. He found her at the cable office, where she hurriedly rewrote her dispatch to include the latest information. That done, they dashed back to the house on Calle San Giorgio through sheets of rain.

"I should have had the stable boy get out the carriage," Sam said ruefully, holding his India rubber poncho over her head.

"It's only a few blocks. I won't melt."

Although she tossed the words off with a laugh, Victoria wasn't completely sure they'd prove true. She'd thought the daily downpours torrential before. Once July had melted into August and the rainy season began in earnest, the brief cloudbursts had stretched to steady, pounding rains. If the sun broke through the clouds at all now, it was only for an hour or two each day.

Alger's order to bring the troops home had come none too soon. As miserable as the rains now made life in the city, Sam said they'd turned life in the camps into torment. There was no escaping the wet. It swelled creeks into raging rivers that washed through the camps. Seeped through canvas tents. Rotted food, tobacco pouches, boots. Some of the men had built platforms on stilts to escape the soggy ground, but they couldn't escape the sickness that came with the rains. Malaria raged like the plague among the troops. They had to leave Cuba, and soon!

Victoria had put off facing the fact that their withdrawal also meant hers, but Sam forced the issue when they reached the house they shared with Max Luna. A clucking Señora Garcia took the poncho, shaking her head at the folly of *yanquis* who dashed about so foolishly in the rain.

"I'd best go change," Victoria said, grimacing at the slap of her wet skirts against her calves. "I'm soaked through."

He caught her arm, staying her for a moment. "There's a steamer leaving the day after tomorrow. The *Sea Cloud*. I think we should book you passage on it."

"So soon!"

"It's time, Victoria."

As much as she longed to exchange this wet, torpid heat for the cool, clean winds of Wyoming, she hated the thought of leaving Cuba. She'd come into her own here, as a correspondent and as a woman.

Even more, she hated the thought of leaving Sam. Particularly now that she'd finally shed her doubts and hurts and come to revel in his touch. The afternoon he'd found her asleep in the bath had opened the floodgates. He couldn't seem to get enough of her, or she of him.

"Do you really want me to go?" she asked, searching his face.

"No. Neither do I want to see you shivering with chills or racked with fever."

"But it could be months or years before you're released from duty here."

"It could." He brushed his knuckles down her damp cheek. "Will you wait for me?"

"Oh, Sam." Curling her face into his hand, she pressed a kiss against the palm. "I feel as though I've waited for you all my life. I'll wait as long as I have to."

When he dipped his head and covered her mouth with his, she thought her heart would burst. And when he scooped her into his arms, strode down the hall and kicked the door to the bedroom shut behind them, she shed her wet clothes and tumbled joyously into bed beside him.

The first time was fast and frenzied, driven by a hunger that seemed to grow more insatiable with each day. The second time was slow and languorous and so deliciously, provocatively wicked that Victoria finally pleaded exhaustion. Curling her sweat-slicked body into his, she dropped like a stone into sleep.

Despite their strenuous activities, Victoria came awake before Sam did the next morning. The realization that this was her last full day in Cuba was as heavy as the deadweight of his arm thrown across her middle.

Thinking of all that had happened between them since she'd stepped off the boat at Siboney, Victoria studied him in the dawn light just beginning to creep through the shutters. His dark lashes fanned against cheeks still hollowed from the weight he'd lost. The night's growth stubbled the lower half of his face. His brown hair stuck up in spikes from their energetic activities of the night before.

He looked more like a scruffy pirate than an officer, and Victoria didn't think she could possibly love him more than she did at this moment. Unable to resist the urge to touch him, she traced her fingers along his bare shoulder in a whisper-soft caress.

"Mmm. Nice."

Her hand stilled. "I didn't mean to disturb you. Go back to sleep."

"Too late," he muttered into his pillow.

"It's not quite dawn, Sam. Go back to sleep."

"Not quite dawn?" One brown eye opened. "What woke you so early?"

"Nothing in particular."

Just the realization that they had only one more night together.

"Ha! I don't believe that." A sleepy grin tugged at his mouth. "It usually takes nothing short of a cannonade to get you to stir."

"Surely I'm not as bad as that!"

"Yes, you are. But now that we're both awake—"

Curling an arm around her waist, he drew her closer. Victoria snuggled against him, her back to his front, content to lie beside him and wait for the dawn. It took only the brush of her backside against his groin to realize Sam didn't intend to waste what was left of the night.

One shift of his hips, and her womb clenched. One probe between her legs, and she was instantly, deliciously wet.

"You know," he murmured, his breath hot in her ear, "I wouldn't mind if we greeted every dawn like this for the rest of our lives."

"Neither," she gasped as he slid into her, "would I!"

Writhing, she arched her back and thrust her hips against his. His hand came up to torment her breast. The play of his tongue in her ear drove her as wild as his fast, hard strokes.

When her peak came, she almost screamed with the searing intensity of it. Sam had to slap a palm over her mouth to keep her from waking the entire household.

When his came, it left them both drenched in sweat and the warm, sticky residue of their pleasure.

Exhausted all over again, Victoria barely twitched when Sam slipped out of bed, washed and shaved, and pulled on his uniform.

"I'll swing by the harbor and book your passage on the *Sea Cloud*," he promised as he bent to brush her mouth with his.

That roused her enough to make a husky plea.

"Come home early tonight, if you can. It's our last together."

"I will."

It was almost noon when Victoria woke the second time.

The realization that she had only a few hours left in Cuba wrapped around her like the dark clouds that wreathed the mountains almost all day now. Sighing, she threw off the tangled bed linens.

She had to go to the market, buy gifts for Señora Garcia and the rest of the staff. Make a final visit to the boathouse hospital to say goodbye to Miss Barton and her staff. Compose a last dispatch from Cuba and put it on the wires.

Yet even as she washed, dressed and consumed the lunch Señora Garcia had waiting for her, regrets pulled at Victoria with sharp, pinching fingers. She didn't want to board the *Sea Cloud* tomorrow. She didn't want to miss reporting on the American withdrawal from Cuba.

She didn't want to leave Sam a day or an hour earlier than she had to.

Surely another day or two wouldn't matter. Just a day or two. With many ships coming into Santiago to begin the troop withdrawal, Sam could find her a place on one of them. She'd talk to him about it tonight. At dinner.

With that thought in mind, she braved the rain to walk to the harbor.

Victoria stopped at the Red Cross hospital first. Drained from her walk and the stifling heat, she plopped down beside Callie May Morgan. All the shutters were closed against the rain, and the air inside the boathouse was stifling.

Flapping a hand in front of her face, she fought for breath. "You'd think by now I'd be used to this climate."

"Does take some getting used to," Callie May agreed, reaching into the basket of just-washed bandages between her feet. With the ease of long practice, she folded one end of the soft cotton rag and rolled it up.

"This constant heat tires me so," Victoria said with a sigh. "It didn't seem to bother me half so much when I first got to Cuba, but now I fall asleep at the oddest hours."

And in the oddest places. Smiling inwardly, she dragged off her wet poncho and sagged back against the wall. Callie May slanted her a considering look.

"Maybe it ain't the heat, miss. Maybe you're breeding."

"Breeding?" Startled, Victoria jerked upright. "Oh, no! I couldn't possibly be."

A chuckle rumbled deep in the older woman's chest. "That's what we all say when it happens."

"No, truly. There must be some other explanation for this...this constant fatigue."

"Well, I'm no doctor, but I have birthed four babies. I near 'bout fell asleep where I stood every day for the first few weeks I was carrying them."

Victoria stared at her, slack-jawed, while the possibility burst like a rocket in her mind. Then she remembered the care Sam had taken to prevent just such an occurrence.

"You don't understand." With an embarrassed glance around, she lowered her voice. "I haven't— That is, the captain and I haven't—"

"You sayin' you 'n' the captain ain't crawled under the mosquito netting together?"

"Yes," she hissed, her cheeks burning. "We have. But Captain Garrett has never— That is, he doesn't—"

"Ahh. I understand. He doesn't pour out his juice inside you."

"No," she got out in a strangled whisper. "He doesn't."

"Me 'n' my Jake tried that, too," Callie May said with another chuckle. "It didn't work for us. Guess it don't work for you 'n' the captain, either." She cocked a knowing brow. "How long since you had your flow?"

Desperately, Victoria tried to recall the last time she'd had her courses.

Dear God! Not since she'd left Cheyenne! Eight, no *nine* weeks ago! Before she took the train to Tampa. Before she and Sam made love for the first time.

"But— But I've been losing weight these past weeks," she stammered. "Not gaining it."

"Huh! Take a look around you. You see anyone here who hasn't shed a good twenty pounds since they come to Cuba?"

Dazed, she let her gaze drift over the crowded ward. Every cot was filled with gaunt, emaciated patients.

"No," she whispered, "I don't."

She *must* be pregnant! Either that, or she'd endured such stress during those weeks at Siboney that it had affected her woman's flow. But stress wouldn't explain her constant drowsiness. Would it?

When she put the question to Callie May, the woman lifted her big shoulders.

"I can't say 'bout that. From the look of you, you plumb wore yourself out up there. Maybe your body's just tellin' you that you need rest." Her black eyes were kind. "You'll know soon enough one way or t'other, won't you?"

Numbly, Victoria nodded.

"Meantime, you sleep as much as you need to.

And if I was you, miss, I'd take that boat home tomorrow. You don't need to be around fever if you *are* breeding.''

Her mind spinning, Victoria walked out of the ward and huddled under the veranda's wide over-hang. Blindly, she stared at the white waterspouts dancing across the bay.

Could Callie May be right?

Was she indeed carrying Sam's child?

She felt like a fool, a complete and utter fool, for not even considering the possibility. How could she have forgotten the unused linen rags still tucked away in the bottom of her valise? How could she have coupled with Sam so eagerly—and so often!—without imagining that a child might quicken in her belly?

Her only excuse was ignorance. Sheer, abysmal ignorance. And the fact that she'd accepted without question Sam's explanation for withdrawing so pre-cipitously each time they'd joined. Evidently he hadn't withdrawn precipitously enough!

Gradually, her shock subsided. Bit by bit, a sense of wonder began to take hold. "A baby," she whis-pered, crossing her arms over her middle. "Sam's baby.''

Until this moment, she'd been sure she couldn't experience any wilder joy than she had in Sam's arms these past weeks. But now...

A baby!

She had to tell him. Had to share this wondrous possibility! Dragging up the hood of her poncho, Victoria pushed away from the protection of the veranda.

She had taken less than a dozen steps before the glow faded and reality set in. There wasn't any question now about leaving Cuba. She couldn't think just of herself. Or Sam. She had to consider the child she might be carrying.

As she slogged through the mud, skirts held high, Callie May's parting advice echoed over and over in her head. Victoria had to board the *Sea Cloud* tomorrow. If she was indeed pregnant, she shouldn't remain around fever patients.

Her mind still spinning, she found a table at a small taverna on the plaza and hurriedly composed her final dispatch from Cuba. Once she'd sent it over the wires, she made a quick tour of the market to purchase parting gifts, then returned to the house on Calle San Giorgio to pack her bag.

Retrieving her personal items from the clothespress, she plopped them on the bed beside her valise. She had made enough purchases over the past weeks to make packing a distinct challenge. Frowning, she overturned the valise and dumped its contents on the bed.

Her stacks of notebooks tumbled out, along with

Richard Harding Davis's now moldy cork helmet, Sam's service revolver and the unused linen rags Victoria had so belatedly remembered. With a shake of her head, she set the helmet and linens aside and picked up the holstered revolver. Small patches of mildew greened the leather, but careful examination showed the Colt itself still glistened with a thin sheen of protective oil.

Chewing on her lower lip, Victoria debated for some moments before returning both the weapon and her notebooks to the valise. Those items alone ate up almost half the available space, but she wouldn't leave them behind. It took only a few moments more to sort through her clothing and cram in what she could.

Once packed, she paced the tiled floors and waited for Sam to return from his duties at the governor's palace.

Of course he had to be late!

Their last night in Cuba. With only hours left for them to be together for God knew how long. And Victoria fairly shivering with wonder, with excitement, with curiosity about how he would react to her news.

Señora Garcia set dinner back twice, but Victoria finally sat down to a solitary meal of stewed chicken served with a spicy sauce of diced tomatoes, onions and peppers. She forced herself to eat every bite. If she *was* breeding, both she and the baby would need sustenance.

After dinner, she retrieved one of her notebooks and tried to compose some reflections on her time in Cuba for a longer article, perhaps a retrospective. She gave up after the fourth or fifth attempt and filled several pages with doodles.

Still Sam didn't return.

The candles had begun to sputter when at last she heard the outer door slam and a low exchange in Spanish. The sound of boots on the tiles brought her around in her chair. Swallowing her disappointment, she welcomed Max Luna with a smile.

"You're quite late this evening."

"I know. I earned my pay tonight, I can tell you. General Wood held a number of meetings with Santiago's civic and military leaders."

Excitement kindled in his dark eyes. Victoria felt it emanating from him in waves as he tossed his hat aside and joined her at the table.

"It looks like the United States and Spain have finally come to terms on a peace agreement."

"Max! Tell me at once! Is the war really over?"

"Apparently. We received a cable from the War Department this afternoon. Spain has agreed to evacuate its forces from Cuba, cede Puerto Rico and the island of Guam to the United States, and sell us the Philippines for an as-yet-undisclosed sum."

A fierce satisfaction shot through Victoria's veins. All those gallant soldiers and sailors hadn't fought in vain. The news reporters who'd covered the rebels' fierce struggle for so long hadn't espoused a hopeless cause. Finally, *finally,* the thousands of peasants who'd been forced into reconcentration camps by the Spanish, decimated by sickness and starved by war would be able to return to their homes.

"Cuba will have its independence at last!"

"Well…" Dropping into the chair opposite hers, Max shook his head. "Not quite yet."

"Whatever do you mean?"

"Evidently a number of influential businessmen with sugar interests in Cuba have petitioned President McKinley. They feel strongly that the island should remain under the jurisdiction of an American military governor."

"For how long?"

"At least until we're assured a native government will protect American economic interests."

Victoria could have cared less about American economic interests at the moment. Her only concern was that Sam would remain indefinitely with the military administrator.

"The rumor is General Wood will be appointed governor-general of all Cuba," Max said, confirming her fears.

"Will he want to keep you with him, do you think? You and Sam?"

"So he's indicated."

"Oh, no!"

Swallowing an unladylike curse, Victoria slumped back in her chair. This was her last night in Cuba. Her last hours with Sam, perhaps for some years to come. They should be celebrating the peace agreement. Discussing the incredible possibility that they might have made a child together. Saying their private, passionate farewells.

"I suppose that's why Sam's still at the governor's palace," she muttered. "No doubt he'll have to remain on duty most of the night."

Max glanced at her in surprise. "He's not at the palace. Didn't he send you word?"

"No."

"I'm sure he meant to, but he must not have had time before he dashed out this afternoon."

"Where did he go?"

"Siboney. He received a message that a friend is down with the fever."

Slowly, Victoria sat up. "Did he mention the name of the friend?"

"Mrs. Prendergast. I believe you know her, don't you?"

She opened her mouth. Tried to speak. Swallowed and tried again. "Yes. I know her."

19

Dark, cloud-covered night blanketed Sam as he spurred his mount along the rutted dirt track that ran from Santiago to Siboney. Mud flew up from the gelding's hooves, spattering both horse and rider, but thankfully the rain had slowed to a drizzle. At least Sam could see more than a few yards in front of him.

What he saw wrung a frustrated oath.

Those lanterns flickering up ahead indicated another damned checkpoint. With close to seventy thousand troops bivouacked in the hills, their tents strung out over every cleared patch of ground between Siboney and Santiago, sentry points seemed to have sprung up every hundred yards or so.

"Halt! Who goes there?"

Gritting his teeth, Sam reined in. "Captain Samuel Garrett. First Volunteer Cavalry, on detached duty with General Wood's staff."

"Come forward, sir."

He moved into the pool of lantern light and dug out the official document he'd hastily written before leaving Santiago.

"Here's my pass."

After being shown to so many other sentries, the ink had all but washed away. Just as well, since Sam had signed the thing himself. The two infantrymen squinted at the soggy paper, but couldn't decipher it any more than they could distinguish his unit insignia.

"Where you headed, sir?"

"To the hospital at Siboney. On a mission of some urgency."

"Must be urgent," one of the men muttered. "Can't imagine anyone going to that charnel house unless they have to."

His companion handed Sam the soggy pass. "You know you'll need a paper from the surgeon to get back through the lines, don't you, sir?"

"Yes."

"Our major gave us strict orders," the soldier warned, stepping aside. "We can't let anyone through from the hospital unless the surgeon certifies in writing they've had no contact with yellow fever patients."

Biting back another curse, Sam pocketed the pass and dug his heels into his mount's sides. Damn Alger and those idiots in Washington. Their fears

about a potential yellow fever epidemic had now
spread to the troops in Cuba. Rumors ran rampant
through the camps. Commanders at every level believed thousands, if not tens of thousands, were
down with the dreaded disease.

From the daily reports coming in to General
Wood, Sam knew the actual count was closer to
three hundred. Yet the paranoia persisted, and Alger's misguided order to segregate the sick from the
well had become carved in stone. Anyone—anyone—known to have contact with yellow fever patients had suddenly become the enemy.

Like Mary.

With every thud of his horse's hooves, the message from the hospital commander drummed in
Sam's head. Brief. Terse. To the point.

Captain Garret had asked to be kept apprised of
Mrs. Prendergast's situation. She was down with
malaria. Only malaria at this point. But in her weak
and exhausted condition, it could well lead to jaun-
dice and complications of the liver. Or worse.

Sam had left Santiago with one purpose and one
purpose only. He wasn't about to lose Mary to malaria. Or to Secretary Alger's order.

By the time he cleared the last checkpoint and
spurred his weary mount up the hill to the hospital,
midnight had come and gone. Flickering campfires
showed specks of red against the dark fields. Long,

silent rows of white tents stretched into the night like sleeping ghosts. Lamps illuminated the interior of the larger surgical tents, displaying dark silhouettes of those still at their work.

Beyond the main hospital, the rolls of concertina wire surrounding the contagion ward glinted in the moonlight. Only a few lamps glowed inside the cordoned-off area. The rest, Sam guessed grimly, had been doused in the hopes the stricken patients might get some rest.

He sat still in the saddle, surveying the isolation unit, noting the sentry posted at the single entrance, working out a tactical plan in his mind. Then he swung down and went in search of the hospital commander.

He found McKenna at his tent. The flap was up, the interior lit by an oil lamp. The gray-haired colonel sat on his cot. Elbows propped on his knees, he dangled his hands between his legs. His head drooped between slumped shoulders. Snores resonated with each rise and fall of his chest.

"Colonel?"

The surgeon's head shot up. "Who? What?"

Blinking owlishly, he searched the tent. Sam stepped into the light.

"Captain Garrett, sir. I received your message."

"Oh. Yes." His shoulders slumped once again. "Come in, man. Come in."

Sam ducked under the flap and forced out the

question burning a hole in his head. "How is Mrs. Prendergast?"

"Delirious, according to the last report."

"When was that?"

"Three, maybe four hours ago. I lose track of time, especially at night." Wearily, McKenna rubbed his eyes with the heel of his hand. "I understand why you've come. You're concerned about her. We all are. But there's nothing you can do for her now."

Yes, there was, Sam thought grimly. He could take her out of the contagion ward. Lessen her exposure to other fevers. Help her fight the malaria. Which was exactly what he intended to do. With a nod to the colonel, he turned to leave.

"Garrett!" The surgeon shoved off his cot. "You're not thinking of doing anything foolish, are you? Like trying to enter the contagion area?"

Sam looked him square in the eye. "No, sir."

Their glances locked. Tension crackled in the air until, at last, McKenna broke it with a harsh sigh.

"I've lost so many of my people. Orderlies. Cooks. Three of my surgeons. Almost half of the volunteers from the Twenty-fourth Infantry. And my nurses." Pain edged his voice. "Fifteen of them dead of dysentery and typhoid so far."

"But not from Yellow Jack."

"No," he said slowly. "None lost to Yellow Jack. So far."

Mary wouldn't be the first, Sam vowed fiercely.

The colonel must have read his thoughts in his face.

"Think before you do something you'll have cause to regret," he cautioned. "Secretary Alger's order is very specific. You risk a court-martial if you attempt to circumvent it."

"You and I both know that order resulted from misinformation and near hysteria," Sam said quietly.

They both also knew that Mary's life was well worth a court-martial. McKenna wouldn't have sent him word of her condition otherwise.

"Mrs. Prendergast has worked in the contagion ward for weeks now," the surgeon conceded wearily. "If she hasn't contracted yellow fever by now, it's clear she's immune. But an order is an order."

"Yes, sir."

With the dragging walk of an old man, he moved to a table tucked under the slope of the tent. It was littered with the implements of his trade. His hand closed around a cardboard box of quinine tablets, the same box that had been issued to every soldier before departing for Cuba.

"Here. Take these. You might need them. The dosage is two every four hours. Now get the hell out of my tent."

"Yes, sir. Thank you."

* * *

Sam decided on a frontal approach. He'd use the hundred or so yards of darkness that separated the contagion area from the main hospital to his advantage. That, and the element of surprise. All he had to do was get close enough to bring the sentry down. Quietly. Efficiently.

Holding his mount's reins in a gloved fist, he walked through the churned up mud and cane stubble. As he neared the entry point, he noted that the man on duty wore khaki instead of regulation blue. Cursing under his breath, Sam recognized one of the corporals from the company commanded by Bucky O'Neill, the mayor of Prescott, Arizona, who'd taken a bullet through the head during the battle of San Juan Hill.

The corporal recognized Sam, too. Not even a coating of mud could disguise the Rough Riders' distinctive khaki pants and spotted neckerchief. Squinting through the darkness, the Arizona miner peered at Sam in surprise.

"Captain Garrett?"

"Yes. It's Peters, isn't it."

"Yes, sir. What are you doing here this time of night?" Concern flashed across his face. "You ain't coming down with the fever, are you?"

"No." Sam dropped the reins and took a step closer. "I've come to see one of the nurses. Mrs. Prendergast."

The man's eyes rounded. "You want to go inside?"

"Yes."

"We're not supposed to let anyone in 'cepting the grave detail. Do you have authorization from Colonel McKenna?"

"No."

"Sorry, sir. Can't let you pass." He shook his head apologetically. "Orders are orders, you know."

"Yes," Sam said for the second time in the past ten minutes. "They are. And I'm sorry, too, Peters."

"'Bout what, sir?"

"This."

Whipping up his arm, he delivered a vicious undercut to the man's jaw.

"*Very* sorry," he grunted, catching the Arizonan before he hit the ground.

Quickly, he dragged him into the shadows.

The nightmare of the ride back to Santiago would haunt Sam for the rest of his life.

He cradled Mary in front of him. Wrapped in his poncho and a thin gray blanket, she alternated between body-racking chills and raging fever. When the fever gripped her, Sam peeled back the blanket and let the rain bathe her burning skin. When the chills rattled her teeth and shook her from head to toe, he hugged her tight against his body to give her what heat he could. She took the quinine tablets without protest, but turned her head away when he tried to get her to swallow the brackish water from his canteen.

Throughout the long ride, he listened for sounds of pursuit. All the while, he detoured around checkpoints and dodged sentries. Twice he had to clamp a hand over Mary's mouth to keep her from moaning while they waited behind thick stands of palmetto for the men marching picket duty to pass by. Once, a vigilant soldier caught the rustle of a palm frond and whirled. His companion spun around, as well, eyes wide and rifle leveled.

"What'd you hear?"

"I dunno. Something." Raising his voice, the sentry called out a thin, reedy order. "Whoever's behind that bush damned well better show hisself!"

With the stealth of a mountain cat, Sam dismounted and gently deposited Mary on the ground. He'd bluff his way through this if possible. If not…

A sudden thrashing stopped him in his tracks. Just ahead, a dog-size creature scuttled out of the bush.

"Shee-it! It's one of them land crabs."

Cursing a blue streak, both soldiers hurriedly backed away. Sam waited, his heart slamming against his ribs, for a full minute before he picked up Mary and climbed back into the saddle.

20

Leaning a shoulder against the window casement, Victoria stared through the open shutters at the moon hanging low above the garden wall. Exhaustion dragged at her limbs and dulled the edges of her mind. She hadn't slept, hadn't so much as closed her eyes. They felt gritty, dry, like patches of sand.

Was it only six or seven hours ago that she'd waited so eagerly for Sam to come home? Only twelve since the possibility that she carried a child had burst on her?

All the confusion, all the surprise and joy and wonder of that amazing possibility was gone. The news from Siboney had buried everything under a thick layer of fear.

Mary was down with fever.

And Sam had gone to her.

Victoria knew in her heart what he would do. He

wouldn't let Mary die in the contagion ward. He'd bring her out, care for her himself, try to save her no matter the cost. She was his friend, his good friend.

All through the long night, Victoria had agonized over whether or not she, too, should make the journey to Siboney. The very prospect filled her with terror. Not for herself, not for Sam. For her baby.

Oh, God! Her baby!

She wrapped her arms tight around her middle. The torment of her choices almost ripped her apart.

She had to think of her child. Had to consider its health and safety. If there *was* a child.

Against that possibility, she had to weigh Mary's life. Victoria had spent weeks at Siboney. She wasn't as skilled as the trained nurses, certainly, but those long days and nights had taught her a great deal more than Sam could possibly know about caring for fever patients.

Hugging her middle, she closed her sandpapery eyes. What should she do? What could she do?

She was still at the window when a rooster crowed, announcing the thin, gray dawn. Still agonizing when she heard the sounds of the household stirring. Still torn when Max Luna left for the governor's palace.

Sam reached the outskirts of Santiago an hour after dawn. Concealed behind the rubble of what had once been a farmhouse, he held Mary against him and surveyed the formidable coils of concertina wire the Spanish had thrown up in anticipation of an invasion. There was no going around the wire, or bluffing his way past the marines guarding the checkpoints.

He'd have to go through it, Sam decided, eyeing the glistening coils. He knew a spot on the western perimeter, close to the harbor, where some enterprising troops had cut a swath through the wire and enjoyed a wild night in town before being marched back to their units for appropriate discipline. If he timed it just right, he could get Mary through the wire between patrols.

He had just turned his weary mount off the main road when a distant rattle of wheels brought his head around. Squinting through the hazy gray drizzle, he made out the shape of an open carriage. It approached the checkpoint and halted for the marine sentries to verify the driver's pass before rolling through. Cursing, Sam nudged his mount back behind the rubble. He'd gotten Mary this far. He wasn't about to allow them both to be detected within sight of the city.

Cradling her limp form against his chest, he watched through narrowed eyes as the driver flicked the reins and urged the single horse in the harness to as fast a clip as the muddy, rutted track would permit. Suddenly, Sam stiffened.

"What the hell...?"

A poncho was draped over the driver's head and upper body, but the red-gold tendrils flying out from under the hood identified her as surely as a signpost.

Sam's stomach clenched. He guessed immediately where she was headed. His mind racing, he tried to decide whether or not to remain hidden and let her drive by. When he'd ridden out of Santiago yesterday, he hadn't stopped to weigh the risk of infection against the ties of friendship. Exposing Victoria to that risk was another matter altogether, however.

Sam had counted on her boarding the *Sea Cloud* this morning. Had intended to wait until she was safely gone before bringing Mary into the house. Even then, he'd planned to keep the sick woman isolated and care for her himself until her fever broke. Now it looked as though Victoria might miss the steamer. She was heading not for home and safety, but straight for Siboney.

With another curse, Sam kicked free of the stirrups, hooked a leg over the saddle horn and slid down. A few quick kicks cleared a spot in the rubble. Gently, he deposited his burden on the ground. Peeling back the blanket, he saw that fever had her again. Sweat pearled her face. Eyes dulled to a flat black gazed up at him unseeing.

"Mary? Can you hear me?"

Her forehead creased. With a small moan, she fought her way through the mists in her mind.

"Sam?"

"I have to leave you for a moment. Only a moment. I'll be right back. I promise."

He couldn't tell if she understood him or not. Her lids fluttered down again.

When the carriage swept past a mound of rubble and a gaunt, mud-brown specter materialized in the road directly ahead of her, Victoria's heart jumped straight into her throat.

Gasping, she sawed on the reins with one hand. With the other, she fumbled open the valise on the floor beside her feet. Her fingers yanked open the flap on the revolver's holster at the same instant she recognized the mud-covered figure.

"Sam!"

Sagging with relief, she fought to bring the carriage horse to a prancing halt. Sam jumped forward to assist her. Wrapping his fist around the leads, he stilled the skittish mare and pinned Victoria with a fierce stare.

"What the devil are you doing here?"

"Max told me you went to Siboney. He said you received word Mary was down with fever. When you didn't return last night, I had to come and see if I could help."

Gripping the reins, she forced herself to ask the question that had haunted her all night.

"How did you find her?"

"Ill. Very ill. But alive."

"Is it— Is it Yellow Jack?"

Sam noted the catch in her voice, understood the fear behind it. His own skin still crawled with the memory of brushing past so many infected patients to get to their nurse.

"No. Malaria. But between the fever and the chills and utter exhaustion, I doubt she would have survived another day in the contagion ward."

The dread squeezing Victoria's chest like a vise eased its vicious hold. Closing her eyes, she uttered a quick prayer of thanksgiving. When she opened them again, she searched Sam's face beneath the dripping brim of his hat.

"So you brought her out."

It wasn't a question, but he answered, anyway.

"Yes, I brought her out."

She crossed an arm over her belly. She was fighting her fear, Sam guessed, just as he had.

"Where is she?"

"Over there, in the ruins."

Sam half expected her to shrink back against the seat again, and had opened his mouth to assure her that Mary was his responsibility and his alone. To his surprise, she blew out a long breath, wrapped the reins around the brake and started to climb down.

"Well, between us we shall make her well. How fortunate that I brought the carriage. We can—"

Sam stepped in front of her, cutting off both her descent and her rapid patter. "Get back in the carriage. I won't have you exposed to infection."

"You said she's down with malaria."

"She's been in contact with yellow fever patients."

"So have you now," Victoria shot back, "but I would no more abandon you than I would Mary!"

The fierce response took him aback. With a sigh, Victoria tried to explain the tangled mix of emotions that had brought her out of the city.

"Mary looked out for me those weeks at Siboney, Sam. She made sure I ate. Forced me to rest. Reminded me constantly to take my quinine pills. She took care of me, just as she took care of all those wounded and ill soldiers. How could I possibly turn away from her now that she needs caring for?"

That brave speech cost her more than he would ever know. Setting her teeth, she fought to keep from wrapping her arms around her stomach again.

She still wasn't positive she carried a child. Hadn't had the chance to discuss the possibility with Sam. Now she *couldn't* tell him. Not with Mary lying only yards away, desperately in need of help. Putting aside every thought but that one, she reached for the valise.

"Thank God I brought this with me, just in case. If we're to get Mary past the sentries, we'll have to get her out of her hospital garb."

"Victoria—"

"Please! Let's not waste any more time arguing. Show me where she is."

21

Even with Sam's warning that she would find Mary much changed, Victoria wasn't prepared for the near skeleton she found wrapped in a thin gray blanket.

Mary's eyes had sunk deep into their sockets. Her skin hung in loose, sallow folds. The once-glossy black hair was a tangle of sweat-drenched rattails, and the starched white apron and gray uniform dress she'd taken such pride in looked as though they'd been used to mop up floors.

Trying desperately to hide her shock, Victoria sank to her knees amid the rubble and groped for her hand. The bones felt as thin and fragile as a sparrow's.

"Mary? Mary, it's Victoria. Can you hear me?"

Her lids twitched. Slowly, so slowly, she opened eyes glazed with fever. "Victoria?"

"Yes, it's me."

"Shouldn't…have…come."

"Nonsense." She swallowed the painful lump in her throat. "How could I leave you to Sam's clumsy attentions? Dear God, you're shaking all over. Let's sit you up, shall we, so we can get you out of this wet uniform and into something dry."

While Sam held her propped against his arm, Victoria tugged at the sash of the soiled apron with trembling fingers, then went to work on the buttons of her gray blouse. Moments later, she peeled away the sodden outer garments.

Shocked all over again by the widow's emaciated state, Victoria saw that her under linens were just as wet. Sacrificing Mary's modesty to expediency, she ripped open the valise and snatched out a clean camisole. Her hand shook as she folded the soft linen and splashed it with tepid canteen water, but she forced a cheerful note into her voice.

"You'll feel better when we've washed the dirt and mud off and bundled you into dry clothes. I've brought you a red silk dress to wear. And a black lace mantilla. They're rather fine, if I do say so myself."

Gently, she removed layer upon layer of sweat and grime.

"The dress will no doubt wrap around you twice, but that can't be helped. We'll tuck it up as best we can. There, you're as clean as we can manage right now. I'll give you a proper bath once we're home.''

Frowning, Mary swiped her tongue along her dry, cracked lips. "Home?"

"Yes, home. Sam has a house in the city. It's quite comfortable and…"

Victoria's voice trailed off. Frowning, she tossed aside the soiled rag and plucked another camisole and a pair of drawers from the tapestry bag.

She'd left Santiago with no thought but to go to Siboney and offer whatever assistance she could. Now that Sam had removed Mary from that swamp of pestilence and fever, maybe Victoria should indeed take her home. Today. On the *Sea Cloud*.

Frowning, she instructed Sam to hold Mary upright and turn his head away while she eased her out of her wet underclothes into dry ones. The red silk dress came next, followed by a fringed shawl that draped from shoulder to knee.

"I'll take her things and bury them," Sam said.

"Under a pile of rocks. We don't want a dog to dig them up."

Or anyone else. Mary showed only symptoms of malaria, but she'd been in contact with yellow fever patients. It would be better to burn her clothes, but they didn't dare start a fire here.

All the while she worked, Victoria's mind spun fast and furiously. The war with Spain was done. The troops would begin pulling out of Cuba soon.

Although the War Department had ordered that the yellow fever patients be the last to leave, Mary had done her duty by them. More than her duty. She should go home.

When Victoria drew Sam aside and suggested as much, however, he immediately rejected the proposal.

"It's too risky. If you try to board in the company of a nurse who's just come from Siboney, the captain will refuse to take either of you aboard."

"Then we don't tell him she's a nurse, or that she's just come from Siboney. We'll say she's my friend. Or my companion. That's it. My companion. A duenna you've hired to protect the reputation of your virginal fiancée during the voyage home."

Shaking his head, Sam pointed out the flaw in her scheme. "And how will you account for the fact that this duenna is burning with fever and so weak she can't hold up her head?"

"I don't know! I haven't gotten that far!"

"Obviously."

"All right. Let me think a moment."

Kicking aside a crumbled adobe brick, Victoria took two paces, whirled back.

"We'll say she was stricken by the heat. Or she twisted her ankle getting out of the carriage and fainted."

The sudden intent look in his eyes told her she'd caught his interest. "It might work."

"We'll make it work! Think, Sam. Think! You were so insistent that I leave Cuba when the rains came. If it's unhealthy for me to remain here during the rainy season, it's doubly so for a woman down with malaria."

He couldn't argue with that.

"It might be weeks yet before the army clears her to go home." Throwing a glance over her shoulder, Victoria lowered her voice to an urgent whisper. "She might not last that long in this climate. I'll take her home. I'll care for her until she's well enough to care for herself. I owe her that much and more. I owe it to you, too."

He reared back. "You don't owe me this."

"Yes, I do."

"For what?"

"For doubting you. For doubting myself."

She stepped up to him and gripped his arm in an effort to make him understand the tangled emotions she was only now beginning to make sense of herself.

"I love you, Sam. And I know you've come to love me. What you feel for Mary doesn't alter that, or diminish it in any way. In fact—"

She summoned a smile, wanting him to understand, needing him to know *she* understood.

"You couldn't be the man you are if you didn't possess the capacity to love us both."

Silence strung out between them—short, tense, charged with the tension that gripped them both.

"You know," Sam said at last, "a month ago I might have agreed with you."

"You don't agree now?"

"Now, my darling, I have to say that's as big a pile of horse manure as anyone's ever shoveled, myself included."

"I beg your pardon!"

Grinning at her offended expression, he dropped a swift kiss on her mouth.

"You fill me, Victoria. Every part of me. My head. My heart. My deepest, most private thoughts. There's no room inside my skin for anyone but you."

"Oh. Well."

"If we're going ahead with your crazy scheme, I'd better carry Mary to the carriage. We've only a few hours before the *Sea Cloud* sails."

If Sam harbored any doubts about Victoria's scheme, they disappeared when the carriage approached the checkpoint. He needed only a glimpse at the marine who strode out of the guard shack to swear a silent oath that he would get Mary out of Cuba on the next boat.

It ate a hole in his gut that he'd had to spirit her away from Siboney in the dark of night. That the army she'd volunteered to serve couldn't protect her. He and the rest of the American forces had come to Cuba to fight the Spanish. Now, because of the near hysterical fear of yellow fever, the face of their enemy had changed.

"Sam?"

He glanced across Mary's limp form and saw Victoria watching him with wide, worried eyes.

"I don't recognize that marine," she whispered. "He's not the same one who waved me through a while ago."

"The sentries do guard mount at nine." He squinted at the sky, trying to gauge the time. "The new detail must have posted."

"Is that good or bad?"

"We'll soon find out."

Surreptitiously, Victoria tightened her arm around Mary's waist and reached up with her other hand to twitch the black lace. To her astonishment, the woman beside her seemed to sense what was required. Slowly, her spine stiffened. Just as slowly, her chin came up. Victoria barely had time to marvel at her incredible fortitude before Sam reined in at the checkpoint and the sentry snapped a smart salute.

"Good morning, sir."

"Good morning, sergeant."

"May I see your pass?"

The well-handled bit of paper almost came apart

in the sentry's hands. Gingerly, he unfolded it and tried to decipher the rain-washed writing.

"You're on General Wood's staff, Captain Barrett?"

"It's Captain Garrett. Yes, I am."

"And these ladies?"

The tale they'd concocted in the rubble of the farmhouse would serve as well as any.

"This is Miss Parker, my fiancée, and her companion."

"I'm sorry, sir. I don't see their names on the pass."

Sam stiffened, sensing what was coming. Although both the United States and Spain had agreed to the negotiated terms for peace, neither side had as yet ratified a treaty or signed the actual protocols. Two hundred thousand Spanish troops still occupied the northern part of Cuba. Seventy thousand Americans had dug in along the southern coast. Technically, the two armies were still at war, and the United States Marines manning Santiago's perimeter defenses took their sentry duties very seriously. Deferential but determined to do his duty, the sergeant handed back the shredding paper.

"I'll have to get my lieutenant and ask him to authorize—"

"Really, Sam!" Victoria clucked her tongue. "I swear this rain has turned all our brains to mush. Have you forgotten? My pass is in my valise."

He shot her a swift look. At her small but insistent nod, he reached between his legs and ruffled through the contents of the bag. Slowly, his hand closed around the leather holster partially buried under a nightdress.

"No!" Victoria gasped. "That's not it! Look— Look in the top notebook."

Shoving the revolver back under the nightgown, Sam pulled out the notebook she indicated. The press pass she'd been issued to witness the surrender ceremony slipped into his hand.

"I think you'll find the pass quite in order," she told the sergeant. "It's signed by General Shafter himself."

His brows soared. "So it is."

"Now, if you don't mind..." Victoria said with a weary smile. "My companion and I are rather tired. We've had to travel for hours to catch our boat." A note of fluttery panic crept into her voice. "Oh, dear, I do hope we'll make it. It sails in less than an hour, Sam!"

Picking up his cue, he answered with patient assurance. "We'll make it."

"We must. All our trunks are already on board. Do hurry! *Please!*"

"All right, all right. Don't fret. I'll get you to the harbor in time. Sergeant, have you finished with that?"

The marine hesitated, gave the general's signature another glance and handed Sam the document. With a hasty salute, he waved them on.

"Well!" Victoria exclaimed with fierce satisfaction. "Thank goodness for General Shafter's ridiculous edict requiring passes for members of the press!"

Shafter's signature worked the same magic at the next three checkpoints, but Victoria was strung too tight with tension by the time the carriage finally clattered onto the dock to appreciate the irony any longer.

"This could well be the most difficult part," Sam muttered as he reined in a short distance from the *Sea Cloud*'s gangplank. Climbing out, he lifted Mary from the carriage and waited while Victoria scrambled down.

"Here, let me cover her face."

With Mary shielded from too curious eyes, Victoria dragged off her poncho and made a futile attempt to tuck up her own straggly hair. Mud soiled the hem of her gray skirt, but her white blouse and short-waisted traveling jacket weren't too disreputable. The gold locket pinned to her lapel gave her at least the appearance of a lady.

"Can you manage the valise?" Sam asked.

"Yes, I've got it."

"All right, let's see if we can pull this off."

Victoria led the way up the gangplank. They

were so close. So very close. Her blood pounded loudly in her ears, almost drowning out the screech of the gulls crying overhead. But not the shriek of a winch. Flinching at the shrill squeal of metal on metal, she gripped the rail and watched as a huge net filled with crates of mangoes was lifted from the quay.

The *Sea Cloud* was a cargo steamer, one of the dozens that had made windfall profits for its owners by hauling supplies and equipment to the American forces in Cuba. Soon, Victoria suspected, it would bring in more profits by hauling the same equipment home.

Breathing in the odors of wet rope, overripe fruit and bilge water, she took the last few steps. A sailor dressed in canvas pants and a red-striped shirt reached out a horny palm to help her step down onto the deck.

"Miss Parker?"

"Yes."

"I'm Joshua Hawkins, chief bos'n's mate. Cap'n said I was to keep a watch for you. I'm to show you to your cabin."

"Thank you."

She moved aside, making room for Sam to step down. The seaman's gaze took in the officer's muddied uniform before fixing on the woman in his arms.

"This is my companion," Victoria informed him

with a charming little pout. "It's quite ridiculous, I know, but my fiancé insisted on hiring her to accompany me on the voyage home."

"The cap'n didn't say nothing about no companion."

"Miss Parker and I just came to an agreement on the matter this morning," Sam said with perfect truth. "I'll speak to your captain about the cost of her passage after I see the ladies settled in their cabin."

"What's wrong with her?" the mate asked, frowning.

"Unfortunately," Sam replied, "she tripped and sprained her ankle just before we left our residence." Hefting her higher in his arms, he snapped out an order. "Lead the way, man."

Still Hawkins hesitated. Victoria was searching wildly for some distraction when Mary dragged her head up. Drawing on her incredible well of inner strength, she gave an embarrassed twitter.

"You must forgive me, *capitán.* To be so clumsy and trip as I did! I...I die of mortification!"

"Yes," Sam said gruffly, "it was certainly clumsy. But we would prefer you don't die just yet, if you please."

Victoria didn't suck in a complete breath until Hawkins showed them to the small cabin, said he'd let the captain know two ladies had come aboard instead of one and left.

"I think we all chose the wrong profession," she murmured as Sam lowered Mary onto the bunk. "We're such accomplished actors, we should have gone on the boards and traveled about with a vaudeville show. Wait, let me get that shawl out from under her before she becomes all tangled up in it."

Between them, they did their best to make Mary comfortable. They didn't dare undress her or tuck her under the blanket, knowing that the captain would seek them out.

He rapped on the cabin door some moments later. When Sam stepped outside, he allowed the man only a glimpse of the two women sitting on the bunk. Victoria's nerves crawled as she listened to the rise and fall of their voices outside the door. After what seemed like hours, Sam stepped back inside.

"It's done. I've made arrangements with the captain to cover Mary's passage. The ship leaves in less than an hour."

"Thank God!"

"She'll drop anchor at Key West to off-load cargo, then dock in Tampa." His glance went to the woman now stretched out on the bunk. "By then, her fever should have broken."

"Let's hope so."

The awesome responsibility she'd taken on

weighed heavily on Victoria's shoulders. What if Mary succumbed to her illness? What if she died before they made Key West or Tampa? She stood silent while Sam made his farewells to the widow.

"You'll be home soon," he promised Mary, taking her hand. "Just rest, sweat out the fever and get back your strength."

The brusque order brought a feeble attempt at a smile.

"Yes…sir."

"Victoria will see to you. She insists she learned to care for fever patients from one of the army's best nurses."

Mary's gaze shifted to include them both.

"She…did…indeed."

With a gentle squeeze, Sam released her hand and drew Victoria outside the cabin to make their farewells.

"Send me a cable when you reach Tampa."

"I will."

"You have my service revolver with you?"

"Yes."

"Keep it handy until you're home safe."

"I will," she said again, sincerely hoping she wouldn't have to put it to use.

"Are you carrying any funds? It took all I had to pay for Mary's passage."

The generous supply of greenbacks her father had given her had dwindled considerably, but suf-

ficient remained in her purse to buy food and whatever else they might need until she could wire for
more.

"I have enough to get us home."

He hesitated, knowing he had to go ashore, hat-
ing to leave her with the burden she'd so calmly
assumed. Amazed that only a few months ago he'd
considered her a mere girl requiring his guidance
and protection, Sam brushed his knuckles down her
cheek.

"I don't know when I'll return to the States. I'll
have to answer for taking Mary away from Siboney.
I might spend the next months on General Wood's
staff—or in the guardhouse."

"Let's hope it's not the guardhouse."

This was no time to tell him she might be breeding, Victoria thought with chagrin. He had enough
to worry about without her adding more. She'd put
the news in a cable when she and Mary were home
safe and she knew for sure she carried a child.

Aching for a last taste, a last touch, she slipped
her arms around his neck.

22

Sam stood beside the carriage while the dockhands threw off the *Sea Cloud's* hawsers and the harbor tug pushed the ship away from the quay. Slowly, her bow swung toward the mouth of Santiago Harbor. Black smoke bellied from her twin stacks as she got up steam. Gray and angry-looking, the waters of the bay churned beneath her stern.

Eyeing the clouds that hung dark and sullen on the horizon, Sam could only grit his teeth and hope the storm held off until the *Sea Cloud* was well away. Victoria would have enough on her hands without heavy seas.

Admiration tugged at him. It had taken a special brand of courage for Victoria to climb into a carriage and start out for Siboney, determined to aid a woman who'd spent weeks in the contagion ward. A woman she'd once considered a rival.

Sam knew now that whatever he'd once felt for

Mary paled beside his fierce passion for Victoria. It went beyond rational thought, sprang as much from instinct as from intellect. No poet, he couldn't put flowery adjectives to his feelings or wrap them up in fine, noble phrases.

She was his, and he was hers.

It was as simple and as all-consuming as that.

He remained on the dock until the *Sea Cloud* steamed past the ruins of Morro Castle, reduced to rubble by U.S. naval bombardment at the start of the Santiago Campaign. Then he returned to the house on Calle San Giorgio, stripped out of his uniform and bundled it into a blanket. Scrubbed clean of mud, he pulled on his only spare uniform. The khaki canvas pants had seen arduous duty during his first weeks in Cuba, and the blue flannel shirt had a bullet hole in both the front and the back right shoulder, but the bloodstains had washed to only a faint rust.

Carrying the soiled, bundled uniform out behind the house, he burned both it and the blanket he'd wrapped it in. Ten minutes later, he presented himself at the governor's palace.

"Sam!"

Max Luna jumped out of his chair. His dark eyes were grave as he hurried around the table he'd appropriated and put to use as a desk.

"General Wood wants you to report to him the moment you show your face."

"I figured as much."

Squaring his shoulders, he started for the door to the general's office. Max stayed him.

"How's Mrs. Prendergast?"

"Weak, but holding her own."

"Where did you take her?"

"Not to Calle San Giorgio."

Anger flashed across the New Mexican's proud face. "Did you think I wouldn't want her at the house? She cared for the men in my company, too, Sam."

"I know."

"If you'd told me what the hell you intended before you rushed out of here yesterday, I would have gone with you to Siboney."

"That's why I didn't tell you. I didn't want to involve you." Seeing that his friend was still offended, he tried to make amends. "I'm sorry, Max. I didn't mean to imply you wouldn't help Mary or have her at the house."

"I only asked because of Victoria," Luna said stiffly. "I knew you wouldn't want to expose her to danger."

"She exposed herself."

"What?"

"I stopped her just outside Santiago this morning. She was on her way to Siboney."

Max gave a soundless whistle. "She's very brave, your woman."

"She is that." Sam glanced at the door behind the desk. "Guess I'd better get this over with. Is the general in his office?"

"Yes. Colonel Roosevelt's with him, going over the order for the Rough Riders' embarkation."

"When does the regiment leave?"

"Two days from now. They're shipping home to Montauk, New York, out on Long Island. They'll stay there until it's clear they're not contagious, then be mustered out."

"So the regiment's being disbanded?"

At Max's nod, regret splintered through Sam. He'd served more than eight years in the regular army and forged many close friendships with his brothers in arms. But his ties to the tough, colorful Rough Riders had been fired by respect and tempered to unbreakable steel by battle.

He would have liked to complete the journey he'd begun with the United States First Volunteer Cavalry. Chances were, though, that he'd miss the final mustering out. He'd be here in Santiago. Or in a ship's brig, awaiting transport with the other misfits and derelicts.

The prospect of returning home, stripped of his rank by a court-martial, wasn't one Sam particularly relished. He spent a second or two imagining what his father would have to say before shrugging the thought aside. He'd done what he had to do. He'd do it again, in a minute.

Squaring his shoulders, he strode to the door.

* * *

With a ruddy-faced Roosevelt sitting to one side, General Wood rose, clasped his hands behind his back and pinned the officer standing at rigid attention before his desk with a cold stare.

"Let me make sure I have the facts straight, Captain. Did you or did you not write out a pass for yourself without authority?"

"I did, sir."

"Did you ride to Siboney and overcome a sentry by use of force?"

"Yes, sir.

"Enter a restricted area?"

"Yes."

"Violate the direct order of the Secretary of War by removing a medical attendant from isolation?"

"Yes."

Wood's jaw worked. Through clenched teeth, he bit out an acidic query.

"Are there any other potential charges that might be brought against you for last night's piece of work, Garrett?"

Sam thought about it for a moment. "I'd say that about sums it up, sir."

"Dammit, man! Why didn't you come to me before haring off to Siboney?"

He gave the general the same answer he'd given Max. "I didn't want to involve you."

"Harrumph!" Clasping his hands behind his back, Wood rocked back on his heels. "I'm not going to ask where Mrs. Prendergast is. I'm assuming she's in good hands."

"Yes, sir. Very good hands. And if it will relieve your mind, she's no longer in Cuba. She and Miss Parker left this morning."

The general looked anything but relieved. "All right, Garrett. You may return to your quarters. Consider yourself under house arrest until further notice."

"Yes, sir."

23

The *Sea Cloud*'s passage from Santiago to Key West took twelve torturous hours.

Gray skies and swelling seas provided the two women aboard with the perfect excuse to remain in their cabin, but as the swells grew rougher, Victoria's stomach began to roll with the ship. Battling bouts of nausea, she somehow managed to bathe away the rest of Mary's mud and sweat and force several doses of quinine down her throat.

After that, one hour blurred into the next. Victoria couldn't have said when day became night. Mary consumed all her attention, all her energy. When she thrashed on the bunk, moaning with the heat, Victoria ripped up a spare pair of drawers, dunked them in the pitcher of water a cabin boy delivered and wrapped her in damp, cooling cloths. When the heat gave way to bone-rattling shivers, she replaced the damp cloths with blankets.

By the time the ship made port at Key West a little past four o'clock in the morning, the wind shrieked like demons from hell outside the porthole and Victoria was so seasick she could hardly stand. She'd retched up most of what she'd forced down of her dinner. Each wild, plunging swing of the ship at the end of its anchor chain threatened to bring up the rest. Thoroughly miserable, she passed almost another hour with her body flung across Mary's to keep her from rolling out of the bunk.

"Miss Parker!"

A hard pounding on the cabin door accompanied the muffled shout.

"Miss Parker! Cap'n says we have to put you ladies ashore."

Staggering across the cabin, Victoria wrenched open the door. "Put us ashore? Why?"

The mate stood in the gangway, drenched to the skin. Bracing his arms and legs, he shouted to be heard over creaking metal and howling wind.

"The storm's blowing up fierce enough to snap the anchor chain. Looks to become a full hurricane. We're taking the *Sea Cloud* to open water to try to ride it out, but cap'n says it's safer for you ladies ashore."

"But—"

"No time to argue. The longboat's ready to be lowered." He brushed past her into the cabin. "You take your grip, miss, and I'll help your friend up to—''

He stopped short, his eyes bugging at his first real glimpse of Mary, and swung around.

''You said she'd hurt her ankle!''

Victoria could hardly deny the truth staring at them with dark, fever-glazed eyes. ''Unfortunately, she's also come down with a touch of malaria.''

Hawkins looked as though he might bolt at any second.

''It's only malaria,'' Victoria insisted. Flinging out a hand, she gestured to the box of tablets at the foot of the bunk. ''I've been dosing her with quinine all night.''

Half-afraid he might run to the captain and have them both tossed into the sea, she tottered to the bunk and began wrapping Mary in blankets.

''Bring me that poncho. Now, if you please! If the captain says it's safer for us ashore, then we'd best get to the longboat.''

Hawkins hovered by the door, uncertain, nervous. The sight of Victoria calmly tending to Mary reassured him somewhat. Still, he refused to lift the invalid from the bunk until she'd been swathed head to foot in the rubber shield.

Making his way precariously out of the tilting, swaying cabin, he carried Mary down the narrow passageway and up two flights of stairs. Victoria lurched along behind them. With every other step, a hip slammed against the bulkheads and her valise banged against her knees.

The moment Hawkins shouldered open the hatch that led out to the deck, she gasped in terror. The entire world outside that small, square opening had become a seething cauldron of wind and rain and gray, crashing waves.

"We can't disembark in this!"

The wind tore her frantic protest away. Either that, or Hawkins chose to ignore it. Slinging Mary over his shoulder, he reached for the safety line strung across the deck.

"Dear God!"

Her heart in her throat, Victoria watched him plunge across the deck toward the lifeboat riding high in its davits. Her fingers fisted around the lifeline, but she couldn't bring herself to take so much as a step until she saw that Hawkins had made it safely across the tilting, sea-washed deck.

Setting his jaw, he fought his way back and relieved her of the bag. "I'll take that," he shouted over the shrieking wind. "Hold on to the rope and haul yourself across, hand over hand. I'll be right behind you."

She was only a few yards from the longboat when the deck seemed to drop out from under her feet. She went down, legs thrashing, arms straining against the pull of seawater that crashed over her. Cursing, Hawkins let go of the lifeline, buried a fist in her skirt and dragged her the rest of the way. Heaving, he tossed her into the longboat. Her valise landed on top of her.

"Wait for the next wave," he shouted to the men at the ropes. "Then lower away!"

Victoria groped about on hands and knees and found Mary huddled in the sloshing water at the bottom of the boat. Blinded by rain and the wet hair that slashed at her face, she could only throw herself atop Mary and pray as she'd never prayed before.

24

Feet planted wide apart, hands fisted at his sides, Sam stood at the window of the bedroom he'd shared with Victoria the past few weeks. The unruffled covers of the four-poster presented mute testimony to the fact that he hadn't slept since she'd departed Santiago yesterday noon.

He couldn't remember a more nerve-racking twenty-eight hours. Putting Victoria aboard the *Sea Cloud* with the desperately ill Mary had drilled a hole right through him. Being placed under house arrest hadn't exactly filled the void.

Now this storm.

Clenching his fists, Sam listened to the wind howl like the dogs of hell. Sheets of rain lashed at the wavy glass windowpanes. Outside, the lemon trees in the courtyard whipped wildly, bowing almost to the ground before the vicious gusts.

The storm had blown in late last night from the

north, which meant it had cut across the straits separating Cuba and Florida. Sam had spent most of the dark hours of the night hoping the *Sea Cloud* had steamed ahead of the gale—and most of today filled with the gnawing worry it had not. The message Max had sent from the governor's palace earlier in answer to his terse note said the navy was already receiving initial reports of damage to ships at anchor and at sea.

Spinning away from the window, Sam paced the room like a caged tiger. One day under house arrest and already he chafed at the enforced inactivity. He hated having to send a note to Max begging for information, hated being cut off from the cables and reports that flowed through General Wood's office. Serving on staff had its drawbacks, but at least Sam had kept a finger on what was happening.

He supposed he shouldn't complain. He wasn't sitting in a damp, subterranean cell in the former Spanish fort overlooking the harbor. Nor had General Wood laid charges against him. Yet. Wood had other matters to deal with at the moment—like coordinating with General Shafter on the units to remain in Cuba as part of the army of occupation and ensuring the orderly departure of the rest.

The gale now sweeping across the island would wreak havoc with the army's departure plans, Sam guessed. At best, the storm would delay sailings. At worst—

He balled his fists again. The navy's initial damage reports indicated the winds and crashing seas had blown the troop transports enroute to Cuba all to hell and back. Several were reported sunk.

Christ! The *Sea Cloud* had to have made safe harbor in Key West!

Not until six o'clock that evening did he receive further news. It came in the form of an order to report to the governor's palace immediately.

The winds were dying as he strode through the streets, but the rain still sliced down. Once inside the palace, Sam pulled off his poncho, shook himself like a terrier and made his way to the general's office. Max wasn't at his desk, but the young lieutenant manning the table jumped up at Sam's approach.

"General Wood's expecting you, sir. Go right in."

Tucking his hat under his elbow, Sam rapped a knuckle on the door frame and entered the ornate salon.

"You wanted to see me, sir?"

"Yes, I did. Stand easy, Captain."

Wood pushed away from his desk, his movements slow and heavy. Like Sam, he looked as though he hadn't slept since yesterday. Fatigue had etched deep grooves at either side of his mouth. His eyes showed more red than white.

"I don't know any way to tell you this but straight out."

Sam braced himself. He didn't know what was coming, but from the look on the general's face, it was bad. Very bad.

"The hurricane tore down every telephone and telegraph wire in Key West, but the navy managed to repair their underwater cable. We've been getting detailed damage reports all afternoon. One of those reports indicates that the merchant steamer *Sea Cloud* went down with all hands."

Sam didn't move, didn't so much as blink. He couldn't. Ice had formed in his veins, freezing everything inside him.

"Captain Luna told me that was the ship you put Miss Parker and Mrs. Prendergast on." The general came around the desk and gripped his shoulder. "I'm sorry, Sam."

He could hear Wood's voice. Feel the weight of his hand on his shoulder. But nothing was real. Nothing could pierce his sudden, icy shroud.

"She went down in sight of the harbor. Evidently she was readying to put out to sea to try to escape the storm when her anchor cable snapped. According to eyewitness reports, the waves rolled her over. She sank within mere moments."

Wood's fingers dug in deep. Sympathy put a raspy edge in his voice.

"Several bodies have washed ashore, but the seas

are still too rough to mount a salvage or recovery operation. Although no survivors have been found, there's a chance, a slim chance, some might have made it to shore.''

Sam nodded. Just once. A small, tight inclination of his head. Without a word, he turned and started for the door.

"Sam. Wait! Where are you going?"

He dragged around, fought the shards slicing into his chest, forced out a reply. "Key West. On the first ship out of Santiago."

"We have some business to take care of first, or have you forgotten that you're under house arrest?"

His jaw locked. "There aren't enough marines in Cuba to hold me here, General, unless you order them to shoot me on sight."

"I've reached the same conclusion. As a result, I've decided not to lay charges against you. Corporal Peters claims he can't identify the man who knocked him out while he was performing sentry duty at Siboney. No one saw you with Mrs. Prendergast, so there's no direct evidence you had anything to do with her removal from the contagion ward. Which leaves only the matter of the pass you wrote for yourself without authorization."

Flinging up a hand, he cut Sam off before he said a word.

"None of the sentries at the checkpoints you went through could say for any certainty whose name was on that pass. The damned paper was too wet to read. But you admitted writing it, along with everything else, and I have to take an officer at his word. Rather than subject you to a court-martial, I'm releasing you from active service, Sam. Mustering you out right here and right now. I won't allow you to desert. Not after your service at Las Guásimas and Kettle Hill.''

Scooping a document off his desk, he shoved it at Sam.

''Here. Take it.'' His bony fingers squeezed the captain's shoulder a final time. ''Let me know how you find matters in Key West.''

25

The hurricane had all but destroyed Key West.

From the deck of the two-masted schooner *Pelican,* Sam stared with stony eyes at the ruin of what had, until three days ago, been Florida's second-largest city. The two-story stone Customs House still stood, but its roof had blown away. Most of the buildings around it had been reduced to rubble. Debris was piled high in the streets, spiked here and there with the trunks of uprooted palms.

Wind and waves had tossed up boats all along the curving shoreline. They lay like beached whales, their rounded bellies exposed to the sun now beating down with a brightness that made the devastation even harder to accept.

It wasn't bright enough to melt the icy shards inside Sam's chest, though. Every breath he'd taken since he'd walked out of General Wood's office fifteen hours ago had stabbed into him like a stiletto.

He hadn't returned to the house on Calle San Giorgio. Hadn't taken the time to send a message to Max or Señora Garcia. He'd made straight for the harbor, boarded the sleek schooner tied up at the quay and promised the captain whatever fee he wanted to set sail immediately for Key West.

After emptying his wallet to pay for Mary's passage, Sam had only enough funds with him to make good on half the amount the captain demanded. As the skipper cheerfully informed him, however, the Rough Rider uniform he wore guaranteed the rest. Sam didn't bother to inform the man that he was no longer entitled to wear the khaki pants and blue flannel shirt.

Sticky with sweat, the shirt now clung to his back. He didn't feel its heat, didn't notice the rivulets tracing down his cheeks. He didn't think he'd ever feel anything but cold emptiness again.

A rattle of rigging and the whoosh of the swinging boom warned that the *Pelican* was about to come about.

"The wharf's all ripped up," the skipper announced grimly from where he stood at the wheel. "I can't bring her in any closer. We'll have to drop anchor here and take the dinghy ashore."

Picking his way through the debris, Sam not only saw the devastation close at hand, he smelled it.

Flies buzzed in thick clouds around the bloated car-
casses of chickens and pigs. Fruit ripped from trees
and bushes rotted in the sun. Every breeze added
the stink of rust, barnacles and spilled bilge water
from the beached boats.

Efforts were already under way to clear the
streets. Blue-shirted seamen from the naval base labored side by side with sweating civilians, grunting
as they heaved aside shattered timbers and odd
pieces of furniture. Sam picked his way over to a
sailor with a long row of stripes disappearing into
his rolled-up sleeve.

"Where can I find information on the *Sea
Cloud?*"

His tattooed muscles straining, the petty officer
tossed aside what looked like a wrought-iron headboard. "The *Sea Cloud?* Don't know her, sir."

"She's a merchant flying the United States flag.
She arrived in Key West the night of the storm."

"Can't help you. You might ask the harbormas-
ter. He's up at— Oh, wait a minute! Is she the
steamer that snapped her anchor cable, went broad-
side to the swells and capsized?"

Sam's throat went tight. "Yes."

"I heard they've recovered most of her crew.
Check at the Customs House. They've set up a temporary morgue in the warehouse."

A few weeks ago, Sam had thought that helping

to recover the bodies of his brothers in arms and readying them to be sent home for burial would be one of the most wrenching experiences of his life. He'd served with those men, respected them, loved them. But walking into the Customs House was like driving nails into his chest.

"Better cover your mouth and nose with this, sir."

The customs officer pressed into service as mortician and graves registrar passed Sam a rag dipped in a strong-smelling disinfectant.

"We don't like to bury the corpses until someone identifies them, but— Well, we won't be able to keep these much longer."

The moment he opened the door to the warehouse, the stench of death rolled out and hit Sam in the face. His eyes watered above the rag. Locking his jaw, he walked into the gloom.

"Worst storm I ever saw," the customs officer muttered as he followed Sam down the narrow aisle between corpses covered by tarps. "And I've lived here going on twenty years now. Thirty-four dead that we know of. More, I expect, when they get a final tally on all the souls lost at sea. Here, these are the bodies we think came from the *Sea Cloud*."

Grabbing the edge of a tarp, he dragged it off to expose a half-dozen bloated corpses. With the rag clamped tight to his face, he glanced sideways, respectfully, hopefully.

"Recognize anyone, sir?"

Sam barely heard him above the drone of the flies and the roar in his head.

"Sir? Do you know any of them?"

"Yes." He fought for breath behind his mask. "That one on the end. He is...was...the *Sea Cloud*'s third mate. I think his name was Hawkins."

Satisfaction flickered across the mortuary officer's face. One more unknown identified and ready for disposal. He gave Sam another moment to check the sightless eyes and pale, swollen faces before flicking the tarp back over the bodies.

"Thanks for your assistance, Captain Garrett. I'll—"

"There were two women aboard that ship. Hasn't anyone found a trace of them?"

"We only have one unclaimed female. I don't think she's from the *Sea Cloud*. They dug her out from under a pile of rubble."

"Where is she?"

"Here, sir."

When the tarp tugged off, relief whipped through Sam, followed instantly by a wild hope. And guilt, razor swift and cutting. He shouldn't have sent up a swift prayer of thanks that the woman was short and stout and well into her middle years, but he couldn't help himself.

"She's not one of the women I'm looking for."

The mortuary officer sent him an apologetic glance. ''Could be their bodies just haven't washed ashore yet. Or they may be trapped inside the ship. The navy's going to send divers down once they finish with their own ships.''

Sam's jaw worked. Nodding, he walked out of the storeroom.

Five days later, he gave up his last shred of hope.

Key West had been rebuilt after a fire in 1886 destroyed most of its buildings. The hurricane of 1898 wreaked considerably more havoc, but, as it had before, the city dragged itself from the ruins. With a civilian population of more than eighteen thousand, an active navy base at the tip of the harbor and bustling sponge and cigar-making industries, the scars healed slowly, but they healed.

Determined teams of citizens and seamen cleared the debris. Temporary plywood structures went up. Divers finished the grim task of retrieving those bodies they could from the sunken ships. The mortuary officer released the unidentified corpses for burial in a mass grave. Business reopened and, incredibly, the mule-drawn trolley resumed operation.

Sam wrote a draft on the local bank to cover the cost of a change of clothes and basic necessities. He spent his five days in Key West checking in at the Customs House, helping with the cleanup where he could and asking everyone he encountered if they had word of either Victoria or Mary.

He spent his nights on a cot in one of the tents thrown up for the homeless, staring up at the musty canvas. Their faces haunted him. Mary's, so flushed and fevered when he'd last seen her. Victoria's, so beautiful and determined. He knew Mary's loss would throb like an open wound for years to come, but Victoria—

Dear God, Victoria.

Regret sliced into him with every heartbeat. He'd done everything wrong a man could do. Blinded by her youth and innocence, he hadn't seen the woman emerging from the girl. Worse, he hadn't known how to handle her when she shed her cocoon and came into her own. He'd blustered, threatened, seduced, demanded. Too late, he'd come to recognize her talent, her tenacity, her courage.

Now, just when he'd come to appreciate the incredible woman who'd given herself to him, he'd lost her.

With an ache that sawed right down to his bones, Sam threw his arm over his eyes and waited for the dawn.

He booked passage from Key West to Tampa the same afternoon telegraph service was restored. With poles and lines blown down all across the island, he hadn't been able to contact his family. Or

Victoria's. Now he had no choice. It was time to tell them what happened. Time to go home.

Time to admit she was gone.

His face grim, he walked into the tarpaper-and-plywood shack serving as a temporary cable office. Two operators, one a scarecrow of a man, the other a woman with her hair bundled up in a puffy chignon, sweated behind upturned packing crates that served as both counter and telegraph station.

A long line had formed—somber citizens, sailors anxious to reassure worried relatives, businessmen in bowlers, their starched collars wilting in the heat. Sam waited his turn, his gaze fixed on a glistening teardrop of tar inching its way down the wall. Finally, he reached the female operator.

Her pencil poised to take down his message, she raised her head. "Yes?"

The breath slammed out of Sam. He stood riveted to the floor, every muscle taut.

"Sir? May I help...? Sir!" Her polite inquiry spiraled to a shriek. "What are you doing!"

Ignoring her startled screech, Sam leaned over the packing crate and wrapped his fingers around the pin dangling above her bosom. One vicious tug ripped it away, along with a good portion of her white blouse. His eyes blazing, he closed his fist around the heart-shaped locket.

"Where did you get this?"

26

"Mary!"

Victoria rapped on the rickety door hanging haphazardly from one hinge. The cotton scarf covering her tangled hair slipped down. Excitement shivered up and down her spine.

"Mary, it's me. Let me in."

She was tired, dirty and so hungry her stomach had long since given up hope of food, but finally—finally!—the end of this awful ordeal was in sight.

When the door opened, she slipped inside. The interior of the small house within smelling distance of one of Key West's turtle canneries stank of wood rot and chicken droppings, yet Victoria barely noticed the odor.

"The telegraph lines are back up!" she exclaimed to the hollow-eyed woman inside. "I put a cable through to Sam in Santiago, and one to my papa. As soon as Papa wires back authorization to draw funds on his account, I'll go to the bank. I'll buy us clean dresses, Mary. Whatever clean dresses are to be had on the island. And food. Real food.''

Carried away by her enthusiasm, she hooked her arms around Mary's emaciated waist and danced her in a little circle.

''We'll get sugar cakes, if there are any. Thick, juicy beef steaks. And cucumbers to take those shadows from under your eyes.''

''Stop! You'll make me dizzy.''

Victoria almost stumbled over her own feet. She could hear the echo of those same words, tossed out laughingly on a snowy February night. Could almost see the yearning in Sam's face as he'd caught this woman in his arms and swung her off her feet.

Dear God, what tortuous roads they'd all traveled since that night!

Grinning, she dropped her arms and tossed aside the scrap of cloth she'd used to cover her hair when she went into town. Although she'd washed away most of the salt and brine with rainwater, she hadn't had the time or the energy to drag a comb through its wild tangles and pin it up.

''I'll be glad to get out of these rags, I can assure you.''

An answering smile lit Mary's face. It was weak and wobbly, but a real smile. She'd managed several since her fever had finally broken yesterday.

"*I'll* be glad to get out of this chicken coop."

Her nose wrinkling, Victoria glanced around the deserted dwelling that had housed them since they'd dragged themselves out of the churning surf and howling winds. It was hardly more than a shed tucked amid the coconut palms, only yards from the beach where the *Sea Cloud*'s longboat had nearly foundered setting them ashore. She couldn't imagine how this ramshackle building had survived the fury that had destroyed so many others in Key West. But it had.

So had she and Mary. Against all odds. Against every probability.

Victoria suspected she would shudder every time she recalled the terror of that boat ride from the *Sea Cloud* to shore. Knew she'd suffer nightmares whenever she thought of the days that had followed, when she'd left Mary hidden while she begged, borrowed and traded the meager contents of her valise.

Fear of disease, she'd discovered, increased exponentially after a disaster of this magnitude. The few times she'd ventured out after the storm, the talk in the streets was all of extreme measures to protect against typhoid. Diphtheria. Cholera. She hadn't dared bring Mary out of hiding until her fever broke. Couldn't risk questions about where they'd come from, or how they'd arrived in Key West.

Disaster relief agencies had provided food and

water. Victoria's few remaining dollars had purchased quinine for Mary. Sam's service revolver had provided protection against the scavengers who crept out at night to pick the bones of the dead.

And just this morning, her gold locket had paid for two telegrams!

"We'll hear from Sam tomorrow," she predicted confidently. "My papa, too. I'll go down to the cable office first thing. In the meantime, I think we should—"

"Quiet!"

Mary cocked her head, her sallow face a blur in the light filtering through the boards.

"I hear something. Or someone."

Victoria's breath hissed out. "Get away from the door."

Her heart hammering, she dived for her valise. Mud, rain and surf had eaten away at the tapestry and rotted its leather handles. Inside, her notebooks had dried thick and almost indecipherable. But she'd meticulously cleaned Sam's revolver and could now hold it steady.

She'd had plenty of practice these past nights. As she'd learned during her brief forays into town, Key West's mayor had appealed to the naval base commander to declare martial law. With no streetlamps, no electric lights, no access or egress through debris-strewn streets, the dregs of humanity who always preyed on the weak had taken to looting. And worse.

Her hands closed around the wood-grained grip of Sam's revolver. It felt smooth. Cool. Lethal.

She'd have to accommodate for the pistol's kick, Victoria reminded herself grimly. It wouldn't produce the same punch as a buffalo hunter's high-powered rifle, but she was damned if she'd end up on her backside in the dirt. Not this time. Not when she and Mary were so close to—

"Victoria!"

The hoarse shout came through the boards.

"Victoria, are you in there?"

She threw a disbelieving glance at Mary. The pistol dropped to the dirt. Leaping for the door, she wrenched it open.

"Sam!"

With a cry of joy, she threw herself into his arms. He gathered her against him in a bone-breaking embrace. Held her mashed against his chest. Shoved her away.

"I thought you were dead."

His fingers gouged into her arms. His eyes blazed a path from her tangled hair to her soiled skirts and back again.

"They told me you'd gone down with the *Sea Cloud*. I thought you were dead."

Before she could say a word, he dragged her against him again and buried his face in her hair.

She felt a shudder travel down his length, heard his ragged, in-drawn breath.

Eyes closed, Victoria sagged against him. After all these days and nights, she wanted nothing so much as to sink into his strength, lose herself in his embrace. Just the feel of his hard chest under her cheek broke the dam of her emotions and she started to cry. Not polite, delicate sniffs, but great, gulping sobs.

"Victoria. Sweetheart." His brutal hold gentled. Remorse flooded his voice. "Don't cry. It's over. It's all over."

Sobs racked her. Her hands clutched at his shirt. Tears streamed down her cheeks.

"How...? How did you find me?"

"I went to the cable office and saw the telegraph operator wearing your locket. She told me she'd taken it in payment for the cables you'd sent. I went through hell tracing your path from the telegraph office to here."

His gaze swept the ramshackle shed, hardened, came back to her.

"I swear, I'll never put you on a ship alone again. Wherever we go, we go together. Whatever disasters we face, we face together."

"And joys, Sam." She smiled through her tears. She could tell him about the baby now. Or she would, as soon as her head stopped spinning. "We'll share the joys as well as the sorrows."

She sagged against him again, safe, sure, home from both war and the sea. A heartbeat later, she tipped back her head.

"Mary's here. Inside. Her fever broke yesterday. She's still weak, but slowly getting back her strength."

Sam nodded and held her. Just held her. He'd see to Mary in a moment. For now, he couldn't seem to bring himself to let Victoria go.

Epilogue

~~~~~

Washington D.C.
February 2, 1901

A cold, damp wind knifed down Pennsylvania Avenue and tugged at the coat skirts of the toddler Sam carried in his arms. Squealing at the wind's bite, she buried her face in the beaver-trimmed collar of his overcoat.

"Hold on, sweet. We'll be inside in a moment."

Angling his shoulder to cut off the wind, Sam snuggled her closer against him while he waited for a uniformed marine to assist Victoria from the carriage. She gave the sergeant a gloved hand and descended. Her cheeks were pink from the cold, her blue eyes alive with excitement.

"I can't believe we're here," she murmured in awe as Sam slipped his free hand under her elbow and escorted her up the carpeted steps. "At the

White House! Invited to witness a bill being signed into law.''

''Not just witness.'' He grinned down at her. ''You've got work to do, remember? I expect your coverage of this event will hit not just the front page of the *Tribune,* but most of the AP papers.''

''I expect it will,'' Victoria answered smugly. After the wildly popular series of stories she'd penned following her return from Cuba, her byline now appeared with regular frequency in newspapers across the country.

Still, to be invited to the White House! By the vice president-elect, no less.

''Oh, how I wish Mary could be here!''

The toddler snuggled against Sam's shoulder lifted her head. ''Me, Mama?''

''No, darling, not you. Your aunt Mary.''

How strange life was at times, Victoria mused as another marine opened the tall doors at the top of the steps. Here she was in Washington, about to witness the signing of a bill recognizing the service of army nurses in the Spanish-American War, and Mary was back in Cuba, working with Dr. Walter Reed and his Yellow Fever Commission. General Leonard Wood was still there, too, as governor-general of Cuba. His surgeon's training and single-minded determination to conquer yellow fever had provided the impetus for the army commission.

For a moment, the glittering lights that spilled

from the massive chandelier in the entrance foyer faded. Victoria could almost see a ring of jungle-covered mountains. The tall, rustling palms. The long rows of tents that constituted Camp Lazear, named for one of the commission members who'd died during the early phases of the study. After almost a year of intensive study, the commission still hadn't pinpointed either the cause or a cure for the dreaded Yellow Jack. But they would. This time they would! According to Mary's last letter, Dr. Reed was beginning to suspect that mosquitoes, not infected sheets or clothing from other patients, transmitted the disease. Now he just had to prove it.

"Garrett!"

The hearty bellow turned every head in the foyer.

"There you are, man!"

The vice president-elect strode down the hallway. In his frock coat and high starched collar, Theodore Roosevelt looked far more like a sleek politician than the scruffy, sunburned colonel Victoria remembered. Wisely, President McKinley had ridden the wave of Roosevelt's huge popularity after the war and named the Rough Rider as his running mate for his second term. She couldn't think of a better man for the job.

He pumped Sam's hand, chucked the wide-eyed two-year-old under her chin and bussed Victoria heartily on her cheek.

"Quite a day, by jingo! I'm glad to see it, I can tell you that. It's long past time this country recognized the contribution of our army nurses. A point you've stressed repeatedly in your articles, Mrs. Garrett."

"Their service speaks for itself, sir. I merely added a few adjectives."

"And very eloquently, if I may say so. Come into the Red Room. Mrs. Roosevelt is there, with Mrs. McKinley. You can shed your coats and warm up with a cup of hot tea."

Tucking her arm in his, he led her through the public rooms of the house he already had aspirations of moving into in the not-too-distant future.

"We've a few minutes before the formal ceremony." His eyes twinkled behind his thick spectacles. "You won't need Sam to wrangle you a special pass from General Shafter to get you into this one."

Victoria threw a laughing glance over her shoulder at her husband. "If I did, I don't have a doubt in the world he could secure it."

"Neither do I," Roosevelt boomed. "Neither do I. He was a Rough Rider, after all."

A half hour later, an aide escorted Victoria and Sam to the chairs lined up in front of the desk President McKinley used for ceremonial signings.

Mary, bless her heart, didn't make a fuss. She rarely did when her father held her.

Victoria pulled a notebook and pencil from her string purse. Her mind was already cataloging the gold fringe on the curtains, the apple-green carpeting, the proud, shining faces of the nurses who stood in a semicircle behind the president. She recognized one from Siboney, a tall, spare woman who, like Victoria herself, had plopped down in a creek fully clothed to wash away the sweat and gore.

For once, she couldn't make her pencil move. To be a part of this momentous occasion was so overwhelming, so humbling. Laying the pencil flat on her notebook, Victoria groped for Sam's hand.

His fingers locked around hers. When he glanced at her, the smile in his eyes tightened her throat. They'd survived a war. Created a child. Braved tropical diseases and hurricanes. Together. Whatever else came, whatever monumental events happened in this new century, they'd meet them together.

With a sigh of pure happiness, Victoria gripped Sam's hand and watched the president's pen scratch across the bill authorizing the United States Army Nurse Corps.

Dear Reader,

I've been wanting to write a story featuring the women who served during the Spanish-American War since I saw a picture of nurses taken aboard the hospital ship, *Relief*, in 1898. That photo captured my imagination and wouldn't let go. Although I have no medical background myself, I became fascinated by their story.

Did you know that more than 1,500 American nurses volunteered to serve with the military during the Spanish-American War? Many worked in stateside hospitals. Hundreds shipped to Cuba and Puerto Rico and the Philippines. All labored under the most difficult conditions imaginable. Their courage and dedication led to the founding of the U.S. Army Nurse Corps in 1901, and U.S. Navy Nurse Corps in 1908.

During my research I also became absorbed by

the fact that this was truly a "correspondent's war." Men like Richard Harding Davis, artist Frederick Remington and novelist Stephen Crane didn't just record events, they plunged right into them. Warring publishers like William Randolph Hearst and Joseph Pulitzer were also right in the thick of things—Hearst even made a few dashes down to Cuba himself.

While Sam and Victoria and Mary are completely fictional, I had fun weaving their exploits in with those of real people like Teddy Roosevelt, Richard Davis and, of course, the indomitable Clara Barton. I hope you enjoyed this excursion into the past as much as I did!

Sincerely
Merline Lovelace

The third in an unforgettable new trilogy by
USA TODAY bestselling author

CANDACE CAMP

SHE NEVER EXPECTED TO LOVE AGAIN...

On the eve of her wedding, Rachel Aincourt tried to
elope with another man, only to be unceremoniously
returned to her fiancé by her strong-willed father.
Burdened by guilt and shame, Rachel got what she
thought she deserved: a loveless marriage to a cold,
enigmatic husband.

BUT FATE HAD OTHER PLANS

Behind her husband's proper demeanor is a man who
thrives on danger and intrigue—and this man plans to
seduce the wife he secretly loves.

Secrets of the Heart

*Available the first week of February 2003,
wherever paperbacks are sold!*

MIRA®

Visit us at www.mirabooks.com   MCC657

From the *USA TODAY*
bestselling author of
Stonebrook Cottage

CARLA NEGGERS

Shattered by her father's murder,
Zoe West fled her hometown of
Goose Harbor, Maine. But now, a year
later, she's back, still looking for
answers, still convinced the murderer
is someone she knows. And to
complicate things further, FBI Special
Agent J. B. McGrath has arrived in
town, "on vacation," he claims.

Zoe isn't sure she can trust J.B. But
as danger mounts, she realizes she
has no choice. Because someone
got away with murder and is
determined to keep it that way.

THE HARBOR

"...brisk pacing and colorful
characterizations sweep the reader
toward a dramatic and ultimately
satisfying denouement."
—*Publishers Weekly* on *The Cabin*

*On sale January 2003
wherever paperbacks are sold!*

MIRA®

Visit us at www.mirabooks.com   MCN651

A breathtaking new novel from bestselling author

DIANE CHAMBERLAIN

Joelle D'Angelo and Liam Sommers have always been friends, but they are drawn even closer together when Mara, Liam's wife and Joelle's best friend, becomes critically ill. One night, seeking solace for the pain they both feel, Joelle and Liam cross the line of friendship.

Now, secretly pregnant with Liam's child, Joelle is desperate to save the man she has come to love. Seeking the help of a mysterious healer, Joelle intends to give Liam back his wife, unsuspecting that she has set in motion events that will change all their lives.

CYPRESS POINT

"As Chamberlain examines myriad forms of love, her complicated novel will bring tears to her readers, but they won't regret the experience."
—*Booklist* on *Cypress Point*

*On sale in January 2003
wherever paperbacks are sold!*

MIRA®

Visit us at www.mirabooks.com

MDC647

USA TODAY Bestselling author

CHRISTIANE HEGGAN

Abbie DiAngelo has the life she's always wanted. Then her stepbrother arrives.

Straight out of prison, Ian McGregor claims to have proof that implicates Abbie's mother in a twenty-five-year-old murder. Proof that Ian will keep to himself...for a price. But when Abbie arrives to pay Ian off, she finds his murdered body.

Homicide detective John Ryan quickly realizes that there's more to the murder than he originally thought and no one—especially Abbie—is telling the truth. But when Abbie's son is kidnapped, she has no choice but to trust him. Because someone is acting with deadly intent....

DEADLY INTENT

"...provocative subject matter, likeable characters and swift pacing..."
—*Publishers Weekly* on *Moment of Truth*

Available the first week of January 2003 wherever paperbacks are sold!

Visit us at www.mirabooks.com

MIRA®

MCH648

Ties of love, ties of blood.
Sometimes they feel like the same thing.

KATHERINE STONE

Along with other family confidences, Dr. Paige Forrester
has been keeping her medical condition a secret from her
family, her friends and her colleagues. When she falls in love
with an old college friend, her life becomes complicated.

Further complications arise when Paige meets Gwen St.
James, a woman who has never known her parents. But
Gwen is a woman with whom Paige experiences a
powerful sense of family, and a woman with whom she
grows close…*as close as sisters.*

*Available the
first week of
January 2003,
wherever hardcovers
are sold!*

THE OTHER TWIN

MIRA®

Visit us at www.mirabooks.com

MKS655

Academy Award®-nominated actress

JANET LEIGH

Eve Handel followed her dreams—all the way to Hollywood. Hired by Utopia Studios to find talented actors and build them into stars, she became one of the most powerful women in an industry run by men. And Hollywood's elite freely unloaded their secrets—and scandals—on Eve.

Now Eve lies in a hospital bed, her life hanging in the balance. Those closest to her are torn between their concern for Eve and concern for their own reputations. Because Eve Handel kept a journal—a journal containing truths that could jeopardize careers and ruin lives.

The Dream Factory

"...her settings ring with authenticity. Ms. Leigh writes...with the authority of one who has been there."
—*New York Times Book Review* on *House of Destiny*

On sale January 2003 wherever paperbacks are sold!

MIRA®

Visit us at www.mirabooks.com

MJL650

MIRABooks.com

We've got the lowdown on your favorite author!

☆ Read an excerpt of your favorite author's newest book

☆ Check out her bio

☆ Talk to her in our Discussion Forums

☆ Read interviews, diaries, and more

☆ Find her current besteller, and even her backlist titles

All this and more available at

www.MiraBooks.com

MEAUT1R2

Merline Lovelace

66871 THE COLONEL'S DAUGHTER ___ $6.50 U.S. ___ $7.99 CAN.
66784 THE HORSE SOLDIER   ___ $5.99 U.S. ___ $6.99 CAN.

(limited quantities available)

TOTAL AMOUNT $_____
POSTAGE & HANDLING $_____
($1.00 for 1 book, 50¢ for each additional)
APPLICABLE TAXES* $_____
TOTAL PAYABLE $_____
(check or money order—please do not send cash)

To order, complete this form and send it, along with a check or
money order for the total above, payable to MIRA Books®, to:
In the U.S.: 3010 Walden Avenue, P.O. Box 9077, Buffalo,
NY 14269-9077; **In Canada:** P.O. Box 636, Fort Erie, Ontario,
L2A 5X3.

Name:_____
Address:_____ City:_____
State/Prov.:_____ Zip/Postal Code:_____
Account Number (if applicable):_____
075 CSAS

*New York residents remit applicable sales taxes.
 Canadian residents remit applicable GST and provincial taxes.

MIRA®

Visit us at www.mirabooks.com   MML0103BL